PRAISE FOR THE WITCHES OF LYCHFORD SERIES

"At once epic and terribly intimate. This is the story of a village, not a city, and all the more powerful for that; not all big fantasy needs an urban setting. Beautifully written, perfectly cruel, and ultimately kind. This is Cornell at the height of his craft."

—SEANAN McGUIRE, *NEW YORK TIMES* BESTSELLING AUTHOR OF THE INCRYPTID AND OCTOBER DAYE SERIES

"Masterfully creepy and sinister, all the more so for taking place in the beautifully drawn English countryside."

—JENNY COLGAN, AUTHOR OF *DOCTOR WHO: INTO THE NOWHERE*

Praise for *The Lost Child of Lychford*

"Cornell weaves together a fast-paced story and engrossing character studies; he paints a setting of a gloomy English countryside, disarming his readers with magic and danger that lurks unseen. Beneath the suspense lies wry humor that buoys the tale along."

—*PUBLISHERS WEEKLY*

"Cornell introduces some genuine existential chills into this ingratiating setting."

—*CHICAGO TRIBUNE*

Praise for *A Long Day in Lychford*

"Cornell's brand of magic is delightfully atmospheric and refreshing."

—*PUBLISHERS WEEKLY*

ALSO BY PAUL CORNELL

THE LYCHFORD SERIES

Witches of Lychford
The Lost Child of Lychford
A Long Day in Lychford
The Lights Go Out in Lychford
Last Stand in Lychford
Gnomes of Lychford

THE SHADOW POLICE SERIES

London Falling
The Severed Streets
Who Killed Sherlock Holmes

Rosebud
Chalk
British Summertime
Something More
A Better Way to Die

The Lychford Collection 1

WITCHES OF LYCHFORD

THE LOST CHILD OF LYCHFORD

A LONG DAY IN LYCHFORD

PAUL CORNELL

TOR PUBLISHING GROUP
NEW YORK

This is a work of fiction. All of the characters, organizations, and events portrayed in these novellas are either products of the author's imagination or are used fictitiously.

THE LYCHFORD COLLECTION 1

A Tordotcom Book
Published by Tom Doherty Associates / Tor Publishing Group
120 Broadway
New York, NY 10271

www.torpublishinggroup.com

EU Representative: Macmillan Publishers Ireland Ltd, 1st Floor, The Liffey Trust Centre, 117–126 Sheriff Street Upper, Dublin 1, DO1 YC43

The Library of Congress Cataloging-in-Publication Data is available upon request.

ISBN 978-1-250-39401-9 (trade paperback)

First Edition: 2025

Printed in the United States of America

10 9 8 7 6 5 4 3 2 1

The Lychford Collection 1

Witches of Lychford

For the Wonderful Folk of Fairlord

1

Judith Mawson was seventy-one years old, and she knew what people said about her: that she was bitter about nothing in particular, angry all the time, that the old cow only ever listened when she wanted to. She didn't give a damn. She had a list of what she didn't like, and almost everything—and everybody—in Lychford was on it. She didn't like the dark, which was why she bit the bullet on her energy bills and kept the upstairs lights on at home all night.

Well, that was one of the reasons.

She didn't like the cold, but couldn't afford to do the same with the heating, so she walked outside a lot. Again, that was only one of the reasons. At this moment, as she trudged through the dark streets of the little Cotswolds market town, heading home from the quiz and curry night at the town hall at which she had been, as always, a team of one, her hands buried in the pockets of her inappropriate silver anorak, she was muttering under her breath about how she'd get an earful from Arthur for being more than ten minutes late, about how her foot had started hurting again for no reason.

The words gave her the illusion of company as she pushed herself along on her walking stick, past the light and laughter of the two remaining pubs on the Market Place, to begin the slow trudge uphill on the street of charity shops, towards her home in the Rookeries.

She missed the normal businesses: the butcher and the greengrocer and the baker. She'd known people who'd tried to open shops here in the last ten years. They'd had that hopeful smell about them, the one that invited punishment. She hadn't cared enough about any of them to warn them. She was never sure about calling anyone a friend.

None of the businesses had lasted six months. That was the way in all the small towns these days. Judith hated nostalgia. It was just the waiting room for death. She of all people needed reasons to keep going. However, in the last few years she'd started to feel things really were getting worse.

With the endless recession, "austerity" as those wankers called it, a darkness had set in. The new estates built to the north—the Backs, they had come to be called—were needed, people had to live somewhere, but she'd been amazed at the hatred they'd inspired, the way people in the post office queue talked about them, as if Lychford had suddenly become an urban wasteland. The telemarketers who called her up now seemed either desperate or resigned to the point of a mindless drone, until Judith, who had time on her hands and ice in her heart, engaged them in dark conversations that always got her removed from their lists.

The charity shops she was passing were doing a roaring trade, people who'd otherwise have to pay to give things away, people who couldn't otherwise afford toys for their children. Outside, despite the signs warning people not to do so, were dumped unwanted bags of whatever the owners had previously assumed would increase in value. In Judith's day . . . Oh. She had a "day" now. She had just, through dwelling on the shite of modern life, taken her seat in the waiting room for death. She spat on the ground and swore under her breath.

There was, of course, the same poster in every single window along this street: "Stop the Superstore."

Judith wanted real shops in Lychford again. She didn't like Sovo—the company that had moved their superstores into so many small towns—not because of bloody "tradition," but because big business always won. Sovo had failed in its initial bid to build a store, and was now enthusiastically pursuing an appeal, and the town was tearing itself apart over it, another fight over money.

"Fuss," Judith said to herself now. "Fuss fuss bollocking fuss. Bloody vote against that."

Which was when the streetlight above her went out.

She made a little sound in the back of her throat, the closest this old body did to fight or flight, halted for a few moments to sniff the air, then, not sure what she was noting, carefully resumed her walk.

The next light went out too.

Then, slightly ahead of her, the next.

She stopped again, in an island of darkness. She looked over her shoulder, hoping someone would come out of the Bell, or open a door to put their recycling out. Nobody. Just the sounds of tellies in houses. She turned back to the dark and addressed it.

"What are you, then?"

The silence continued, but now it had a mocking quality. She raised her stick.

"Don't you muck about with me. If you think you're hard enough, you come and have a go."

Something came at her out of the darkness. She sliced the flint on the bottom of her stick across the pavement and made a sharp exclamation at the same instant.

The thing hit the line and enough of it got past to bellow something hot and insulting into her face, and then it was gone, evaporated back into the air.

She had to lean on the wall, panting. Whatever that had been had almost got past her defences.

She sniffed again, looking around, as the streetlights came

back on above her. What had it been, to leave a smell of bonfire night? A probe, a poke, nothing more, but how could even that be? They were protected here. Weren't they?

She looked down at a sharper smell of burning, and realised that had been a closer run thing than she'd thought: the line she'd scratched on the pavement was burning.

Judith scuffed it over with her boot—so the many who remained in blissful ignorance wouldn't see it—and continued on her way home, but now her hobble was faster and had in it a sense of worried purpose.

It was bright summer daytime, and Lizzie was walking by the side of the road with Joe. They were messing around, pretending to have a fight. They had decided on something they might one day fight about and they were rehearsing it like young animals, she knocking him with her hips, him flapping his arms to show how useless he'd be. She wanted him so much. Early days, all that wanting. He looked so young and strong, and happy. He brought the happy, he made her happy, all the time. A car raced past, horn tooting at them, get a room! She feinted at his flailing, ducked away, eyes closed as one of his fingers brushed her cheek. She shoved out with both hands and caught him on the chest, and he fell back, still laughing, into the path of the speeding car.

She opened her eyes at the screech and saw his head bounce off the bonnet and then again on the road. Too hard. Much too hard.

She woke slowly, not suddenly with a gasp like in the movies. She woke slowly and took on slowly, as always, the weight of having dreamed about him. She recognised her surroundings, and she couldn't help but look over to what, until just over a year ago, had been his side of the bed. Now it was flat, and there were still pillows, pristine, and he still wasn't there.

She found the space in her head where she prayed and she did that and there was nothing there to answer, as there hadn't been for a while now, but after a minute or so she was able—as always—to get up and begin her day.

Today there was a parochial church council meeting. In Lychford, judging from the three she'd been to so far, these always involved whizzing through the agenda and then having a lengthy, intricate debate about something near enough to the bottom of it to make her think that this time they'd get away early. Before this afternoon's meeting she had a home communion visit with Mr. Parks, who'd she'd been called to administer the last rites to last week, only to find him sitting outside his room at the nursing home, chatting away and having tea. It had been a bit hard to explain her presence. Vicars: we're not just there for the nasty things in life. Before that, this morning, she was due to take the midweek Book of Common Prayer service. She looked at herself in the mirror as she put on her crucifix necklace and slipped the white strip of plastic under her collar to complete the uniform: the Reverend Lizzie Blackmore, in her first post as new vicar of St. Martin's church, Lychford. Bereaved. Back home.

The Book of Common Prayer service was, as usual, provided for three elderly people with a fondness for it and enough clout in the church community to prevent any attempt to reschedule their routine. She'd known them all years ago when she was a young member of the congregation here.

"I wouldn't say we're waiting for them to die," Sue, one of the churchwardens, had said. "Oh, sorry, I mean I *can't*. Not out loud, anyway." Lizzie had come to understand that Sue's mission in life was to say the things that she, or indeed anyone else, wouldn't or couldn't. Just as well Lizzie did little services like this one on her own, except for the one elderly parishioner out of the three whose turn it was to read the lessons, boomingly and haltingly at the same time, hand out the three prayer books and collect the nonexistent collection.

When Lizzie had finished the service, trying as always not to interject a note of incredulity into "Lord . . . save the *Queen*," she had the usual conversations about mortality expressed through concern about the weather, and persuaded the old chap who was slowly collecting the three prayer books that she'd do that today, really, and leaned on the church door when it closed behind them and she was alone again.

She would not despair. She had to keep going. She had to find some reason to keep going. Coming home to Lychford had seemed like such a good idea, but . . .

From the door behind her there came a knock. Lizzie let out a long breath, preparing herself to be the reverend once again for one of the three parishioners who'd left her glasses behind, but then a familiar voice called through the door. "Lizzie? Err, vicar? Reverend?" The voice sounded like it didn't know what any of those words meant, her name included. Which was how it had always sounded since it and its owner had come back into Lizzie's life a week ago. Despite that, though, the sound of the voice made Lizzie's heart leap. She quickly restrained that emotion. *Remember what happened last time.*

She unlatched the door, and by the time she swung it back she had made herself seem calm again. Standing there was a woman her own age in a long purple dress and a woollen shawl, her hair bound with everything from gift ribbons to elastic bands. She was looking startled, staring at Lizzie. It took Lizzie a moment to realise why. Lizzie raised her hand in front of her clerical collar, and Autumn Blunstone's gaze snapped up to her face. "Oh. Sorry."

"My eyes are up here."

"Sorry, only that's the first time I've seen you in your . . . dog . . . no, being respectful now—"

"My clerical collar?"

"Right. That. Yes. You . . . okay, you said to come to see you—"

Lizzie had never thought she actually would. "Well, I meant at the vicarage . . ."

"Oh, yes, of course, the vicarage. You don't actually live here at the church. Of course not."

Lizzie made herself smile, though none of her facial muscles felt up for it. "Come on in, I won't be a sec." She made to go back to the office to put in the safe the cloth bag that didn't have a collection in it, but then she realised Autumn wasn't following. She looked back to see the woman who'd used to be her closest friend poised on the threshold, unwilling to enter.

Autumn smiled that awful awkward smile again. "I'll wait here."

They'd lost touch, or rather Autumn had stopped returning her calls and emails, about five years ago, just after Lizzie had been accepted into theological college, before Lizzie had met Joe. That sudden cessation of communication was something Lizzie had been astonished by, had made futile efforts to get to the bottom of, to the extent of showing up on Autumn's doorstep during the holidays, only to find nobody answering the door. She'd slowly come to understand it as a deliberate breaking of contact.

It made sense. Autumn had always been the rational one, the atheist debunker of all superstition and belief, the down-to-earth goddess who didn't believe in anything she couldn't touch. The weight of being judged by her had settled on Lizzie's shoulders, had made thoughts of her old friend bitter. So, on coming back to

Lychford to take up what, when she'd come here to worship as a teenager, had been her dream job, she hadn't searched for Autumn, had avoided the part of town where her family had lived, even. She had not let thoughts of her enter her head too much. Perhaps she would hear something, at some point, about how she was doing. That had been what she'd told herself, anyway.

Then, one Friday morning, when she'd been wearing civvies, she'd seen a colourful dress across the Market Place, had found the breath caught in her throat, and had been unable to stop herself from doing anything except marching over there, her stride getting faster and faster. She'd hugged Autumn before she knew who it was, just as she was turning, which in Lizzie's ideal and desired world should have been enough to begin again with everything, but then she had felt Autumn stiffen.

Autumn had looked at her, as Lizzie had let go and stepped back, not as a stranger, but as someone Autumn had expected to see, someone she'd been *worrying* about seeing. Lizzie had felt the wound of Joe open again. She'd wanted to turn and run, but there are things a vicar cannot do. So she'd stood there, her best positive and attentive look locked on her face. Autumn had quickly claimed a previous engagement and strode off. "Come to see me," Lizzie had called helplessly after her.

Lizzie had asked around, and found that the guys down the Plough knew all about Autumn, though not about her connection to Lizzie, and had laughed that Lizzie was asking about her, for reasons Lizzie hadn't understood. She'd looked for Autumn's name online and found no contact details in Lychford or any of the surrounding villages.

Now, Lizzie locked up, and went back, her positive and attentive expression again summoned, to find Autumn still on the threshold. "So," Lizzie said, "do you want to go get a coffee?" She kept her tone light, professional.

"Well," said Autumn, "Reverend . . . I want to explain, and I think the easiest way to do that is if you come to see my shop."

Autumn led Lizzie to the street off the Market Place that led down to the bridge and the river walk, where the alternative therapy establishments and the bridal shop were. Lizzie asked what sort of shop Autumn had set up. She was sure she'd already know if there was a bookstore left in town. Autumn just smiled awkwardly again. She halted in front of a shop Lizzie had noted when she first got here and stopped to look in the window of. Autumn gestured upwards at the signage, a look on her face that was half "*ta daa!*" and half kind of confrontational. Witches, the sign said in silver, flowing letters that Lizzie now recognised as being in Autumn's handwriting, *The Magic Shop*.

"*You* . . . run a magic shop?" said Lizzie, so incredulous that she wondered if the gesture might mean something else, such as "Oh, look at this magic shop, so against everything I've ever espoused."

"Right," said Autumn. "So."

"So . . . ?"

"So I'm sure this isn't the sort of thing you'd want to associate yourself with now that you're a reverend."

Lizzie didn't know if she wanted to hug Autumn or slap her. Which was a pretty nostalgic feeling in itself. "If this is the new you," she said, "I want to see it. I'm happy to step over *your* threshold."

Autumn gave her a look that said "yeah, right" and unlocked the door.

Inside, Lizzie was pleased to find herself in a space that said her old friend, scepticism apart, didn't seem to have changed all that much. The displays of crystals, books about ritual and healing, posters and self-help CDs were arranged not haphazardly, but in a way which said there was a system at work here, just one that would make any supermarket customer feel they'd been slapped around by experts. Crystal balls, for example, which Lizzie thought would be something people might want to touch, rolled precariously in plastic trays on a high shelf. Was there an association of magic shop retailers who might send a representative to tut at the aisle of unicorn ornaments, their horns forming a gauntlet of pointy accidents waiting to happen? She was sure that, as had been the case with every room or car Autumn had ever been in charge of, she would have a reason why everything was as it was.

Autumn pulled out a chair from behind the cash desk for Lizzie, flipped over the sign on the door so it said "Open" again, and marched into a back room, from where Lizzie could hear wineglasses being put under the tap. At noon. That was also a sign Autumn hadn't changed.

"You can say if you're not okay with it," she called.

"I'm okay with it," Lizzie called back, determinedly.

"No, seriously, you don't have to be polite." Autumn popped her head out of the doorway, holding up a bottle. "Rosé? Spot of lady petrol? Do you still do wine? I mean, apart from in church when it's turned into—if you think it *does* turn into—"

"Do you have any tea?"

Autumn stopped, looking as if Lizzie had just denounced her as a sinner. "There's an aisle of teas," she said.

"Well, then," Lizzie refused to be anything less than attentive and positive, "one of those would be nice."

Autumn put down the bottle, and they went to awkwardly explore the aisle of teas, arranged, as far as Lizzie could see, in order of . . . genre? If teas had that? "So . . . this is . . . quite a change for you."

Autumn halted, her hand on a box of something that advertised itself as offering relaxation in difficult circumstances. "Look who's talking. You were Lizzie Blackmore, under Carl Jones, under the Ping-Pong table, school disco. And now you're a . . . reverend, vicar, priest, rector, whatever."

"But I always . . . believed." She didn't want to add that these days she wasn't so sure.

"And I always thought you'd get over it."

Lizzie nearly said something very rude out loud. She took a moment before she could reply. "Autumn, we are standing in your *magic shop*. And you're still having a go at me for being a believer. How does that work? Are you, I don't know, getting the punters to part with their cash and then laughing at them for being so gullible? That doesn't sound like the Autumn I used to know."

Autumn wasn't looking at her. "It's not like that."

"So you do believe?"

"I'm still an atheist. It's complicated."

"You don't get that with craft shops, do you? 'Will this fitting hang up my picture?' 'It's complicated.'"

"Don't you dare take the piss. You don't know—!"

Lizzie couldn't help it. The sudden anger in Autumn's voice had set off her own. "You dropped me when I went away. You dropped me like a stone."

"That was complicated too. That was when things got . . . messed up."

Lizzie felt the anger drain from her. One facet of Autumn's character back in the day had been that she came to you when she needed something. She was always the one who knocked on your door in the middle of the night, sobbing. Had something bad happened to make her come to Lizzie's door again today? "Did you stay in Lychford back then? Or did you go away too?"

"A bit of both." A clenched grin.

"Where did you go?"

Autumn seemed to think about it. Then she shook her head. "I shouldn't have come to see you. I'm sure you're busy, Reverend, I've just got to . . ." She gestured towards the inner door. "You see yourself out."

Lizzie desperately wanted to argue, but just then the shop bell rang, and a customer entered, and Autumn went immediately to engage with her. Lizzie looked at the time on her phone. She needed to go to see Mr. Parks. "If you need me, Autumn," she called as she left, and it was on the verge of being a yell, "you let me know."

The following evening, Judith decided to do something she had never deliberately done before. She was going to participate in the civic life of the town. Which meant that first she had to negotiate getting out of her house. She went to put the recycling out, having spent a relaxing five minutes crushing cans with her fingers, and found that her neighbour, Maureen Crewdson, was putting hers out too. Maureen had found herself running for mayor, unopposed, because nobody wanted to do it. "By accident," she'd said, having one night had a few too many Malibus down the Plough. Of all the people Judith had to put up with, she was one of the least annoying. She had, tonight, the same weight about her shoulders that Judith had seen for the last few weeks. "I'm coming to the meeting tonight," Judith told her, and watched as, imperceptibly, that weight increased.

"I didn't think you'd be bothered with all that. Are you for or against the new shop?"

"I've decided I really don't like it." Since summat had had a go at scaring and then attacking her for considering voting against, that was.

The weight on Maureen's shoulders increased again. "Oh. It's going to bring so many jobs to . . . sod it, can we please not talk about it?"

There was some strangling emotion wrapped around her, something only Judith could sense, that would take a bit of effort to identify. Judith didn't feel up for poking into her business that much at this point. She knew better than to go rummaging into private pain. "Looks like it's going to rain, dunt it?" Judith felt the relief as she left Maureen to it, and went back inside to make herself a cup of tea while considering her exit strategy. She waited until a few minutes before she had to go, then took a deep breath and called up the stairs. "I'm off to the meeting." Silence. That was odd. What had happened to the noise from the telly? "Arthur? You hear what I said?"

This silence had something aware in it. Mentally girding her loins, Judith set off up the stairs.

Arthur was sitting where he always sat—in the bedroom, in his favourite chair, which he'd had her haul up here, the sound of his ventilator sighing and heaving. It was normally obscured by the constant noise of the telly, but the mute was on, and Arthur was fiddling with the remote, trying to get the sound back. He was watching some quiz show. That and ancient whodunits were all he watched, the older the better. Judith kept the Sky subscription going just for him. He didn't acknowledge her arrival. "Arthur, I said—"

"I heard you, woman. You're leaving me again."

She didn't let her reaction show. "It's only for an hour, and your programme's on in a minute." *Waking the Dead*. He loved gory mortuary dramas. Of course he did. She took the remote off him and tried to find the button to unmute it, which was hard in this light.

He looked up at her with tears in his eyes. "You'll be sending me away soon. Your own husband. You'll be putting me where you don't have to see me."

"If only I could!"

His face contorted into a sly grin, his cheeks still shining. "Will your boyfriend be there tonight, full of Eastern promise? Oh, that accent, he's so lovely, so *mobile*!"

She kept on trying to work out the remote, not looking at him. "You don't know what you're talking about, you old fool."

"That'd make it easy to send me away, wouldn't it, if I was going mental? You reckon he can make you feel young again? You're planning to get rid of me!"

"I bloody can't, though, can I?" Judith threw the remote at somewhere near him, turned on her heel and marched out of the door, only for her conscience to catch up with her, along with his howls of laughter, on the first step of the stairs. With an angry noise in her throat, she went back in, managed to switch the sound back on, slapped the remote back into his hands, and then left the cackling old sod to it. She put on her coat. As she got to the front door she heard his laughter turn to stage sobs, or real sobs, but still she made herself get outside and close the door without slamming it behind her.

2

The town hall was packed. A table had been placed at the front of the stage, under the Union flag and the Gloucestershire coat of arms. Displays on easels to the left and right showed artists' impressions of Lychford with a new superstore at the heart of it, lush greenery surrounding it, children playing and adults waving to each other outside it. Judith looked around her awkwardly, aware that she'd had various issues in the past with several of the locals who'd gathered here to voice protests against the store being built. She caught the eye of Eric and Sheila Parker, the couple who'd led the anti-superstore campaign on Twitter and had leafleted the town about it. They were here in matching "Stop Sovo" T-shirts. Judith realised, with horror, that they were heading over to talk to her, and couldn't find, at a quick glance, anyone else she knew well enough to get into a conversation with. There were, just occasionally, drawbacks to being a nasty old bitch.

"Judith!" called Mr. Parker, reaching out both hands as if to hug her. "You've seen the light."

"You could say that."

"I can't believe Sovo's gall, trying again," said Mrs. Parker. "This is how all the supermarket chains do it. Lose the first public vote, work out what they can bribe the locals with, win the appeal. This meeting is the bribery part of the process. The council votes next week."

"How are 'our side' doing?" asked Judith, wincing silently at having used the verbal speech marks. She never could force herself to bloody *join* anything. From the look of the crowd in the room, divided very cleanly in twain, each side having sat with those who agreed with them, the feeling of the town was about evenly split.

"I think we're going to win. Just. Every vote counts."

Maureen, looking just as burdened as earlier, walked up onto the stage and took a moment to prepare her papers. "Ladies and gentlemen," she said, "I'd like to introduce you to David S. Cummings, Chief Executive in Charge of New Development, Sovo Superstores International. I hope you'll give him a fair hearing."

A heavily built man with strong shoulders and nice eyes, dressed in a very expensive suit, took to the stage. There was a mixture of applause and catcalls.

"That's their fixer from head office," whispered Mrs. Parker.

"We've heard the bribery has become literal," said Mr. Parker. "The word is that the mayor has taken some sort of backhander."

Judith realised, with a sudden ache in her chest, that now she understood what she had felt around Maureen. She made the effort to look more closely, as only she could, and found weakness and fear and betrayal caught in the folds of the mayor's cardigan like smoke. Maureen looked up from her papers and made eye contact with Judith and the conflict in her eyes confirmed everything. Judith had to turn away, and found she was looking at Shaun, her son, in his uniform. He was pointing at her in surprise.

"You're here. You've taken a side."

"Yes."

"Because I was very much hoping—"

"That I wouldn't."

"Just so we're clear—"

"I won't throw anything."

"See that you don't. I don't want to have to arrest you. Again." He pointed to his eyes and then to her, and, with another glance at her over his shoulder, marched back to his place at the back of the hall.

Judith found a seat next to the Parkers as Maureen brought the meeting to order. She made a few more words of introduction, then gave the floor to Cummings, who stood and held out his hands, palms up, asking for the audience's indulgence. There were again boos and cheers in response. He smiled. "Being booed in a town hall. Now I've really made it as a pantomime villain." His accent was middle class, straight down the middle. "Good evening, everyone, your honour, councillors. Sovo are back here, having opted to go through the appeal process, because our research indicates fifty percent of you want us to build a store in Lychford."

"And half of us don't!" called Mr. Parker.

"The town council, I'm sorry to say, are also split down the middle. So, as most of you will be aware, next week they're going to put this to a final vote."

"You're tearing this town apart!" yelled Mr. Parker. Mrs. Parker put a hand on his arm, but he shook her off.

Cummings gestured towards a flipchart. "We've heard your concerns and adjusted our plans. I hope the changes may persuade a few more of you towards our point of view. We aim to meet challenge with investment. Investment in people. The creation of over two hundred new jobs. Yes, our new facility would change the shape of Lychford. But we hope it's for the better." He turned the first sheet, and revealed an even more lovely painting of an idyllic store in local surroundings. Below it was a more detailed map.

It took a moment for Judith to understand what she was looking at. She took her glasses from her pocket, stuck them onto her nose, and stared at what had been revealed. She had wondered if there was any connection between the fleeting poke of mystical energy she'd run into and the proposals about the store, but she'd never imagined *this*.

"By diverting these roads," Cummings indicated on the map, "the proposed new store would actually bring *more* traffic to local businesses."

Judith suddenly found she was on her feet. Beside her, the Parkers grinned and urged her on. "You'll cut off Compton Street?"

"Yes, and that will mean—"

"That the streets don't cross at the Market Place!"

"Which is why we'll be building, free of charge, a new Market Place parking zone—"

"You bloody fool!" shouted Judith, before she could help herself. "You'll open the gates to the other worlds!"

There was silence, followed by a little awkward, embarrassed laughter. Judith heard, from the back of the hall, Shaun make a little groan of anguish.

She looked down to see the Parkers staring up at her in amazement, but she had her opportunity, they were listening to her, she couldn't stop now. "This town is shaped like it is for a reason! The roads, north south east west! The walls that protect us, seen and unseen, follow that pattern, use it as their foundation! The ancient boundaries, our defences—!" She could hear both sides of the audience starting to catcall now, shouting for her to sit down. She'd actually united the town in something. But she had to say this, they had to know, it was so important. "We've already lost the tree line on Maiden Hill—"

"That was kids playing with bonfires!" hissed Mr. Parker. "For God's sake, sit down!"

"There'll be nothing to stop it! Don't you understand? I understand now why I felt something trying the defences! If you do this, then the things that are out there, that want to get in—!"

The doors to the hall burst open. A great wind blew leaves in and sent papers flying. There were screams. Everyone, Judith included, turned, to see a figure standing silhouetted against the streetlights outside. The figure halted, seemed to realise that he'd made a big entrance, and turned to grab the doors and heave them closed behind him. He was, his actions revealed, a thin, long-haired youth in a leather jacket. He turned back to the crowd and looked awkward. "What?"

Relieved laughter swept the audience. Judith looked helplessly around her. The moment had been lost.

Cummings was watching her, sizing her up, obviously wondering how dangerous this lunatic was. "I'm sure," he said, "that this lady's views are something we all want to give . . . *appropriate* consideration to." Which made the audience laugh once again.

Judith sat down, lost.

She made it through the meeting, despite the Parkers hissing icy comments at her, and then had to head for the door—away from where Cummings was shaking Maureen's hand, away before more people could tell her what a stupid old woman she'd been. They were right. She shouldn't have blurted it all out like that, should have found some reasonable way to say it. If she knew people here better, if she'd had some more friends to call on—! Stupid old woman, stupid! Shaun intercepted her before she got to the door. "Mum, it's okay."

"No it isn't, boy. It isn't for any of us."

"Oh, thank you so much for that, Judith." Mr. Parker caught up with her. "Use a spell and magic this away, won't you? You made our case look ridiculous!" The horrible thing was, he was right. At the end of the meeting there'd definitely been more applause for David Cummings than abuse.

Shaun stepped up to him. "See you later then, Mr. Parker."

After a moment he took the point and marched off, finding his wife. They, and many others, gave Judith baleful glares as they headed out.

"Thank you, people who don't understand metaphor." Judith turned at the welcome sound of the new voice, to find Sunil at her side. He was smiling in his usual wry, understanding way. He was wearing his spectacles tonight, which, she knew, would have been a big decision for this handsome seventysomething man who took such good care of himself. She reflected again that there were just a few things about which Arthur was entirely correct. She appreciated Sunil's support, but she really didn't want to have this conversation with him now. Still, she let him take her arm and escort her to the door.

PC Shaun Mawson had become aware at an early age that his mum believed in some weird stuff. Not that she'd ever shared the details of it with him. He'd asked about the details several times and been told he couldn't know about it because he was a boy. Judith's reputation for fearsome confrontation had helped him through school, where the teachers had seemed as nervous of her as his classmates were. As an adult, with her getting on a bit, he'd gotten increasingly fearful that her mouth might one day get her into something she couldn't get out of. So it was with a sense of relief that he watched her leave the hall. He wasn't sure what he thought about Sunil taking her arm in public like that, mind you. Yet another reason for people to talk about Mum. His thoughts were interrupted by a hand grabbing his shoulder and spinning him round. He found he was facing the long-haired stranger whose dramatic entrance had caused such laughter, who was now appraising Shaun with a piercing stare. "You know her, don't you? Tell her well done for having a brain. She's the only one who talked any sense." His accent was hard to place, perhaps Irish, perhaps the sort of cockney who'd been in America too long.

"Very kind of you, sir, now we're trying to empty the hall . . ."

The man made a guttural sound at him, then marched off into the crowds that were flooding past, trying to stop and persuade them. "Why didn't you listen to her wisdom? Damned *people*! Don't you value your short little lives?" Which Shaun didn't like the sound of, but when he tried to catch up with the man, he found he'd lost him in the crowd.

Sunil walked with Judith through the quiet of the car park. She was heading back towards his car, she realised, without either of them having commented on or thought about it. His concern didn't annoy her, which was unique. He was someone in this town who wanted to understand her, who even liked her, and that was unique too. After a moment they were alone under the trees by the bridge, at his car, with no bloody Parkers or anyone else to see them. Judith let out a long breath of relief. She'd only just realised, but she was still so angry and frightened for the future that she was shaking. She found she was hoping Sunil might put an arm round her, but no, he was far too decent to do that. "If only they'd understood," he said, "as you say, the shapes of things are important. When I start a new business, I look at demand, at where the customers are—"

"Oh, stop being so bloody kind. You know I meant it literally."

"I know you believe in . . . well, I don't know what the proper name for it is, but such seriousness is fascinating. How about you tell me everything? Over dinner tomorrow night, say? Not at my restaurant."

"Why?" She couldn't help teasing him. "Is it the food?"

"Because my staff would laugh at me, being on a date." That

twinkle in his eye. Here it was, a specific invitation. He'd never previously gone that far.

She had both hoped for and dreaded this moment. "Sunil, you're very nice, but . . ." She didn't want to finish the sentence, to say out loud that she just couldn't do this.

He sighed. "You still have your whole life ahead of you. Please, think about it." He very gently touched her arm, and smiled supportively again, and went to his car. Judith watched him drive off and thought about what could never be and then swore at herself for doing so. She had to drive such thoughts from her mind. It was time for battle.

The next morning, having unlocked the church, Lizzie found herself pausing at the point where she normally bowed in front of the cross on the altar. Mr. Parks had been once again surprisingly full of life at his home communion, but had said *she* seemed off her game. She hadn't slept. She was still so angry at Autumn. Had she come back home hoping for the relief—a reconciliation with her best friend? She so much wanted to tell her about Joe, about his death, about her own part in it. Everyone at the time had been so quick to tell her it was an accident. She and Joe had been caught on CCTV camera, she'd been told, though she hadn't wanted to see it. The police had—horribly quickly—cleared her of blame. Maybe what she really wanted was for unpersuadable, sceptical Autumn to listen, to ask questions, to believe her. That Autumn, though, would never have owned a business she didn't believe in. That Autumn would never have said anything was "complicated."

Maybe Lizzie was stuck now. Stuck here, with no faith in her head, no relief. She'd alienated her best friend years ago, and killed the love of her life, and couldn't bring herself to ask for help, because maybe she was committing the sin of not thinking she deserved it. "Oh, what's the bloody point?" she said out loud. She looked from the cross to the beams in the ceiling. "Is there anybody there?"

There was a sudden noise from behind her. Lizzie spun, to see that a man had entered the church and was looking at her apologetically. "Sorry. Only me, as they say." He extended a hand. "Dave Cummings. You may have heard. I'm the man from Sovo."

"Oh. Hi." Lizzie managed to control her breathing.

Cummings wandered further in, looking around at the architecture. "Oh, dear no," he said, "it'll have to go." He saw her startled reaction and laughed. "Joking. Sorry, I always assume that's what people imagine I'm thinking, wherever I go in this town. I'm the Antichrist."

"I'm strictly agnostic about all that," Lizzie assured him. "I have to get on with everyone." In truth, the battle lines had been drawn before she got here, and she could see good points on both sides, and apart from caring for those involved, it wasn't a conflict she was much invested in.

"It's actually a lovely church. Cotswold stone, tower in the perpendicular style, all funded by wool merchants, but built around a considerably more ancient original, am I right?" He saw that he was, and was pleased with himself. "Excellent. Could do with a rood screen, most churches round here once had them, very few left. Font and pulpit placed a bit awkwardly for everyone to see. Oh, you must have thought of that, I'm teaching my grandmother to suck eggs. I hope we can bring more people in here."

"Oh? Is that something your company are into?"

"Well, it's part of the fabric of British life, isn't it? A bit like we are, these days. Community, reliability, togetherness. All very pleasing. Sovo head office donates to a lot to Christian groups."

"I'll take your money. We have a local charity that runs a food bank."

He raised a hand to urge caution. "Such donations being facilitated through organisations like Only Way and the Truth and Light Alliance."

"Ah." Those names meant, to Lizzie, a very particular brand of extremity.

He must have seen her expression. Her attentive and positive face was utterly beyond her at the moment. "Not your sort of people?"

"It's just they're rather more . . . controversial . . . than—"

"Oh, I'm sure they'd say the same about you. It's a pity you judge them and find them wanting. I thought you might want to get some real energy in here, change things around. It's all a bit . . . quiet."

Lizzie wanted to say he should see it on a Sunday morning, but she was trying to find an appropriate manner of speech. He'd caught her at exactly the wrong moment.

"Or perhaps you like the quiet? Like it being just you? Gives you time to think, I suppose. Lots of time alone to dwell on . . . well, whatever."

Did he know something about her? "Why are you talking to me like . . . ?"

"Like what?" He looked suddenly concerned.

"Nothing. Sorry."

"Have I said something to offend you?"

"No," she decided. "No, I think . . . sorry, we seem to have got off on the wrong foot."

"No, no, it's my fault. You mentioned your food bank . . ." He went over to the collection plate that last night's youth service had left out on the side altar, reached into his pocket, and placed on it an enormous wad of cash. "There."

Lizzie was too astonished to say anything.

"See you again soon, Reverend," said Cummings. He headed for the door.

Lizzie waited for a decent moment after he'd left, then went and stared at the roll of fifty-pound notes. There was enough there to keep the food bank charity going for . . . well, years. She hadn't even said thank you. She reached out with the aim of taking the elastic band off the money, to count it, to get it into the safe as quickly as possible, but then she stopped.

For some reason she didn't understand, she couldn't bring herself to touch it.

Autumn had resolved to open the shop on time, despite her lack of sleep. She'd had quite a few customers in over the last few days, ones she hadn't met before, all of them, it seemed, seeking specifically or including in their orders ingredients that were supposed to be able to allow one to hide or vanish. It was as if the New Age community in this and the surrounding towns was bigger than she'd thought and was preparing for some sort of conflict. Their grim faces and refusal to engage with her careful counselling about the proper uses of what they were buying matched her mood. She didn't believe they were actually capable of changing the physical world with what she sold them—that lack of belief was the bedrock of who she was—but from all the years of research she'd done into magic, she knew the rituals they were about to enter into had meaning for the customers themselves, could change who they were. She'd tried, when she couldn't sleep, her own rituals about calmness and sanity, to no avail.

As she unlocked the cash register, her hands fumbled angrily with the keys. Why had she bothered to go and see Lizzie? What had she expected to get out of that, exactly?

All those years ago, her friend had announced out of the blue that she was taking up a major role in a belief system responsible for so many horrors, and when Autumn had paused, needing time to think about this sudden enormous change, Lizzie had started sending her passive-aggressive emails, demanding Autumn answer. Then . . . well, then had come the moment when everything had fallen apart.

Maybe Autumn had gone to see her hoping she could share what had happened, hoping she'd understand, Lizzie being a professional believer. Maybe Autumn had thought she might see her story in a way that Autumn herself couldn't. That look on Lizzie's face, though, that had told Autumn she could never understand the atheist owning a magic shop thing, never mind the . . . the cause of that seeming contradiction. Her going to find Lizzie had been, she decided, the result of desperation, her reaching out for old comfort that wasn't there any more, in the face of . . . a threat which wasn't real, which couldn't be real.

Autumn realised she could hear something again now. In the same instant she went through what was now a familiar process—thinking what she was hearing was just in her awful memories, but then realising that it wasn't.

It was music, or something like music.

A couple of years ago, she'd made herself learn enough musical notation to attempt to write it down, but even then she'd failed. It was a high, repetitive, six-note strain, followed by a recurring three-note sound that seemed like a . . . summons, that circled, floated, repeated, pure liquid sound.

She'd read many accounts of people who claimed to have heard the same sounds, and some of them had such good explanations of what it might be: wind blowing through gaps in stone, shifting quartz scree, even the sound of killer whales through the canvas hulls of boats. None of those could explain why this sound she associated with a horrifying period of insanity had returned, a couple of weeks ago, right outside her shop.

Her hands started shaking uncontrollably, and she dropped the keys. She put a hand to her mouth, looking around wildly, trying to find the threat that might come from any direction. It was coming this time, she realised, from just behind the back door.

She forced herself to walk, step by shaking step, towards the sound. Was it him? As if she was sure there had *been* a him. She had struggled so long with what she'd started to see as mental illness. Now she was closer to the door, she could hear it clearly: the same music that had been blaring into her ears in the chamber of his . . . his father. She shook her head, trying to push the memories, the stories she'd told herself, the symptoms of her illness, whichever, out of her mind. She was looking at the frosted window at the back door. A shape stepped forward. There was someone . . . something there.

Then it was gone.

Autumn had blinked, and perhaps there'd been a blur of movement, perhaps not. At least the music had stopped. Only then . . .

. . . she slowly turned. It was coming again, this time from near the front of the shop. She closed her eyes, and could only find images from the past, or from her imaginings, crowding in on her. Her walking hand in hand with . . . him . . . no, *it*. The clearing in the forest to the east of here—he'd led her into it, and she'd been so amazed to see the line of flowers strung between the two enormous trees. That music had been everywhere, lighter then, inviting. In her memory, she could taste it somehow in the air. He'd raced towards the bower, gesturing happily for her to follow. She'd hesitated on the edge of the two trees, struck suddenly by what deep shadows they cast. He'd come back round behind her, put a hand on her shoulders and had suddenly . . . pushed her—

She didn't want to remember anything after that. It was impossible. It was *all* impossible. Lizzie was saying all the time with her bloody collar that she knew everything about what happened in heaven and earth, only that didn't include what had happened to her, to Autumn. The music was getting louder, or was that just in her head? "You're not real," she whispered, "you're not real."

After a while, the repeated words seemed to work. The music faded again. Then it was definitely gone. Autumn was left shaking. She thought of Lizzie, thought of running back to that damn church, into it . . . but no. All the learning she'd done, all the research . . . perhaps it had all been to deal with this moment when she came to question her sanity again. She had to find some way to protect herself.

3

Judith had decided to check on all the ancient boundaries, so that lunchtime she had her usual going-out row with Arthur, before making her way to the Market Place, then up the street that led eastwards out of it. This had traditionally been the way sheep had come from the hill farms into Lychford on market day.

The dry stone walls along the way weren't in a good state of repair, but as the houses gave way to the edge of the forest, they didn't look like they were going to fall over any time soon either. These stones had been laid with care by those who knew that all the old crafts had a hidden dimension to them, that the placing of a bonder stone changed everything.

Out this way there was the lonely last pub, the Castle, which now had an angry chalkboard sign up that said "drinkers welcome" to indicate its dissatisfaction with other establishments' fads like pub quizzes, bands, food, and, presumably, conversation. Beyond it the road got dark, but that was where the darkness was supposed to be.

Judith looked up at a noise and saw that an enormous Sovo lorry was approaching, cutting through Lychford when traffic was light rather than using the bypass, she presumed, on its way to deliver to a Sovo store in any of a dozen nearby towns. However, as it roared past her, she heard another noise, and watched as the stone in a section of the wall shuddered, a couple of "batter" stones from the top falling away. Furious, she grabbed one of them, turned and flung it helplessly after the lorry.

Which it missed by a mile.

Hopefully the driver had at least registered, in his rear-view mirror, her impotent protest. These people were such fools, they had no idea what they were risking. She raised her index and little fingers at the driver, just so he got the point. Then the lorry was gone around the corner. To Judith's surprise, a car following it skidded to a halt and out of it sprung Mr. Parker, his face florid. "What the hell are you doing now?" His wife was getting out behind him, looking more worried than angry. "Did you really just make a . . . magic sign at that lorry? After throwing something at it? It all gets reported back to head office, you know. You should see some of the stories they've planted in the local media. It's going against us now. We're actually losing support. Thanks to you!"

Mrs. Parker caught up with her husband. "Eric, please don't—"

"How dare you make a laughingstock of us? After all I've done!" He poked his finger into Judith's face.

Judith, not used to being lectured by the middle-aged, had glanced away, back to the wall, and what she'd seen there had made her afraid in a way Eric Parker never could. Standing at the edge of the woods, by the now slightly diminished wall, was an extraordinary figure. It had the shape of a man, but was almost a silhouette, a few lines of a sketch, stark white against the shadows of the trees beyond. It had no features, and yet Judith knew it was looking at her. It took a purposeful step forward.

Eric Parker and his wife stepped forward in that moment too, as a passing car made them get out of the road. "Look at me when I'm talking to you!"

"Eric, for God's sake!" Sheila was getting scared for reasons unconnected to the thing only Judith could see.

Judith looked back and called desperately to the figure. "You can't get in. Not yet. No matter how strong you are. Go! Now!"

Mr. Parker shoved Judith right up against the remains of the wall, sending another stone falling from it. "No, I won't just do what you say because you're magic, you ridiculous old cow! Have you thought about supporting the other side? How about making them look stupid too?"

Judith looked back again to where the figure, now inches away, was regarding them all calmly, purposefully. She caught a familiar scent. This was a more physical form of the probe she'd felt from one of the worlds beyond the borders. Creatures like this were rarely seen in the world of people. Surely it should take longer for them to become this confident?

"Oh, is there something there we can't see? Are the voices talking to you again?" Parker grabbed the collar of her coat, making Sheila cry out for him to stop. Judith raised her stick, against which threat she wasn't sure. She twisted and saw the figure consider for a moment. It reached out.

Its hand slapped onto Mr. Parker's shoulder. He spun at an impact he could obviously feel, and his expression contorted into shock as, suddenly, he could *see* it too. The figure let go. Mr. Parker stumbled back, his face suddenly flushed. His hand dropped from Judith and grabbed at his own chest.

"Eric!" shouted Mrs. Parker. "Eric, where are your pills?"

Judith looked back again. The figure was holding something between thumb and forefinger: a bottle of pills.

The damn demon! Judith made a grab for it, but the intruder had already stepped back. As Mr. Parker fell and Mrs. Parker started screaming, knowing that now Judith didn't dare clamber over what remained of the wall and follow, it calmly walked off into the trees and was gone.

Judith tried, though she had no knowledge of first aid, to help. She yelled at Mrs. Parker to call 999. Shaun, of course, was first on the scene, and he kept up heart massage on the utterly still Mr. Parker until the ambulance got there. All Judith could do was hold Mrs. Parker's hand, which she accepted, sobbing. As the Parkers were driven away in the ambulance, Shaun looked concerned at her. "There wasn't anything more you could have done, Mum."

"No," muttered Judith, looking back to where the wounded wall still stood, a breach that would take more than a simple replacing of bricks to fix. "That's the trouble."

Autumn had spent the morning checking her shop's defences. She'd chosen which empty shop to rent on the basis of its proximity to running water. She'd salted every threshold, had buried witch bottles and the treated bones of cats in holes she'd dug in the supporting walls. As she'd done all that, she'd said the incantations that focussed all one's consciousness on protection. Now she went back to those defences, said all those calming words again. She did not believe, she told herself, in the power of the objects, or that she was changing the physical world, but instead that she was setting up the shop/fortress as a metaphor in her mind, hacking her own brain to withstand the possibility of a relapse. The music was a symbol of mental illness, and she could use her own symbols against it.

She did honour to the four compass points, raised the three forms of the goddess within her, as she'd done hundreds of times over the last few years, and found some slight calm in the familiarity of the ceremony. She had chosen, all those years ago, to investigate that which had harmed her, to understand it and encompass it. She fought her mental illness on its own territory. Now it was early afternoon, and her serotonin levels would be low, and, as she thought she might, she thought she heard the music begin again, at the edge of her perception. However, now she was ready. She took up the yoga stance she'd selected, closed her eyes, and addressed her own illness.

"I know you're not real," she said. "You're a false memory I created, something to punish myself with." She clasped in one hand the protective pentagram on her necklace, that she'd selected after much consideration, for its shape, feel, and materials. "I bring to the surface all the strength of the woman I am. I gather everything that can help me, I summon those forces to me. There is no such thing as an evil force that can harm me."

"Well, that's bollocks."

Autumn's eyes snapped open. She saw that a customer had entered somehow without ringing the bell, an angry-looking old lady it took a moment for her to recognise.

"Are you going to stand there spouting New Age wankery," said Judith, "or are you going to help me?"

Judith was someone Autumn had heard about from her other customers ever since she'd opened the shop—someone who might have been in her core customer base, an actual local practitioner of . . . well, what Judith was actually into varied depending on who was telling the story. She had, it seemed, been thrown out of every local coven and circle from Swindon to Cirencester. "Aleister Crowley in a frock," as one white witch had put it, letting out a long sigh of recalled exasperation.

The fact that, despite that, Judith had never actually ventured into the magic shop had long been a source of nagging worry to Autumn. So her being here now was perhaps actually a positive sign, a synchronicity showing that the universe and Autumn's mind were now on the same upward path. Judith slapped a shopping list into her hand and marched round after her, grabbing each item off the shelves as Autumn found it. Judith seemed to share the occasional feeling that some of her customers expressed, that Witches was perhaps not arranged for browsing.

The old woman seemed to have an urgent desire to assemble a collection of items and ingredients that indicated a need on her part to shortly practice the craft in a rather worrying way. Autumn had tried and failed to communicate with her many other customers recently who'd also come here looking for troubling items, but this was different. Having Judith Mawson here was both a major coup and the chance to help an old lady who might be scared, lonely, confused even. "You seem," she said, as Judith threw another sprig of herbs into her basket, "to be seeking protective ingredients, protective crystals. It's all about protection for you today."

Judith grunted.

"So is there some new situation in your life, some new problem which has made you seek such protection?"

Judith stopped, as if realising she wasn't going to get away without being talked at, and seemed to consider for a moment. "Nothing you can help with. I've found my materials in nature rather than in this jumble sale of a shop because you don't believe in magic. Now things have gotten to a bloody terrifying point where I need everything you've got as well as everything I've got. You're asking because you want to know if *you* need protection. The answer is yes, girl, loads of it, right now."

Autumn found her nails had dug into the palms of her hands. She made herself breathe. "Whatever *seems* to be happening, with the proper mental adjustment—"

"You won't save yourself with frigging aromatherapy. You at least have the sense to be wearing that." She pointed at the pentagram around Autumn's throat. "The sealed nut can work wonders, with sacrifice and whatnot. What you do with that nugget of actual useful info is up to you." Judith opened her handbag and dumped everything from her shopping basket into it with one chuck, then reached in her pocket, immediately found the exact money needed, and slapped it into Autumn's palm. "Magic is real," she said. "Stop running away. You've had some contact with the fairies of the Summerland, whether you're aware of it or not. I can smell it on you. If they come back, now the borders are wobbly, don't accept any invitations or cheques. If they say they can take you to meet royalty, they don't mean at Buckingham Palace, and you're not prepared for what you'd see." Autumn was too shocked by her words to speak, and before she could muster urgent questions, Judith was marching out. "I might have to come back," she called, "even at these prices."

Autumn was about to follow, but then she heard once more, distantly, from behind the shop, the music. She'd just been told everything she'd fended off was true. It was like the sound was laughing at her.

That morning, Lizzie had found Mr. Parks asleep in his nursing home, his breathing shallow, his son and daughter taking turns at his bedside. She had taken the opportunity, when his consciousness had surfaced briefly and he'd greeted her, to pray with him and administer the last rites. She'd done all this, not feeling the words herself. She'd been there as he'd passed away, holding his hand. Then she'd gone to the church, looked again at the wad of cash on the collection plate, and still not been able to touch it. She'd finally grabbed the plate, and hidden it under a duster inside the organ stool. She'd gone home to the vicarage and found she was too tired to make tea. She'd slumped onto the sofa, and soon she was asleep.

In her dream, Joe walked beside her again, on the road where she'd killed him. "Take the bloody money," he said, "give it to the poor. They don't care about what's going on inside your stupid head."

"I know," she said, luxuriating in being arm in arm with him, knowing it was all going to go wrong, but—in a dream—not knowing why or how.

"Maybe faith doesn't suit you anymore."

"This isn't actually you, is it?"

"Right. I'm just the sensible bit of you. I'm not 'watching over you from the other side.' There probably *isn't* an other side."

Lizzie's feelings on the afterlife had always been complicated. The Bible was actually much stronger on the idea that everyone was going to be resurrected together, physically, at what sounded like the end of the universe, than it was on the idea of heaven. "I never thought you were playing guitar with Jimi Hendrix."

"Do you want me to stop meeting you in dreams?"

She shoved him playfully. "Of course not!"

He staggered into the road just in time for the car to hit him again.

Lizzie woke slowly, every muscle aching. She felt too lost in grief to cry. One year gone, and she still felt like this. One year was how long people thought you were allowed to grieve. Maybe something had to give. Maybe that thing was her. The money was just money. She would write and post her resignation letter to the bishop, then go and get the money and pay it directly into the food bank charity's account, and then she would go far away. That row of decisions, falling silently in her head like demolished tower blocks, made her feel the closest to contentment she had in weeks. She hauled herself to her feet, and stumbled towards the first of them.

Autumn stood by the counter, shaking, listening to the increasing volume of the music outside. Judith had arrived in her shop, like something out of the writings of Jung, at the very moment Autumn had been calling in everything she could to help her. What she'd said had matched what was in Autumn's head. Everything in her rationalist readings of magic said she should listen to the words of the wise woman who'd stepped over her threshold.

She had to face the possibility that what had happened to her was true. It was that or collapse, break down, curl up into a ball.

She made her decision. She went to the aisle of unicorn ornaments and found the most pointy of them. She strode to the back door and flung it open. She marched out into the car park her shop shared with the hot stone massage place and the accountancy business. The music was clear out here, blaring, terrifying. Other shop owners must have heard it. If they had, though, why weren't they out here complaining? "Where are you, you bastard?" she yelled, aware that she was giving her neighbours plenty to talk about.

He walked out into the light.

She had to take a step back. She had no idea of what he'd walked out of, if there had been a shadow there or . . . but no, now she couldn't do anything but look at him.

He was real.

He was exactly the same as he'd been all those years ago: so achingly thin, like a skeleton in leather trousers—leather jacket, hair down his back, eyes that looked every moment like he was going to take some sort of immediate and drastic action. He was carrying a radio straight out of the 1950s. It was playing the music—the music that had suddenly become absolutely clear and played by instruments no human had ever played: utterly impossible in the way it was constructed and yet obviously natural and terrifying on that basis alone, as if the sound itself opened up possibilities beyond this world. Autumn felt dizzy. She was breathing too fast. Was she hallucinating?

He switched off the radio and she nearly fell with relief at the silence. He was looking at her. Like she was the object of his next immediate and drastic action. "Digital," he said, pointing to the radio. "Better than the old panpipes, eh?" His accent was, as always, impossible to place, an accent they didn't make anymore.

She could find no response.

"Can I come in?"

"No!" She hated even talking to him, that acknowledgement he was really here. She had her defences. She was not going to let them down by inviting him in.

"You're looking lovely today."

She was frozen with anger.

"I've been trying to make you come out and see me. I didn't think you were going to pay attention to my summons. I wondered if you'd forgotten the music."

"I tried to."

"What?" He looked startled. "Why?" He took a step closer, those eyes searching her face. She made herself stand her ground. "Oh. You thought I . . . wasn't real." She remembered how he could read things like that from faces. "You actually thought all the beauty I showed you, all the treasures I shared with you . . ."

He sounded like he was actually getting angry, like he was the injured party. That gave her the right sort of anger to allow her to speak. "All you took from me!"

"Took? That's damned ungracious. You held my hand willingly. You entered my nation willingly—"

"You shoved me in!"

"Well, okay, yes, but only because you were hesitating. And what did I say to you immediately afterwards?"

If this was all true, then she remembered that, and she didn't want to. "That's not the point."

He roared at her. "*What did I say?*"

She stumbled *backwards,* feeling the force of his voice in her head. She used everything she'd learned to put a boundary around who she was and shoved him back out again.

He leapt back, as if he'd been slapped. He stared at her, sizing her up once again. "Oh, you've been studying. Interesting *flavour* to it. Practical. Different. A bit . . ." he gestured to his radio, "modern, like."

She had actually faced him down. The relief and exultation inside her threatened to make her start laughing or sobbing, and if she started she felt like she might not stop. If these were memories, not dreams or imaginings, then she remembered what had happened and she had to keep the moral high ground. "You said that every step I took was of my own free will. But I don't know how much you were influencing me to stay."

"Not at all, because you actually bloody left in the end, didn't you? I told you what you had to do to go home—"

"To let go of you . . . of your hand . . . for more than a hundred heartbeats. That's also true. But again—"

"You put it to practical use. You tried it. It worked. You ran out on me." He stopped, suddenly realising. "Are you saying I forced myself on you, influenced you to—?"

"Did you?"

"No. Because I'm a prince of the blood, not some human cowson, out for whatever he can get in his short lifetime. As if I'd soil such honour for you." She swore at him. He looked pleasingly outraged. "I didn't even lie to you, did I?"

"You didn't tell me where we were going."

"You still don't believe it now, so you wouldn't have believed it then."

"I'm talking about informed consent here."

"You consented *after* you saw the Summerland. Several times."

"You kept me—"

"I did not keep you."

"I was in there, in the kingdom, for—"

"A weekend."

"A year! It was a weekend for us in there, but for me it was a year away from home! Thanks to you, I lost my job, my family thought I'd run away or been murdered—!"

He stared at her. She couldn't read his face. "I can navigate across the border, I could have brought you back to the right point, but you ran—"

She didn't want to hear it. "I got out of your bed, I . . . I went for a walk, and I kept counting heartbeats." She remembered . . . she had to accept that was the right word now . . . she remembered her awe at the clusters of what she now knew to be magic ingredients growing all over the building, a tree or cave or something which had seemed like part of the landscape, the bright fields of what her reading had since told her were things of value to her craft seen through circles and gaps, the sheer *meaning* everywhere. She had thought since, on those few occasions when she'd allowed herself to imagine the experience to be real, that what they called magic in this world was just a gathering of scraps from that one. Then, however, came the part of the dream that hurt her. The curiosity about how all the corridors and branches and breezes led one way, to an enormous door that was open just a crack. How she had run, knowing her time was short, to that door, and had looked inside like a child expecting to see a secret. She had seen . . . her memory shied away from it still. "I saw . . . I saw your father, on his throne. I saw . . . !" She didn't want to remember the sight, slammed the door in her mind now.

"You saw what he 'really' looked like?"

"Yes!"

"What I must 'really' look like, whatever this *really* word means?"

"Yes!"

"And you ran from the sight of my father, leaving him furious at such judgement of him on your part, offended to the depths of his pride, which is why he—who is, himself, the land and also thus the border—made you arrive back a little late. When he didn't have to let you go at all."

So . . . so that had been deliberate? She just shook her head. Couldn't deal. "You make it sound like I should be grateful."

"You ran away because you realised I wasn't so attractive without my makeup. Because I'm not a young white male."

Something felt sick inside her. She checked her own defences, found he wasn't trying them. "You're twisting my words. This is what you do, you trick people."

"People trick themselves and blame us. Whatever 'us' is the latest us."

"You . . . you can't be saying . . ." She needed to make clear to him the tremendous hurt he'd caused, what the shock of what she'd seen and the time away had done to her. She needed to tell him about the harm done by the stories she'd made up for herself and others about where she'd been in that missing year, stories that she'd come to half believe herself, about the distance the experience had put between her and her family, between her and Lizzie. She found she had no words to do that now, but she would have some one day. Now, though, there was something more urgent to ask. "Listen. Why have you come back? Why are you here?"

"Because trouble is coming. You can help."

"I'm not going to help you." She indicated the pentagram at

her throat, remembering what Judith had said. "This protects me from going with you."

He looked hurt. "You'd need cold iron for that, I could walk through that thing. Not that I intend to. Not with me being so disgusting to you. And as for that—" He gestured vaguely towards the unicorn ornament she'd forgotten she was clutching, "it's only just occurred to me that it's meant to be a weapon and not a vastly inauthentic gift. Listen. My father—"

"I don't want to hear about your father!"

"My father is considering going to war. Those old fools at that town meeting last night, they don't know what they're up against. Only one of them seems prepared, and nobody was listening to her, so I came to you."

Autumn found herself wrong-footed. Again. "Your father is considering going to war against a supermarket?"

"You've all spent decades ignoring it, but the shape of this town, the magic you call 'planning permission,' it's vitally important. This town is the lynchpin that holds all the barriers in place."

"The barriers?"

"Like the one you stepped over."

"Was *pushed* over!"

"Don't start that again."

"If I could do that, how is it a barrier?"

"Well, obviously the barriers allow a certain amount of traffic, passage to those who know what they're doing, at the proper times and places. Did you ever go looking for that border again?"

"No."

"Oh, and I see that's actually true. Weird. If the barriers collapse completely, there'll be chaos, disaster, as everything from the other worlds tries to rush in and plunder at once. Rather than allow that, my father will intervene to establish order, with sword and spear and glamour. By 'glamour,' I don't mean he'll be—"

"I *know*."

"To human beings it won't look or feel like a war, it'll be more like . . . one of those modernist paintings you lot do, if it melted. Inside all your brains. Forever. That's the message I came to deliver: you have to get your people to vote the right way or, failing that, find some other way to stop this happening. If you don't sort this, we will."

It boggled Autumn to think cosmic powers from other worlds paid more attention to local news than she did. "I can't deliver some mad message to the whole town. They won't . . . believe me." Again. He was trying to put her through her ordeal again.

He looked disappointed in her. "I don't mind if my father goes to war," he said. "I get to take heads. I haven't had that pleasure in a while. I came back here because I was worried about you. About all of you." He sighed. "Look at you. Shaking. Furious. But if I asked you to come with me—"

"No. I can resist you now."

"I said 'ask.' And I won't ask. But you would." He switched his radio back on, and Autumn flinched, but now instead of the unearthly sounds of his home, it was playing smooth jazz. "Nice," he said. "We don't have that at home." He took a sudden, deliberate stride and once again, without her seeing where he went, he was gone.

Autumn slumped against the wall, breathing hard. It was all true. It was all true, and she had completely failed to deal. She needed help. No. No. They *all* needed help. Who was going to believe her? Could she even make herself try to convince . . . ? No. It didn't matter what happened to her, for everyone's sake she had to try. First she had to find Judith and tell her they were now on the same side. Because they'd make a great PR team: the mad woman and the old lady everyone hated. But where else could she start? Clasping her unicorn ornament to her, she rushed back into the shop and locked the door behind her.

4

Judith ran a line of silver paint, with several of the ingredients she'd bought from the magic shop in it, around the edge of her window sill. This was the last one. It was getting dark outside. She'd spent a couple of hours covering every entrance to the house, making sure she at least had a redoubt, somewhere to run back to if things tonight went pear-shaped. She had been thinking about possible allies, and had realised there was only one possibility, and that was going to be a bloody awkward conversation, but if she was going to go on the attack, she needed all the help she could get. She looked up at the sound of a knock on the door.

"That'll be your boyfriend," Arthur called from upstairs.

"If only!" Judith yelled back. She went to open the door, checking as she did so that the line she'd painted around it earlier was still intact. She opened the door to find nobody there. A meaningful absence of person. A sharp smell made her sneeze, a different scent to that of the figure who'd come from the woods, but just as troubling. She saw what she was smelling: in the middle of her front door had been painted, in red, the three lines of a downwards-facing triangle. She realised immediately what the shape signified. All you needed were white letters in a reassuring font across it and you had the Sovo brand logo. She grabbed her coat, called out to Arthur that she was just popping out for five minutes, and was out the door before he could say anything scathing in reply.

Autumn had marched around the town in the late afternoon dark, trying to find Judith, having realised that she had no idea where she lived. She'd hoped to find someone who knew her. She was about to look in on the Plough and ask Terry, who worked behind the bar there, when she saw, across the Market Place, Lizzie. She was standing beside the post box under the streetlight, a letter in her hand, and visibly hesitating. She was crying. Perhaps yesterday—earlier that day even—Autumn would have made sure Lizzie didn't see her and gone on her way. Now, feeling as vulnerable as she did, she didn't seem to have room for resentment. She knew now that the impossible things she'd studied were real. It didn't matter what Lizzie thought was true. As Lizzie seemed to be making herself raise the letter towards the slit in the box, Autumn found herself running across to her. "Hey," she shouted, "Lizzie, wait!"

Lizzie turned, startled. "I was just going to post this letter," she said, quickly wiping her eyes.

"Well . . . don't!"

"You don't even know what it is."

"No," and as she said it, Autumn found huge relief in still understanding her old friend, "but I know you don't want to post it."

Lizzie let herself be led into the Plough. They found the snug was empty and they could talk in private there, the only sound being the quiz machine. Autumn got them two pints of Arkell's 3B, the first sip of which was very welcome. "A lot's happened to me today," she said, sitting down facing Lizzie.

Lizzie found herself actually laughing. That Autumn could have dragged her in here having found her in that state and then led with what *she'd* been doing . . . that was very her. Very her was good right now. "Me too," she said, "I've come to a big decision I'm sure will please you—"

"No, listen. This is what I wanted to tell you before, only . . . has anything impossible ever happened to you?"

Lizzie had to take another drink and consider this change of pace for a moment. "I suppose the moments when I've . . . *thought* . . . I was having some sort of communication with God—"

Autumn waved aside the religious stuff. "I mean something that made you feel bad?"

Lizzie opened her mouth in exasperation at having her subtext run over yet again. Then she closed it again as she realised there *was* something. "Once I'd posted my *letter*—" Autumn gestured at her to get past that. "I was about to go back to the church and try to force myself to touch a large sum of money given to me as a donation for the poor."

Autumn's eyes narrowed, as if this wasn't quite what she was after, but she was too interested to let it go. "Why can't you?"

"I don't know. I've started to feel . . . that perhaps the world is just . . . chairs and tables and physical objects and that's all."

Again, Autumn didn't follow through on the implications of that. "So that means it's just money."

"Yes. I know. That's what I don't get about my own brain. Well done on putting your finger on that. Cheers." Lizzie took another deep gulp of her pint.

"Listen, this psychologist once asked a group of people if they'd sit in a chair that had belonged to a serial killer, that had been in his house—"

Lizzie shook her head. "No."

"Why?"

"I'd want it cleaned."

"It's been cleaned."

"Steam cleaned?"

"It's clean, okay?"

"Still, no."

"Because?"

"Because: euw."

"And almost everyone says that. When it's just a chair. I think that reaction is hardwired into peoples' brains, like they *know* there's something more to the world. I used to think that was just a sign that symbols were important."

Lizzie found herself astonished. "'Used to?' I thought you didn't believe in—?"

"That's the impossible thing that's happened to me today. Okay, listen . . ." Autumn started to tell her story, and Lizzie found she was going to need another pint.

Judith strode quickly through the twilight streets of Lychford, seeing the Sovo symbol painted, at uneven intervals, on roughly half the doors. One of the marked doors opened as Judith approached, and she realised the figure emerging was someone she vaguely new from the quiz nights, a woman called . . . was it Lydia something? In Judith's head she was labelled as "annoying woman who talks only about false teeth."

"Have you seen the state of your door?" Judith called.

"What?" said Lydia, turning to look. "Paint's peeling a bit . . ."

Judith realised she couldn't see the mark. "You're against Sovo, aren't you?"

Lydia confirmed that she was. Before she could ask any questions or find a way to mention her dentures, Judith continued on her way, matching marks on doors to "Stop the Superstore" posters in the windows. These were surely the addresses of everyone planning to vote against. She turned into Ford Street, heading south out of the Market Place, and stopped, then stepped back into the shadows when she saw what was up ahead.

A young woman in a business suit, who Judith vaguely

remembered from the meeting, had a paint pot in her hand, and was checking something, presumably addresses, on her phone. She confirmed her latest target, then walked up to the door and marked it with a well-practiced three slashes. Judith wondered if anyone else but her could see this job being carried out. Then she became aware that she was not alone, that someone stood at the corner with her. She didn't give the new presence the satisfaction of a reaction. "What are you really?" she asked.

David Cummings stepped from the shadows. "I've been very clear about my job title."

She couldn't see anything extraordinary about this man, any more than she had when he'd been on stage at the meeting, but, ah, there, now he wasn't concealing how big he really was. She could suddenly feel the gravity of him. He was holding himself back, even, letting only a little of himself extrude into the world. His true scale would cause panic in the streets. Judith had only twice in the past been anywhere near one of the great powers. She now had a primal urge to get down on her knees and beg for mercy. Well, sod that. "So it's not just foolishness on your part. You're doing this deliberately. Is Sovo some sort of front for—?"

"We're exactly who we say we are, doing exactly what we've told everyone we're planning to do."

"Apart from the bit about painting on opponents' doors."

He chuckled, entertained by her. "If they can't see it, what's the difference?"

"What are the symbols on the doors for?"

"You know, I've got tons of money to throw around. How would you fancy a Saga tour of the Caribbean for yourself and a friend, whoever that might be? Chance to get away? Start a new life? Before it's too late?"

She was pleased that he hadn't felt able to tell her what the symbols were for. "It would be too late, though. The world would have a bloody hole in it. Why do you *want* the barriers around the town to fall?"

"There's a word people in business use a lot: *disruptive*. The market can never be stable, the best it can be is falling apart in useful ways. Like the universe in general, really. To disrupt the market in your favour is now seen as being the ultimate achievement. Create a climate of absolute uncertainty, continual fear about enormous change, and you'll see people's . . . well, I was about to say 'true selves,' but they don't really have true selves, they're continually falling apart too . . . you'll see people concentrate on looking after themselves and their own, grabbing for familiar symbols. The right . . . *brands*, shall we say, can prosper hugely then, in the ultimate disruption."

"Oh, you'd enjoy that."

He looked genuinely hurt. "I'm not sure *enjoy* is the right word. I'm just doing my job. Looking forward to some time off, honestly, after the end of the universe. Now, are you sure we can't interest you in coming onside?"

Judith knew he could kill her with a glance. He was limited, though, by the role he'd taken on, by the rules of the game he'd decided to take part in. "Sorry, love," she said. "I'm too old for shop work." She marched off before he could tempt her with anything else. She didn't want him to see how much he'd scared her. She had to find her only ally, but before that, she had to have a go at getting rid of that symbol on her door.

After I came back to the . . . the real world," Autumn was saying to Lizzie, "I was in a psychiatric hospital for a while. I made the mistake of trying to tell people about the impossible beings I'd met."

"That's why you never got back in touch," whispered Lizzie. She didn't know what to make of what she was hearing. It was clear that, from what Autumn had told her about her "visit" from some sort of supernatural being today, and the dire, if vague, warning he'd delivered, her friend now believed utterly in the story she'd just told about where she'd been all that time. Was the bit about the psychiatric hospital the only thing that was true? Were their roles now going to be reversed, with Autumn the believer and her the sceptic? Her training had given her insight into how to deal with mental illness, but she didn't like the idea of having to apply that training to Autumn.

Autumn smiled the wry and somewhat bitter smile that Lizzie had seen when she'd come to see her, earlier—when she'd failed, she realised, to tell her about all this. "When you told people about the impossible beings *you'd* met, they gave you a job."

"Is this why you didn't want to step inside my church? Oh. You're not going to tell me you've become a . . ." She'd started to say the word and realised she had to finish, making sure she did so with every ounce of her attentiveness and positivity. "A vampire?"

"What? Of course not!"

"Of course not. Right."

"You're the one who thinks wine turns into blood!"

"Well, I don't, didn't, actually, in my brand of . . . and *now*—"

"It's just there's something about your church. When I walked up to that threshold, I . . . felt something. In those moments when I let myself believe in it, I've sometimes felt my time in that other world changed me, *tainted* me—"

"Oh no, oh no, that's so the opposite of what we . . . I . . . stood . . . stand for. You felt welcome when you stepped in, didn't you? Please tell me you did."

"I felt . . . like that building is . . . connected to something, and I can feel it. I sometimes feel it at other places in Lychford."

Lizzie blew out a long breath. She didn't know what to believe. "Perhaps I should show you this money."

"Was it maybe something to do with Cummings himself?"

"Well, he is a being of tremendous power and evil," said Judith, sitting down beside Lizzie and placing her pint on the table in one movement. "You get on your way, shopkeeper, I need to talk to the grown-up." By which she meant Lizzie.

"Sorry," said Lizzie, "we're in the middle of—"

"No time for that. My name, Reverend, is Judith Mawson. Did your predecessor tell you much about this town? Did he mention my name?"

"No." Lizzie had heard of the old woman, from a number of terrified parishioners. She was, she assumed, someone whom Autumn would have had as a customer, but the look on her friend's face was desperate, thankful.

"Listen," said Autumn, "I've been trying to find you—"

"You're talking over her thinking more seriously about my question."

Actually, Lizzie *was* thinking about it. Her predecessor, Frank, had left a very terse note, giving her the bare minimum of information. She'd asked the churchwardens about everything from the organist to the accounts, until she was sure no surprises awaited her. They had always had, though, she realised, a look on their faces as if they were waiting for someone else to tell her something awkward. "No, but—"

"I know it's all true," said Autumn. "A prince of the blood came to warn me. He says something terrible is going to happen."

Judith looked to Autumn with new interest. Lizzie was sure she was about to see the start of a beautiful folie à deux, and she wasn't sure she wanted that inflicted on her friend. "I'm afraid I'll have to insist—"

"Sorry about this," said Judith, "but we need to get past all that time-wasting incredulity." She grabbed Lizzie's nose between her fingers and viciously twisted before letting go. Lizzie yelled, blinded by tears of pain, furious.

Judith was looking at the blood on her fingers. She put them in her mouth, tasting it. "You never thought," she said, as if reading from a book she didn't understand, "that Joe was playing guitar with Jimi Hendrix."

Lizzie found the anger draining from her, replaced by sheer vertigo and rising fear. She looked to Autumn, who nodded, willing her to believe it. Lizzie found blood was running from her nose and fumbled for a tissue.

"No floundering," said Judith, "no arguing. Good. That's how a vicar of Lychford should be. Some of your predecessors found a packet of Oat So Simple an intellectual challenge. Now, come on, you too I suppose." She nodded a little reluctantly to Autumn. "It's time you knew everything." She threw back her pint in one long swallow, slammed it back onto the table, got up and headed out of the pub without looking over her shoulder.

"I'm going with her," said Autumn. "Lizzie, I have to know."

"Yeb," said Lizzie through the tissue. "I hab do doo."

Judith led them through the darkness to the church, which surprised Lizzie, because she couldn't imagine being taught anything about a space she'd already explored. On the way, she listened to Autumn's story, asking at intervals for more detail. Autumn only hesitated at the threshold of the building for a moment this time. Lizzie switched on the lights and Judith took them over to one of the enormous displays of blooms that the flower ladies provided to decorate the nave. "I should have come to see you when you first got here. I'd sort of guessed Frank hadn't done his duty in explaining the extra responsibilities of someone officiating here. It didn't seem urgent."

"You could have pinched her nose," said Autumn. "How does that work, anyway? Is there information in the blood, in the DNA maybe—?"

Judith stopped and visibly winced. "'DNA' my arse. If you're coming along, I don't want you coming out with bloody science all the time. You'll be looking at everything through the smallest window."

"The smallest window," said Autumn, "might have the clearest glass."

"It doesn't. It's muddy."

"But the other windows will stay as they are, but this window could be replaced by . . . a big set of French windows, when science catches up with magic."

Judith rolled her eyes. "I'm trying to show you the ineffable and you're planning an extension."

"Ibe reddy do libben," Lizzie said through her hanky.

"The flower ladies," said Judith, turning back to the display, "keep these refreshed for a reason, which they probably think these days is just about good taste." She picked up the enormous vase and hauled it aside.

Behind the flowers, Lizzie was surprised to see revealed a painting, faded colours on a surviving remnant of the original plasterwork of the church, part of what, for most of the building's life, would have been a vibrant background of many hues. The painting was a map of the town. It looked ancient.

Around the central crossroads of buildings were family names of outlying farms, some of which were still familiar. There was the church itself, there was the forest and the river.

Outside all of that, however, were rough borders in different colours that didn't correspond to anything Lizzie knew about the shapes of parishes or counties. Inside those areas were painted what looked like demons, strange dancing humanlike figures, even chaotic swirls, like storms. "This map of Lychford," said Judith, "dates back to when the church was built, in Saxon times, replacing a stone circle, which replaced a longbarrow, the remains of which are under the crypt." Lizzie knew of no records of such a barrow. "Here"—Judith pointed to the outlying features of the map—"are what borders Lychford—other realms, of the foul and the fair, the horrible and the wonderful, and some stuff beyond understanding." She said that as if it were a phrase that had been repeated to her. "You won't find these on a sat nav."

Lizzie looked to Autumn. She was staring at the map, her expression half relieved, half horrified. She had a hand on the end of a pew, as if she continually had to reassure herself of reality. Lizzie took that hand in hers.

"As the town grew around the river crossing," continued Judith, "and became a point where the farmers could sell their produce, locals who knew the craft realised that by building here they were upsetting a delicate balance that had been sorted out long before people came to Britain. That balance protected a very rare, perhaps unique crossing place, from which all these different worlds could be reached. Perhaps the people back then were skilled enough to work that out themselves, perhaps they were visited and given some sort of ultimatum. At any rate, they planned the town with that balance in mind, worked out exactly where to build, using the shape of what they made to seal off the borders and prevent any accidental blundering about. The church, when the Saxon shire reeve decided one was needed, was designed as a major part of that effort. You could say it's one of the pins that keeps things fastened."

"That's what I can feel," said Autumn.

"Ah, something rubbed off on you in fairyland. As well as the other way round."

Autumn stepped forward, and pointed at the place on the

map with the dancing figures. "*That's* where I went. That's . . ." She peered closer at one of the figures. "Oh my God. That's him. That's Finn."

Judith tutted. "And after meeting him, she still didn't believe! Is it really that hard to pay attention to what's shagging you?"

Autumn looked back to her, furious. "I could have used this bloody map a few years back. I could have used your help when I got home."

Judith's expression remained absolutely fixed—something that meant, Lizzie knew from dealing with many ladies of the older generation, that big emotions were moving underneath. "If I'd known," she said, "I'd have come to see you." She looked back to Lizzie before she was forced to register any further emotion from Autumn. "Because the church is part of the defences, the vicar and the others who know the secrets have always worked together."

"De ubbers?" asked Lizzie.

"Well . . ." Judith looked suddenly troubled. "Your churchwardens must know what the last vicar's traditionally meant to have told you, but if they believed it they'd have made sure. So, since old Mrs. Hitchmough moved to Bournemouth I suppose it's just me. I'm not the most sociable person. I've got issues I don't talk about and others wouldn't want to hear. Which, when summat terrible's about to happen, is just my bloody luck."

"Dabid Cubbings," said Lizzie, "he said—"

Judith grabbed her nose again and just as Lizzie was about to yell from the pain again, she realised that the pain had actually stopped and that her nose had stopped bleeding. She lowered her handkerchief. "He talked about changing the shape of the church."

"Makes sense."

"You said he was a being of tremendous power and evil, but I've looked him up. He's got a wife and family. He's on LinkedIn."

"Those are the worst sort. He's had himself incarnated. His wife and family probably aren't aware of what he is."

"Which is?"

"There are lots of names, none of them pleasant, some of which could lead you astray." She marched towards the door. "You'll learn a lot more where we're going."

As Judith led them down to the river walk, then under the bridge, picking her way with more enthusiasm than skill along the narrow path in the freezing dark, Autumn started to feel more and more afraid. Suddenly, without even a torch to help her, Judith veered off into the darkness of the forest. She immediately fell over a branch, but was pushing herself up using her stick before Lizzie or Autumn could reach her. "This path should be safe," she said. "It's changed, but only a bit. I still know it."

"Is there some rule," said Lizzie, her breath billowing in the air, "against using a torch?"

"Of course not. I just . . . thought I could do without." She allowed Lizzie to find an app that made the screen of her iPhone light up, and, having been shown how to hold it, kept going, keeping Lizzie and Autumn close enough to catch her if she fell.

"I haven't been out here much," said Autumn, "not since . . . you know—"

"Since you became a Fairy Wife. As they call it."

"—but this footpath only goes to Borton."

"If you walk it the usual way, it does. Look." Autumn followed her pointing stick and saw, in the light of the moon that was now rising over the hill, that a crossing with a wooden signpost lay ahead. She felt nauseated to see it.

"That's . . . not usually there," said Lizzie. She went up to the sign and touched it, like it was something out of Narnia. Autumn hated seeing that reaction. That was what she'd felt on the way in, too. One of the direction indicators on the old sign said "Borton," pointing in front of them. The other, going off at an angle, was blank. Or was it? Autumn felt she could see something there, but it was like when you looked at the stars and saw the fainter objects only out of the sides of your eyes. When you looked directly, they vanished again, and so did this.

She saw Judith looking appraisingly at her. "I can't see it," she said.

"At least," Judith said, "you know summat's there. There are three ways to walk the old paths. One is by sacrifice." She pulled a pin from her hair, and struck it across her own thumb like striking a match, a worryingly practiced gesture that produced a flick of blood. She squeezed her hand into a fist, then put the bloodied palm flat on the pathway that led off at an angle. "Or there's an appeal to a higher power," she nodded to Lizzie. "What you do. Or you can use what's already there, manipulate it, like judo or summat. I've heard that if you live where there are lots of people there are other options too, but that's all for a hedge witch like me."

Autumn couldn't help herself. This stuff was like a lifeline for her rationality to cling to. She was, she realised, going to have to keep using logic to deal with it, as she always had before, or she'd be lost. "That's all really interesting. If there are rules, then didn't you ever want to work out *why* there are rules, how it all connects—"

"To science? That was going to set us all free, but here we are, free to buy the latest gadget, free to be watched on CCTV and Google Whatever It Is." Judith was suddenly in Autumn's face, animated by an anger Autumn hadn't seen in her before. "This stays secret, for the people who don't have much, who live in the gaps, who have to find some way to get by. If you start blabbing about what I show you today—"

"No, no." Autumn held up hands, not wanting to hear whatever threat Judith was about to come out with. She'd already spent so much of her life being scared by magic, she hated that the old woman was scaring her too. "Out of respect to you, okay? I will deal with this my own way, but I won't go calling up the *Sun* and trying to get them to believe it. As if."

"You say," said Lizzie, who'd been following, looking fascinated, "that big companies shouldn't have this, but aren't Sovo a big company?"

"Sovo are just doing what they always do, unaware. Dave Cummings is riding them. You still don't really believe, do you?"

"It's . . . a lot to take in."

"Never mind, our next stop will sort that out." She led them round two turns through the trees, and stopped at the edge of a clearing. She struggled to switch off the iPhone light until Lizzie showed her how to do it, then as their eyes adjusted to the dark, she pointed. "There."

In the clearing stood a well. It looked simple, ancient. Autumn felt a great weight to it, like she had at the threshold to the church. There was no winch, but on the ground sat a metal bucket with a rope. "This is where," said Judith, "I lost my innocence. I was shown this by my mates, the older girls who played in the forest and had come to see the ways. Over the years they've all gone. Stupid old woman, never passing it along like I should have done. If I'd had a daughter—" She stopped, shook her head. "My mother knew, and she tried to stop me learning. She was scared, poor soul. My friends brought me here one summer night, and I wish it was summer now, but those that have no choice have to make do."

She went to pick up the bucket and threw it into the well, letting the rope trail behind it. It turned out there was a lot of rope in that coil. It kept going as Autumn looked incredulously at Lizzie. Finally, there was a distant splash. Judith began to haul it back up again. "This," she said, "will let you see things like I do. I had an inkling of it, like Autumn does, but this opened my eyes." She brought the bucket to the lip of the well. "Right then. Clothes off."

"What?" said Lizzie.

"No." Autumn shook her head.

"I'm really not up for—"

"It's bloody freezing!"

Judith sighed. "All right, all right. This water is from the river that runs between the worlds. It lets you see the truth. Is that what you want?"

"Yes," said Autumn.

"I want," said Lizzie, "to understand what's going on. So, okay, do you want us to drink it, or—?"

Judith threw the bucket of water over them.

Autumn shrieked at the shock of the impact. The cold went right through her coat, into her clothing. She was about to yell like Lizzie was doing when all of a sudden . . . it was like a curtain had fallen away from her vision. What had been a bare old stone well was now shining with symbols in golden inlay. The forest, stark and leafless, pulsated with the deep, hidden warmth of every tree. The moon was enormous, full of detail that was so fascinating it felt like it threatened to draw her up into it. The stars beyond it had infinite complexity, each with an individual life. Autumn had taken her fair share of illegal substances, back in the day. This was different to all of them. This was the drug that was everyday vision being cleansed from her body. This was what where Finn had taken her had been like, and with that thought didn't come fear, but enormous relief. The strange water in her clothes had become not a horrible burden but warming. She could feel it not evaporating, exactly, but sinking into her skin, becoming part of her, vanishing from the cloth as it sought out her flesh.

"That's why I said take your clothes off," said Judith. "For the next twelve months or so you'll see like I do. Then, if you want to, you can come back for another dose. Assuming any of us are still here."

"It's real, Lizzie," whispered Autumn.

Judith laughed at their expressions. "Just like my first time," she said. "Only without the lesbianism. Probably no time for that now."

"No," agreed Autumn, alarmed.

"Right," nodded Lizzie quickly, then seemed to feel compelled to add, "not that there's anything wrong with that."

"You don't have to, I found out, afterwards," said Judith. "But they didn't tell me at the time. It was the sixties."

Lizzie looked like she'd suddenly realised something that troubled and excited her at the same time. "If I can see this . . ." She came to a decision. "I'm sorry," she said, and she turned and ran back down the path.

"Lizzie!" Autumn shouted after her.

"It's all right," said Judith. "I know where she's going."

5

They found Lizzie in her church, walking back and forth, desperately looking around. She turned to look at them almost accusingly. "Nothing." She took them over to the organ stool and opened it, and Autumn was startled to see just how much money she'd been talking about. She'd found that the miraculous detail and sense of hidden wonders had faded a lot when they'd returned to the normal path and especially in the town, but she'd still felt a sense of additional meaning and gravity at certain places, this church included. There was no divine presence here, though, not that she could feel, and the money was just money.

Judith put a hand on Lizzie's shoulder. "The higher powers choose when to show themselves."

"If you worked with my predecessor—"

"I don't know whether or not what you believe in is true, love. All I know is, it's your job to help protect the people in this town."

Autumn watched Lizzie take a deep breath, then nod. "What do you want us to do?"

Lizzie tried to keep a calm expression on her face as Judith led them into town. She wanted to jump every time she felt the presence of an underground river or saw some extra dimension to someone's expression as they trudged past. It would take some getting used to. The trouble was, as Judith had realised, it hadn't dealt with the enormous holes at the centre of her life. Indeed, it had emphasised them. "Can we see . . . dead people?" she asked. Which got a puzzled look from Autumn.

Judith took a moment to answer. "Sometimes," she said carefully. "But now I need you to see this." On random doors down the street, red symbols were shining. The symbols . . . it was like they stank. They had the same feeling about them that made you recoil from something that had been in your fridge too long.

Judith told them about her encounter with Cummings, and Lizzie felt glad she could at last bring something useful to the table. "It's like the Passover," she said, "the story in the Old Testament. The Angel of Death kills the firstborn of everyone who hasn't obeyed God's instructions to put a marking in sheep's blood on their door."

"God wanted that?" said Autumn.

"Yeah. He's changed a lot. But this is the other way round, right? It's a threat to the people *with* markings, if these are the ones who are against Sovo. It's a reversal, like an upside-down cross."

They went up to one of the houses that didn't seem to have anyone home. Lizzie was acutely aware that here she was, in her clerical collar, in which she didn't even allow herself to have more than a couple of pints, standing with two well-known local "characters," staring at people's doors. She could feel, actually literally now, the curtains twitching. The paint on the door felt warm to their faces. None of them wanted to touch it. "What if we got rid of the marks?" asked Autumn.

"Oh," Judith said brightly, "I hadn't thought of that."

"Sarcasm," said Lizzie, "about what is and isn't possible: not allowed now."

"I scrubbed my door," said Judith, "with every magical cleansing agent I could think of. *And* Cillit Bang! I just ended up burning my Brillo pads."

"I guess just painting over it—?" began Lizzie. Judith was silent. "Aha!" said Lizzie.

"You said sarcasm wasn't allowed," said Judith. "You two had better watch out about your own doors when you get home. Now we can see this stuff, we can be burned by it too. Sometimes ignorance is bliss."

Lizzie felt a little awkward. "I had to keep a bit above it all, no sign for me."

"I, erm, was *for* the store . . . ," Autumn said. "It's not like they were going to sell magic stuff. Although maybe *now* . . ."

Lizzie decided there was something she could do. She looked around to make sure nobody was out on the dark street at this moment, then stepped up to the door. "In the name of the father—" She'd raised her hand to make the sign of the cross, but she found that she just couldn't complete it. What was this? Was some powerful force stopping her? No, just a feeling of . . . absurdity. Weakness. She *knew* it wouldn't work.

"This mark is made of actual paint," said Judith, gently, "no matter how weird and special that paint might be. If you could get a mark off a door by raising your finger—"

"That would be an actual miracle," said Lizzie. "I never was sure what I thought about those."

"We need to take a scientific approach," said Autumn. "No, wait, hear me out. You say it's actual paint. So let's try to find out more about it." She looked around, as if for inspiration, then found it. She pointed at the "Stop the Superstore" sign in the window of the house. "Can we get hold of one of those posters?"

Jade Lucas felt she was doing okay, and with how things were at the moment, okay was better than okay. Okay meant she was just about up to the limit on her credit cards, but she paid the rent, and she wasn't in trouble with logbook or payday lenders like a lot of her mates. She'd been junior management at Sovo in Slough when Mr. Cummings had visited one lunchtime to give a pep talk. They'd all expected it to be the usual bollocks, but he'd been funny, and kind of harsh, and everyone agreed after that he'd been straight with them.

He'd talked about austerity not as something politicians talked about, something that'd be gone when the economy got better, but as a way to live your life. If you looked after number one, then you'd do better, and you'd be able to look after the people you loved. Jade didn't love anyone in particular, and he'd made her feel better about that, so she'd decided to take him up on one of his points about seizing every advantage. She'd walked beside him as he headed to his car and had said she'd do anything to get higher up in the company. He'd nodded, unsurprised, like this had happened before, and had asked her to get in with him, saying he'd clear it with her boss. In the back of his car, she'd been startled when he'd asked her to literally kiss his arse, but had hesitated only a moment before doing so, wondering how much further he'd want to go, and whether she'd really meant "anything." He'd been satisfied at that, however, and had offered her a contract, which she'd signed immediately.

She'd been moved, at the company's expense, to a nice new house near a local hub in Swindon, where she'd become part of an unusual sales strike force. They were called upon to do the weirdest things, most of which turned out to be a laugh, like today, where they'd been drawing the company logo on people's doors. Alec, her immediate boss, had said nobody would mind or notice, and they hadn't. Jade felt she'd learned a lot about human nature since joining the strike force. Now she was doing one last sweep before they all went back to the hotel, then off to a club in Gloucester, where hopefully there'd be some snort to be had, because she was knackered.

She'd finished her list, and she'd been told to also look out for houses not on it which now displayed anti-Sovo posters, the floating voters. There was one now, to her annoyance, in the window of . . . a shop that sold magic things. Used to the idea that nobody would object, Jade opened her pot of paint that smelled like the most gorgeous coffee, dipped in her brush, and made to mark the door.

Which was when some black girl in an amazing dress and a bomber jacket opened the door and grabbed the pot and brush. "Not today, thank you," she said, and before Jade could react, her tools had been snatched inside and the door slammed in her face. Jade hammered on it, horrified at the thought of what might happen to her if she had to go back and tell Alec she'd lost her tools.

"Any trouble here, ma'am?"

She turned to see a policeman looking at her, a wry look on his face. She considered for a second saying she'd had some things stolen, but then she'd have to explain what she'd been doing. Alec didn't have to know. They just threw the stuff into a bin bag anyway, to be taken back to central office. Not telling him: that was looking after number one. "No trouble," she said, and headed off, wanting to put distance between her and that shop, and looking forward to her night out.

Lizzie was looking around at a workshop full of bubbling test tubes and beakers with things dripping into them. There were what looked like ancient diagrams Blu-Tacked to the walls, but the back room of Autumn's shop looked more like a school science lab than a wizard's chamber. A moment ago, Autumn had returned triumphant, the pot of paint and brush in hand. They'd had to wait an hour, the lights on the shop front turned off, before someone had taken the bait. Lizzie applauded, and Judith nodded, one eyebrow raised, in appreciation. "So," Lizzie went up to her, gesturing to the equipment, "this is where the magic happens."

"How long have you been waiting to say that?"

"Since you told me you owned the shop. But, you know: trauma."

"I had the workshop set up in my old house before I had the shop. I like making my own potions."

"It's all too scientific," said Judith.

"What do you use? A cauldron?"

"Obviously."

Lizzie picked up the brush, sniffing the red goo. The pungent smell made her cough. "We need to do some sort of chemical analysis," she said, "find out what's in this stuff. I can't . . . see . . . anything weird, not with my new senses, I mean."

"It's mostly red paint," said Autumn, "with a few herbs I stock in the shop."

Lizzie was impressed. "How did you work that out so quickly?"

Autumn held up the tin and pointed. "List of ingredients."

Lizzie saw she was right. "Wow. The powers of evil are kind of thorough."

"And it turns out, according to this, that the same herbs which went into my invisibility potion really can make something invisible."

"With the proper incantations and sacrifice during mixing," said Judith, "and the force of belief, which you wouldn't have been able to add."

"You sold an invisibility potion?" asked Lizzie.

"It was designed to provide solace, comfort, a sense of getting away from it all . . ."

"But not *invisibility*," said Judith.

"There was a disclaimer on the bottle," said Autumn. "Can we get on?"

Judith picked up a piece of paper and began to draw. "If what's in this stuff is just to make it invisible, then there has to be summat else going on to add other effects, like harming anyone who's got it on their door. Sacrifice and incantation will have gone into setting that up. The shape of the symbol might be important." She held up a drawing of the Sovo logo. "It has an unsettling aspect."

"Meaning—?" asked Lizzie.

"That's the sort of thing I say when I have no idea what I'm going on about."

"We can't get rid of the marks," began Lizzie.

"And painting over them won't make any difference," said Judith.

"And if this isn't about the paint, no amount of analysis can help us," said Autumn.

"We've got three days until the meeting," said Lizzie. "Sovo seem to be going to do something terrible to those planning on voting against, or maybe just stop them leaving their houses. If Dave Cummings gets his way and the new store gets built, it sounds like it might literally be the end of the world. So . . . what can we do?"

They looked at each other. None of them had an answer.

The following evening, Shaun Mawson decided he'd go to sample one of Sunil Mehra's excellent chicken dansaks, and also perhaps two or three Cobra beers, rude not to, and at the same time, have a chat with the proprietor. So they found a table, and Shaun, while liberally distributing lime pickle on his papadum, made his position clear. "Okay, so she might be mad as toast, she believes a lot of weird stuff, her cooking's terrible, and she wears the same cardigans for weeks, until they smell like diesel, for some reason—"

"You're talking to me about your mother? Oh, dear." Sunil raised a hand to his waiter. "Keep the Cobra coming for PC Mawson."

"I'm here to say I think Mum *needs* something more in her life. Even more so at the moment. I'm here to say . . . don't get discouraged. Okay?"

Sunil looked as if he was having trouble formulating a response, but before he could, someone else arrived at the table. It was Maureen, the mayor. Shaun had noted her on the way in, eating on her own, looking like she hadn't slept in days. She'd barely acknowledged his greeting. These days, every such hello must for her be either a gesture of support or the start of a row. "Excuse me," she said, "I couldn't help overhearing. This is difficult—"

Sunil had a chair brought over. "Please," he said, "it's everyone's night for difficult conversations. If you'd like me to leave you two to talk . . . I'd be delighted."

"No, because, well, I gather you and Judith are great friends, Mr. Mehra, and like Shaun I'm glad to see that. I just wanted to ask . . . oh dear, I shouldn't—"

Shaun had heard what everyone else in town had, that Maureen had taken money to support Sovo. He'd waited for anyone to allege it to him or to his superiors on an official basis, but the lack of such an approach had presumably meant that those opposed to the store had failed to find anything solid they could offer him. He'd always liked Maureen, because his mum had, to the tiny degree she liked anyone, but now he wasn't feeling especially gracious toward her. "If you've got something to say about Mum—"

"I saw her yesterday evening, going around town, looking at people's doors. Just going right up to them and staring at them. She was dragging the new vicar and that girl from the magic shop around with her, like she was trying to persuade them about something. I've seen her talking to someone who wasn't there—"

"I'm not sure I want to hear this." Mum hanging around with those two fitted in with her usual eccentricities, and when she'd called him about the magic shop the other day, there really had been someone trying to get in, though it had taken Shaun's eyes a moment to adjust to the gloom and see her, just like Mum had, oddly, said it would.

"No, please, I'm not saying she's like that all the time, I know she isn't, she's just . . . tough and a bit eccentric, and I like that. I just think . . . it's getting to all of us. So many people in this town are breaking under the strain, and I . . . I don't know what to do. What I'm saying is, she needs someone to talk to right now, and the way she looked at me the other day I know I can't . . ." She trailed off, then closed her eyes, as if trying not to cry, then had to quickly get up. "Excuse me," she said. "I've left some money." Then she was off and out the door.

Shaun looked carefully back to Sunil. "Now, that made what's happening with Mum sound a bit more serious than it is . . ."

Sunil sighed. "How long have I known your mother? Business as usual, by the sound of it."

Shaun made himself smile, but he wondered—given what he'd seen in the town just lately, with rows breaking out in the queue for the post office, people getting hate mail, postings on the town's website forum that had for the first time made the webmistress decide on a moderation policy—if whichever way the vote went, any of them could look forward to business as usual.

Lizzie took time, in the days before the meeting, to go and see her parishioners, particularly those she knew had symbols painted on their doors. What she most heard was a formless anger about how things were changing so fast, how someone had to stand up to the big companies who thought they ran everything. With her collar on, Lizzie still didn't feel able to agree out loud.

Those she talked to who wanted the store to come here had hardly embraced evil. They talked about how hard things were, how they needed to shop more cheaply without spending a lot of money on petrol, how they and their relatives needed the jobs Sovo would provide. There was something of a class divide there. Those who weren't well off tended to back the store on the basis of economic survival.

As Lizzie had seen so many times with victims, the harder your life had been, the harder it was to give yourself room for ethical choices.

So were born cycles of abuse.

Both sides had friends across the divide, people they were having trouble talking to. Lizzie went door to door, causing many raised eyebrows about her sudden presence on the doorsteps of especially the elderly. Everywhere she went, she asked people to keep talking to her.

She saw occasional wonders, with her new senses, in peoples' homes: animated love of beloved teddy bears, figures of departed loved ones with stony or caring faces. Those had scared her, though she hadn't shown it. She'd gone back to the vicarage, after leaving Autumn's workshop, wondering if she'd see Joe there, almost hoping. He hadn't been there. Something had changed, though: she now had a Sovo symbol on her front door.

They listened closely, and they worked fast.

She kept in touch with Autumn and Judith, heard they were both researching, trying to discover what exactly Sovo was attempting to do. All Lizzie could think of was how useless research would have been in the week before Passover. All she herself could do was attempt to pray, and she found she still didn't have it in her to do that. She wanted to go and take the money that still sat untouched in the collection plate and give it to the poor. She still couldn't, though Joe, in her dreams, was now yelling at her that she should.

"Are you my conscience now, my whole religion?" she angrily asked the memory of Joe, when she woke on the day of the council meeting and the deciding vote. "Is a single push of my hands why I do things now?"

Perhaps she hoped that the catastrophe to come, or preventing it, would confirm her faith, though she knew that was a selfish thought. The letter to the bishop remained unsent, but still sat in the out tray on her desk.

Judith was getting increasingly desperate. She found the strain of it getting to her old body, making her shoulders ache, making her want to weep. The combination of incantation, purpose, shape, and whatever sacrifices had gone into the symbols on the doors was a code she couldn't crack. Nor could she think of anything which might get, for example, everyone who was for Sovo to leave town before the vote. It would take power beyond hers, and what little the novices could add, to get people to act against their own fervent wishes.

Sovo seemed to be doing only one thing, hinging everything on the mundane matter of tonight's vote, and presumably trying to influence it, exactly the sort of drama one expected from the major powers.

She had extended, through potion and ritual, all her senses, and found nothing sinister about the company or their representatives, apart from Cummings. So whatever they were doing depended on him. There were three approaches one could take: sacrifice, appeal to a higher power, or manipulation. She tried some experimental sacrifices: she pulled a tooth from her mouth and gave the pain to the forge of the fates. She prostrated herself before the aspects of the Goddess, before Lugus of the Skilful Hand, before, in final desperate gestures, T.S. Eliot and Ringo Starr. She could not think of any means to achieve manipulation.

She would pull some ancient thought out of her feeble excuse for a brain, then find it connected to nothing useful. She had made the mistake, for so many years, of keeping her knowledge in her head. So this morning she had decided she had almost certainly forgotten something important, and had gone up into her attic and found her old trunks containing the diaries she'd kept as a youth. She'd indexed them, she remembered. She was pretty sure that everything in the index had long ago become second nature to her. Certainly there was nothing under P for Protection that she didn't now do offhandedly, and nothing that could be applied to those doors to counteract whatever nastiness Sovo had planned for those inside. She ran her finger down the alphabet, and stopped at K.

K for Kill.

She found she was holding her breath. She flipped to the entry, and found something pressed between the pages. A twig. She'd remembered, she'd realised, somewhere at the back of her head. She'd tried to forget the boy, what he'd done to her. His name had been Robin. It was his fault . . . she didn't want to think about the curse he'd placed on her. She didn't need to. She lived with it every day. Robin had been from Lancaster, and he'd boasted of what he could do, and she'd been so bloody impressed, hadn't she? She'd gotten him to show her. They'd buried the squirrel together, buried it deep.

Could she do this? She had only this day left, and no other ideas. No time for second thoughts, no time for conscience. She came down from the loft and went to get a spade.

On her way out, the implement over her shoulder, she checked in with Arthur. He was on the verge of his afternoon nap. She wondered, distantly, what an invasion of all that was impossible would mean for him. "What would you do tonight," she asked him, "if you were me?"

"Stay home and look after me, you old cow."

"Right. Now I know what not to do." Before he could start to yell, she was out the door and heading for the woods.

Autumn had felt that the most obvious way to learn about the Sovo symbol was to experiment on the one on her own door. She used every incantation and aid to focus she knew about, now with, she had to admit, an added expectation that they might have results in the physical world. Nothing changed the marking. She tried to cool it, using everything from ice to fragrances that suggested winter. Nothing worked. She had a sudden thought of corporate espionage, hacking into Sovo's computer, like in the movies, though she didn't know anyone who could do that, and looked up where the label said the paint was made, but it turned out to be somewhere in Taiwan, with a website that defied Google translation. The ingredients listed on the tin were reasonably rare: amaranth, Spanish Moss, mullein, valerian root, vetivert . . . you could find galangal in Waitrose, and a few of the others in Holland & Barrett, but most of them in processed form, not the originals that the recipe seemed to demand. In parts of the United States you could go out and pick Spanish moss, but that wasn't true in Britain. Still, the Internet would bring everything to one's door.

She checked her ingredient wholesalers online, and found to her surprise that supplies of several of the herbs had been reduced to zero, with the red "reordering, more soon" lettering beside the checkboxes. She made a couple of calls and found that bulk purchasers had raided all the major depots. Would Sovo really need that much of this stuff to daub even every door in one small town? It wasn't like they were doing this all over the country. Judith had gone on about how unique Lychford was. She checked her own shelves: there were only small amounts of a few of the relevant ingredients.

Then she realised. All those new customers in the last couple of weeks, all seeming to want the ability to vanish. They hadn't been here as individual shoppers, they'd been Sovo workers, buying up her stock to write invisible signs on doors. She slumped on the work bench, annoyed at how that had gotten past her, but then a new thought came to her. Sovo didn't need this stuff themselves. They just didn't want anyone else having it. Which meant there must be some way it could be used against them.

She went to the paint pot, and found almost nothing left in it. She'd used up a lot of it in her experiments. Still, it didn't matter how much she had if she didn't know what to do with it. The idea of what she could actually do, and the idea of where she might get the ingredients to do it came together in her mind in one terrible moment. She had to put a hand onto the bench to support herself. How could she even be contemplating this?

Judith had said this working, whatever it was, had required sacrifice. So sacrifice could be used against it. There was an obvious sacrifice she could make.

If she was going to do it, it had to be done today. She didn't see she had a choice. She pulled on her coat and headed for the door, and after she'd locked up, she called Judith and then Lizzie and left messages, sharing her discoveries and her plan. It was possible she wouldn't see either of them again.

6

Judith found the place in the woods surprisingly quickly. Every tree had its history visible, and golden threads of information shone between them, leading her down the years to her memories. He'd been so beautiful. Ridiculous. Nasty. Spouting such bollocks. He'd told her he loved her and she'd just said that must be great. He didn't get the words he was after, but she didn't leave him with anything to complain about. Or so she'd thought. He'd stormed off, and it was only later, when she met Arthur, she'd discovered the curse he'd placed on her, what she'd lived with ever since. That had made her how she was, she supposed, if that was how personalities really worked.

She found the place they'd buried the squirrel. It was still a black pit in the world of her greater senses, still stank of contamination. She'd protected herself with silver, dabbed on her wrists, but to her eyes a halo of shining armour. She dug hard and swiftly, her old body screaming at her, her willpower letting her ignore it.

She found the squirrel. It was a skeleton, but it was still being killed by what Robin had infested it with from that twig. It hissed its little skeletal mouth at her, in torment. She harvested the black tarlike stuff with a spoon from the back of her cutlery drawer, one she was willing to throw out, and gathered it into a velvet bag that squealed and squirmed in her hands. Then she contained the velvet in several ziplock sandwich bags and was finally satisfied that death couldn't escape.

She gave the squirrel all the peace she could with water and words of release, but still couldn't quiet it. She hadn't expected to be rid of her old sins that easily. She covered it again with earth as swiftly as she could, and, propped up by her stick, headed home with her awful prize.

She wondered, as she often had, what had become of Robin. Those who played with such magic usually got eaten by it. She stopped at the signpost that indicated the way back to Lychford and read the sign which Autumn hadn't been able to make out on the way to the well: *All Other Routes*. All of them, they had that right.

She realised there was something standing in the bushes nearby, and turned to look at it. It was the thing that had killed Eric Parker—that had also been the wisp that had first tried the town's defences. It was now fully formed, a silhouette of a man, a pit in human form, a whole demon. It smelled of piss and broken promises.

Judith prepared herself for it to attack, but instead it simply raised an arm and indicated she should proceed. From the bushes around it stepped many others of its kind.

They were biding their time, she realised. They could afford to wait. Sometime after 7 p.m. tonight they'd be able to walk into Lychford and harvest as they pleased.

Unless Judith could bring herself to do a terrible thing.

Autumn had never before felt such fear as on that early afternoon, as she ventured into the woods. She hadn't gone by the paths Judith had shown them, but into the parts of the forest she remembered mainly because she'd taken care never to go back there. With her new senses, it felt even more like she was stepping into a nightmare. The forest loomed over her and confirmed with every stride that she was deliberately walking back into what had destroyed her life.

She found herself fighting to stop jogging downhill, her boots slipping on the carpet of decaying leaves, as, after a point, every angle of the forest floor led to what was ahead. She fell just as she saw it and scrambled back onto her feet. Here was what those without her new senses could never find. Across two stark and leafless trees was hung a garland of blossoming flowers. In the gap between the trees it was summer. Blue sky shone there, and here was the smell of heat and nature that took her stomach right back there, and . . . oh, God, there it was, very quietly, that music.

She made herself walk right up to the edge of it, feeling the volume increase as pressure fell away in her ears, as if she were taking off in an aircraft. She could see, over the low garland, lost in a summer mist, the shapes of buildings beyond. She knew what lay inside those buildings. She knew the way back to the centre of her nightmare. "Finn!" she called.

No reply.

She was sure, with her new senses, that he must have heard her. She'd felt that shout connect. She knew what he wanted her to do, what she had to do if she was going to save everything. "Let me come back with enough time to do it," she said, and she didn't know who to, maybe to Lizzie, to the higher love Lizzie represented. "Let me come back." And she stepped, of her own free will, over the border.

Lizzie spent the afternoon going round the pubs, in her collar, gauging opinion. She saw Autumn had left a voicemail on her phone, but when she listened to it, it was just static that, to her new hearing, seemed to have a mocking tone to it. The sound of it chilled her. Had they done something to harm Autumn? The Sovo workers had taken up a corner in the Railway, and were politely declining offers of drinks and ignoring punters who wanted to have a go at them. The meeting was due to start at 7 p.m.

Lizzie went and stood on the steps of the town hall as people headed in, the whole town, it looked like, including those she knew were planning to vote against, a bleak-looking Mrs. Parker, in the midst of her grief, among them. So the symbols on the doors hadn't stopped them leaving their houses or, so far, done them harm.

Suddenly, she saw Judith. The old lady had a forlorn look on her face, shaking her head at whatever her son, walking beside her in uniform, was trying to say to her. Lizzie arrived as he left to resume his post as crowd control. "Why haven't you called? Isn't there anything we can do? Have you seen Autumn?"

Judith licked her lips, moistening them against the cold. She seemed not to want to meet Lizzie's gaze. "I got a message from her, which I couldn't hear. They'd done something to erase it."

"Judith, what's wrong?"

"Forgive me, Mother, for I have sinned."

"Okay . . . but we really should do this in private—"

She finally looked at her, with some of her old wryness. "I wasn't talking to you."

"What's going on? What's the plan?"

"I'm going to do the only thing I can do, and you mustn't have anything to do with it."

Lizzie grabbed her arm. "I'm not going to step away. Not after all you've shown me."

Judith looked angry, but then a sad smile appeared on her face. "On your own head be it, Reverend."

Maureen Crewdson sat on stage and made herself watch as everyone she knew in town, everyone she didn't know, perhaps everybody, filed into the hall, and filled every corner of it. The local media, such as they were, had turned out—a couple of reporters and someone from Radio Gloucestershire carrying a microphone. Even the teenagers who sat on the roundabout at the park were here, presumably lured by the possibility of violent conflict. Or perhaps this was all Sovo's doing. Mr. Cummings had smiled when he said he expected a big turnout. When Maureen had become mayor it had seemed like a reasonably fun thing for a community-minded person to take on. All she had to do, she thought, was keep her sensible hat on, and the challenges were all issues she knew very well from her voluntary work. Then Sovo had arrived.

She had genuinely been onside at first, and so when David Cummings had offered to pay her "expenses," which had sorted her worries about keeping her old mum in the care home she liked, she'd only hesitated a moment: she was being paid to support a cause she supported anyway. They could waste their money on her if they liked. This was obviously just how grown-ups did things.

However, as it became clear the issue was tearing the town apart, she'd started to have her doubts. She'd started to worry about how she could tell those in the anti camp that she was listening to them when she'd been paid not to.

When she put some difficult questions to Cummings, he'd said they had to be very careful who knew about the bribe. He'd actually used that word. If people gossiped, he'd said, she could lose her job, even go to prison, and what would happen to her mum then?

She'd gradually become sure that word had gotten out, that people were gossiping, from the looks on the faces of her former friends, and her colleagues in the town council. The last straw had been when Judith Mawson—her neighbour, who everyone thought of as this rude old battleaxe with mental health issues, but who had started knocking on Maureen's door when Maureen's husband had died—had suddenly gotten that awful look on her face. Now here Maureen was, trying to keep a calm expression, while everyone who hated her sat down in front of her and waited for her to be the Judas they expected her to be. It wasn't as if the other side loved her for what she'd done either.

Beside her, she felt David Cummings sit down. She knew he was smiling. She didn't turn to look.

She watched as Judith entered, the new vicar with her. The reverend seemed to be urgently asking her about something, with such a fearful expression—not something you ever saw on a vicar. She was obviously horrified about whatever Judith had told her. That terrible look on Judith's face too. All the horror of this moment, she was wearing it. Sunil had come in at the other end of the hall, looking around for Judith and failing to find her. She wished desperately that those two might find some happiness, that at least she'd done some good trying to bring them together. Two rows back, there was Sheila Parker, already crying, comforted by supporters who were glaring at Maureen, as if Eric Parker's death was her fault too. She had to look away. She had to run this meeting the way Cummings had told her to, had to let all the other bribes he'd doubtless made have their influence, had to keep up the pretence of democracy. She had no way out. She got to her feet.

"Everyone," she began, "thank you for coming. If you look around you, I don't think we're missing anyone with an interest in this matter. Does anyone know anyone who hasn't got here yet, who ought to be here?" This was the wording Cummings had insisted on.

"My Eric!" shouted Sheila Parker, and there was applause.

It took Maureen a moment before she could continue. She ran through the usual business of a council meeting, with thankfully nothing much in the way of reports or other motions, the councillors having for once realised the crowd would get restive if someone started grandstanding about drainage at the cricket club. Finally, they got to the matter at hand. "Since we're all here, I have to tell you, the council have been having a series of . . . sometimes fraught . . . meetings about the matter of Sovo building a store here." Cheers and yells. "It's time for the vote, though I think I know which way it's going to go." She read out the official wording of the proposal and asked for a show of hands for those in favour. Six of the twelve councillors on stage beside her raised theirs. She took a deep breath. "The council are divided equally, so the deciding vote comes down to . . . me." There was, as Cummings had told her there would be, a roar of disapproval. She talked over it, kept saying it until they listened. "But I don't want to make my . . . my choice overrule the will of the people of this town. Okay?" They were listening now; this was odd. "Since everyone's here, I'm going to ask all of *you* to vote, a simple show of hands, and I'm going to cast my vote with whichever side has the majority. I hope in so doing I will put an end to the conflict that's done us . . . done us so much damage." They gradually started to make approving noises. They thought that was fair. Of course they did. That was the plan. She risked a glance across to Cummings. He was acting, doing his best to look shocked, his fingers making nervous shapes at high speed. How many of this audience had he bribed? How could he be so sure the knife-edge vote wouldn't go against him?

Judith nudged Lizzie in the ribs and whispered, "Look what he's doing with his fingers. Can you feel it? Whatever he's planning with those symbols on the doors, it's happening now."

Lizzie could feel it. Something was gripping the room, coming and going in waves. She realised she was seeing the rhythm as she felt it, to the same rhythm as Cummings moved his fingers. She could feel it in herself, too, a little intrusion in her gut with every flex, that was moving its way up her shoulder, making the top of her arm twitch, a feeling of pins and needles gripping her, and with the feeling that her arm wanted to move, a feeling that she genuinely wanted to move that arm, because she genuinely wanted to vote, to vote for . . . "He's using the symbols to control the vote," she said.

"As simple as that," said Judith, sounding oddly calm. "Look around, he's doing it to about half those who were going to vote against. It's all he needs."

"I hope that now you can see you're free to choose." Cummings had got to his feet, still flexing his fingers, as if nervous. "You'll see that voting for our store will bring the community together again." He sat down, and one of the councillors got up to make the case against, but Lizzie could see even she was rubbing at her arm, feeling the same thing many of those against did.

"I have to do it now," said Judith as the councillor finished speaking, a great sadness in her voice. "I'm sorry." Before Lizzie could stop her, she was on her feet, and had pulled from the pocket of her coat a blackened twig, which to Lizzie now looked like the most terrifying thing she had ever seen. Judith pointed it at Cummings. "Out out out, death to you, death!" she screamed.

Lizzie tried to grab the twig from her, certain as she did so that touching it would harm her hands, but Judith pushed her aside and sent her sprawling into the aisle. As the audience yelled and screamed—obviously thinking Judith had some sort of weapon—Lizzie felt the horrible potential of the twig suddenly release itself. For a moment she was sure she could see it, a jagged rip of blackness that consumed the world between Judith and

Cummings, murder thrown at him from what had immediately become Judith's hopelessly blackened heart, the short circuit of hatred bringing a stench that burst across the hall. Lizzie was aghast. Whatever they thought Cummings was, he was also a person, with a real wife and children. She hauled herself to her feet and stared . . . at Cummings raising a bemused eyebrow.

The audience had turned to Judith, some shouting their anger, some now laughing in relief and mockery, some still crying out in fear. She lowered the twig, a confused, desperate expression on her face, a helpless old woman.

Lizzie took Judith's arm and tried to steady her as she rocked on her feet. She could see she was crying, her fingers numbly still trying to extract an ounce more hatred from what had become just a twig. As Lizzie watched, the wood crumbled in her fingers. Judith curled over, weeping, and sat down.

Lizzie could only sit beside her, horrified. That had been their last chance. Where the hell was Autumn? Had she run away?

"Well . . . ," the mayor, looking ashen, took a moment to bring the meeting to order, glancing in their direction then away again. "Let's . . . let's go ahead and have that vote, then . . ."

Lizzie desperately wondered if she could make any difference with some sort of speech, at least delay things. Suddenly, she heard a welcome, familiar voice from someone who'd sat down beside her. "Let it happen." She turned to see Autumn, a calm, serious look on her face. Lizzie opened her mouth to protest, but Autumn shook her head. She looked changed, somehow . . . no, she looked more like the Autumn she'd first known: grounded, strong. Lizzie looked to Judith and saw that the old woman was blinking, wondering where Autumn had found such hope.

"All those in favour?" said Maureen.

Lizzie grabbed her own arm, relieved she was able to use her willpower to do that, and feeling . . . actually no urge to raise her hand. The sensation in her arm had remained there, failing to move her arm as if the muscles were too exhausted to carry a weight. She looked around the room. About half of those present had raised their hands, the ones who'd supported Sovo. Some who had previously were keeping their hands down, one or two of those who'd been against had their hands up. It was what you might expect from a free vote. She looked to Cummings, who was staring at the audience in genuine shock now, his fingers working feverishly, fury starting to show on his features.

"Oh," said Judith, her hand over her mouth in relief and amazement. "Oh."

"I tied the knot to activate it," said Autumn, "just before I walked in. Sorry to leave it so late." She held up a sprig of some sort of herb, knotted and daubed with red paint.

Maureen finished doing a head count and checked with the councillors and the secretary that they all agreed with the number. "And those against?"

Another free show of hands. Lizzie put hers up, as did Autumn, a proud grin on her face, and Judith, astonished. About half the room joined them. There was more counting, which led to a whispered debate on stage. Finally, Maureen looked up from the notepads. "It's a tie," she said.

"That's . . . that's impossible," said Cummings. Lizzie was delighted to hear those words from him.

"So it really is down to me," said the mayor. The room became angry again. Lizzie realised that if what she'd heard about Maureen was true, then they were going to lose anyway. Cummings had obviously realised that too, looking urgently to her. Maureen didn't meet his gaze. She was instead making eye contact with Judith, who was blinking back tears, urging her on. "I . . . I've hated the way this debate has ripped us apart. You all know . . . I took their money." There were gasps from the crowd, then angry shouts. Cummings was staring at her. Judith smiled, amazed as if she couldn't believe in this much good. "My friend Judith . . . you just saw what this has done to her. It's been stressful for all of us, but it's sent her over the edge, and . . . and I just can't stand it anymore. I vote against."

The crowd leapt up around Lizzie, Autumn, and Judith, a roar of triumph blotting out anything Lizzie might have wanted to say. She grabbed Autumn, and they held each other. After a moment, they looked to Judith. The smile had faded. She was looking extremely offended.

While the townspeople in the hall were still celebrating, commiserating, and debating, and Shaun was asking Maureen urgent questions, in answer to which she was sadly nodding, Autumn led them out of the hall. "I risk my soul, or whatever you want to call it," Judith was saying, "with forbidden magics, and she thinks I've gone doolally!"

Lizzie saw Cummings, flanked by Sovo workers, leaving the hall at speed, hoping to avoid the local media. He was stumbling, limping, waving away employees who were trying to offer him assistance. It almost looked like he'd been physically harmed. "I'd prefer to say that she felt sympathy for you and that pricked her conscience."

Judith just glared at her, then looked to Autumn. "What did you do?"

Autumn led them to a door in the Market Place, a coffee shop that was home to a couple who'd been against Sovo. The symbol still burned bright, but now it was different, Lizzie saw, the triangle having been turned into a pentagram. Autumn took a coffee jar full of paint from her coat pocket. "You were right, Judith. The shape of the symbol was the important thing. We couldn't erase them, or paint over them, but with enough of the right sort of paint, I added to them. I made them into this." She held up the symbol on her necklace. "It takes doing. Four more triangles on each and a fiddly bit in the middle. Some of them went really wrong. I'm glad that didn't, you know, turn anyone into anything."

"A manipulation," said Judith. "You found a way."

"Where did you get the paint and that herb knot thing?" asked Lizzie.

"From us," said a voice nearby. They all turned to see what Lizzie took to be Finn, clad not very sensibly in a vest and jeans, his breath not visible on the air like theirs were. He was also holding a pot of paint and a brush. "I helped."

"Is that him?" asked Lizzie.

"Oh, thank God, you can see him," said Autumn.

"Bloody fairies," said Judith. "You went to the lands again, then?"

"I went to see his father," said Autumn, and there was again a tremor in her voice. "I apologised for offending him. I . . . managed to look at him. He replied, and his voice was . . . I didn't understand what he said."

Finn sighed. "He accepted your sacrifice of fear."

"And you made a sacrifice," said Judith, "having appealed to a higher power. It took all three."

"I'm not clear on what happened after that. Things went into a kind of blur. I think something happened with time."

"Dad," said Finn, "had all the Summerland gather what you needed and sent you back to be his sword and shield and save the way of the worlds and made sure you arrived back way before the meeting started, and sent me with you to do the bit with the doors in record time, without anyone seeing."

"Yeah," said Autumn, "I thought it must be something like that."

"I have to report back," said Finn. "Will I see you again?"

"Maybe."

"Annoying. But also . . . excellent. Nobody ever plays hard to get." He walked into a shadow and after a moment Lizzie realised he wasn't there anymore.

"So," she said, "that's a fairy."

"Yeah," whispered Autumn.

"He didn't look like a fairy."

"What were you expecting?"

"For him to look like a fairy."

Judith looked to Autumn and sized her up for a moment before finally nodding. "That was . . . all right." She paused for a moment and seemed to decide on something. "I'm not getting any younger. Despite everything I've tried. You two . . . you're not on my list of what I don't like. The great powers find failure in their incarnations very hard to deal with. They tend to withdraw their influence, leaving their human forms a bit ill and angry, but you know what it's like dealing with a dying wasp. He might well have another go. Or sneak in to cause havoc in some other way. And other things in the darkness out there, things like I've met recently, might have seen how shaky the walls of Lychford are getting, and right now will be thinking about having a go, whether or not they've got Cummings to help them. If you two are willing, perhaps it's time for me to take on an apprentice, and to take more seriously the traditional relationship between the local wise woman and the clergy."

"Are you saying you could use our help?" said Autumn.

"Don't push it."

"Because I was going to say I could use your help in the shop."

"Your wisdom, she means," said Lizzie. "To make the shop into what it needs to be."

Judith glowered, but held out her hand, then looked away and almost imperceptibly nodded as Lizzie and then Autumn took it. After a second, she shook away their touch. "Lychford is going to need us," she said.

"The only thing is," said Lizzie, "I'm not sure what good I'll be to you. I . . ." She was going to say that nowhere in all this had she found her faith. Cummings was certainly some sort of evil supernatural power, but that didn't seem to imply to her the presence of a God, any more than it did in the movies. Looking at Autumn's ill-concealed pleasure, however, she didn't feel like raining on her parade. "I . . . didn't do anything to help."

Judith actually smiled. "You will," she said quietly. Then, declining Lizzie's offer of help, she pushed off with her stick and marched off unsteadily towards her home.

Autumn and Lizzie ended up in the Plough, where a number of those from the meeting had congregated. From what Lizzie could overhear, it seemed shared jokes about the mayor's confession and Judith's eccentricity were starting to once more pull the town together.

"What were you trying to tell me earlier?" asked Autumn.

So Lizzie, haltingly at first, proceeded to tell her at first just about Joe, but then, unable to stop herself, about everything.

"Oh," said Autumn. "Oh, no." She took Lizzie's hands in her own. "I'm sorry I wasn't there for you. And . . . I'm sorry you're having a wobble about your faith."

"Really?"

"Yeah. I got to find out how real my impossible beings were. I even got to show them to other people. But you—"

"That's something I'd have gone through even if all this hadn't happened."

"We should catch up. We should catch up right now," decided Autumn. "Until closing time."

She was pleasingly shocked when Lizzie took off her collar.

Judith made her way slowly back to her house, feeling the exhaustion brought on by using the dark stuff. She'd only done it twice before in her whole life. The sense of potency it gave you . . . well, she could see why it was so addictive. That was why Robin had turned out to be someone who could do . . . what he'd done to her. She might have known, though, that Cummings would have been immune to her ultimate weapon. That darkness was what he breathed.

"Judith!" The voice as she reached for her keys made her jump, but it was just Sunil, catching up with her. "I tried to find you after the meeting—"

Judith didn't want to deal with this now. Her being so shaken up, she felt like she might give in to how she felt about him. "I'm sorry, I'm very tired."

"But you're all right?"

"Not quite gibbering, if that's what you mean."

He took her hand. She felt how cold her hand was in his. "I know you believe in this. And so, I'm guessing what you did back there was pretty extreme. Judith, come back with me, let me get you some food, sit by my fire. Don't go into that cold house all alone."

She looked to the upstairs window, and saw the light of Arthur's television. She was so tempted. "I can't."

"It's your husband, isn't it?"

"Yes," she whispered.

"Judith, I know Arthur was your whole world. He was my

friend too. But it's been ten years since he died, ten years since the funeral."

"I know," she said quietly. She let go of his hand, and he let her, and she didn't look at him again, but instead went inside and closed the door behind her.

Epilogue

That Sunday, despite a hangover which had lasted all of yesterday, Lizzie got to her church early and unlocked everything and lit the candles with half an hour to go before the early service. She was now, she realised as she stood looking towards the altar, a priest who believed in fairies but wasn't sure if she believed in God. She could feel the gravity of this building, the way it was connected to everything, and that felt good, but there was still nothing beyond that. She went to the flowers that stood in front of the old map on the wall and moved them out of the way. People would ask questions. That was good.

She was now also friends, once again, with the town's most obvious pagan. That was a friendship that was going to cause fewer mutterings in the congregation than one might expect. Anglicans were, when it came down to it, generally tolerant types with ecumenical interests. Having Autumn back in her life was a source of great joy. Joy enough to make up for the damage it was going to do to her liver. She missed a greater joy, though. She missed it very much and wondered if having Autumn around might somehow prevent her from ever finding it again.

She went to the organ stool and found once again the hidden collection plate, still with the money on it. She lifted it out. She'd have a big congregation coming in later this morning for the main service. She didn't feel like hiding anything now. So, what was she going to do with this money?

She felt the presence of him beside her, and turned, quite calmly in the circumstances, to find him there. "Mr. Cummings."

He looked rough around the edges, like he'd slept in his suit. Even with her new senses, she still couldn't feel anything strange about him. She couldn't now, though, quite imagine him going back to one of the hotels on the ring road. "Do the poor know you allow yourself such luxury?" he said, pointing to the collection plate. He sounded a little desperate. He stumbled, had to grab at a pew to hold himself up, and as he did so, he let a little of his remaining power show. It was like hearing distant thunder. The size of it made Lizzie gasp and take a step back. She was suddenly scared for herself, if not for her town. It felt to her now like this wounded beast might do anything.

"What luxury?"

"Doubt. Why haven't you taken that?"

Now she had an answer. "Because I'd owe you something."

"Oh, come on now. When you think I'm . . . whatever you think I am? You still feel you'd have to repay me?"

After everything that had happened, why had he chosen to come back here? What did he want with her? She failed to speak, and then managed it, not quite knowing from where inside her the word came. "Yes."

"But I want to do something good! Please, just this one small thing. I hereby declare to whoever is listening that I will not seek any recompense for you taking that money. No bargains. Nothing. It is a gift."

She was almost crying again, and she had no idea why. "You just want me to do what you tell me."

He was suddenly yelling. "It's not *my* ego that's the problem here! Lizzie, if you asked anyone in your congregation, they'd say take that money and give it to the poor. What else are you *for*? What else is the institution you belong to for, if not to walk the walk rather than all the talk talk talk? That's what you've said yourself in the past, though it seems you didn't mean it. It would be laughing in my face now for you to take that money. Joe would have wanted you to *take that money*."

Lizzie made herself meet his gaze, and suddenly realised that in it she'd found everything she needed. She went and grabbed a candle and before he could say anything else she thrust the flame into the bundle of notes. It burst into flame, perhaps more quickly and more powerfully than money should? She wasn't sure. She'd never seen money burn before.

Cummings began a slow handclap. "Oh well done. Bravo! Wait until the newspapers hear. What is the Church of England coming to?"

"I'll find the money myself. Every penny."

"That's the spirit! How long do you think that'll take you? Until you retire? Not even then?" He stepped forward, into her face, smiling an enormous, desperate, demanding smile. "I could pop back every now and then, offer you some useful ways of making extra cash. What do you say?"

"I say . . ." Lizzie put her fingers to the crucifix on her necklace. "Though I walk through the valley of the shadow of death, I will fear no evil."

He didn't hiss like a vampire in a movie. He stumbled back a couple of steps. He looked at her like a child who'd had his magic trick spoiled. "Well," he muttered, "now you know." Suddenly, he was gone. He just wasn't there anymore. He left a slight smell of dust in the air. It felt to Lizzie like something had finally fallen apart.

Lizzie blinked. She took a hesitant step forward into the space where he'd been. She found she had inside her a feeling she'd misplaced for so long. In a moment, she would go and kneel. She looked back to the plate where all that remained of the money was ashes. Her heart sank at the sight, but now there was only so far it could sink. "We'll hold a bingo night," she whispered. "An enormous bingo night."

In the early afternoon, Lizzie got back to the vicarage, having preached a couple of—perhaps a bit too emotional—sermons, the personal aspects of which had made the churchwardens raise an eyebrow. She was going to have to have a word with them, to find out the details of what they'd found too unbelievable to tell. "Well," Sue had said as she was tidying up the church, "you've got into your stride. Finally." Lizzie found the letter she'd written to the bishop, ripped it up, and threw the pieces into the bin. She needed to tell Judith and Autumn about Cummings.

Later for that. She went and flopped onto the sofa, exhausted. She allowed her thoughts to drift, and she fell asleep in the low light of the autumn afternoon and dreamed, as she'd expected to, of Joe. They walked again in the sunshine beside that deadly road. "You wanted me to give that money to the poor," she said.

"You *never* bloody did what I said."

"I've gotten my faith back, and more. There's even more to the universe than I thought there was."

"Brilliant."

"Goodbye, Joe," she said.

The Lost Child of Lychford

For the staff and customers of the Plough Inn, Fairford. (This surely gets me one on the house, doesn't it, Rob?)

1

The Reverend Lizzie Blackmore slowly blinked awake, and found, to her surprise, that she was already furious. She was furious as if she'd been angry in her dreams, oppressed and confined by something she couldn't recall, and waking up was just one more damned thing. But why? It must be the sound, she decided, an irritating, whiny sound that was wheedling itself into her brain and then poking it.

She looked over at her clock radio and swore at it. "It's still two weeks to Christmas, and you're playing Greg Lake?!"

"The song 'I Believe in Father Christmas,'" she continued to Sue and Oliver, her elderly churchwardens, twelve hours later, at their weekly meeting round the vicarage kitchen table, "should be banned. It should be a crime to play it. What else has he recorded? 'Valentine's Day Is Just to Sell Cards'? 'Look Out for Wasps, It's Summer'? Radio stations only play it because it's got that nice bit with the jingle bells, but he's doing that *sarcastically*. He's doing *sarcastic* jingle bells."

"I did like him in Crosby, Stills and Nash," opined Oliver, who knew what he meant. "I'll miss him."

"Wow," said Sue. "We're still two weeks out. And you're already that far gone."

Lizzie realised the two of them were looking at her with new-found wariness. This was going to be her first Christmas as vicar of St. Martin's church, Lychford. The churchwardens, however, had a long experience of working with her predecessor. All vicars had a rough time of it at Christmas, but she was obviously setting off their alarm bells already. "Chris de Burgh can sod off as well," she said. "And I liked The Pogues the first eighty-nine times, but come on. Anyway, why are we talking about this? We've got a lot to do. Can we please get on?"

They did indeed have a lot to do. Lizzie most of all. She'd expected to feel daunted. She'd spent the year trying to attract new members into the congregation, and Christmas was traditionally the time when a whole bunch of people who wouldn't otherwise cross the threshold of a church came piling in. The challenge was to somehow keep them afterwards, while running an ecclesiastical assault course. She'd already gotten over the first few hurdles of the season. The Advent Carol Service, which she'd insisted that this year was going to be by candlelight—despite Oliver's misgivings that this would result in what he called a "*Towering Inferno* scenario"—had turned out to actually be problematic in other ways. Lizzie had had to lead the plainsong while not being able to see anything. The congregation attracted by the poster hadn't really sung along, and, as they filed out, Lizzie found them to be a bit bemused that the songs they'd just awkwardly picked their way through were what the Anglican Communion regarded as "carols." "I like 'Silent Night,'" one young woman had said, "but perhaps that's a bit too popular for you." Lizzie had nearly replied there was a little number by Greg Lake she'd probably enjoy.

Then there had been Christingle, which had meant more fire—and this time children were handling it—and which brought in very few people who understood why there were oranges with candles stuck in them. At times, Lizzie had wondered if the best way to deal with the added numbers might be some sort of video prologue. "Previously, in Christianity . . ."

But what she was feeling went beyond daunted, beyond useless, beyond stressed. There was a sort of . . . background anger, a feeling of being downtrodden. She really didn't understand it, and it was getting in the way of what should be a season of joy. That's what Christmas had always been for her in the past.

The morning after the churchwardens' meeting, she went into the church to check the stocks of wine, wafers, and hymn sheets, ready for the forthcoming onslaught. There were fourteen more days of frantic organisation and hopefully passionate delivery ahead of her, as well as all the other matters of life and death which, in the normal course of parish life, kept her really pretty damn busy. On top of all that was the sombre fact that Christmas killed people. Old folk tried to hang on for one last Christmas lunch and found that took a bit too much out of them. Or just about managed to hold on, but then immediately expired. So she had a larger number of funerals than usual to attend to as well.

And still, beyond all that—the star atop Lizzie's personal Christmas tree of stress—there was the wedding. For the last few months, she'd been meeting with a couple from Swindon who were deluded enough to believe that to get married on Christmas Eve was to be the stars of one's own festive rom com. She'd tried to dissuade them, saying spring was so much nicer. She'd pointed out that other parishes were available. She'd shown them just how many other services she had to fit in on that day. She'd shown them around the church, pointing out how small and drafty it was. But no. They were set on it. So that was yet another damn thing.

On the way to the vestry, she dipped before the altar, stopping a moment to recheck the Advent dressings placed on it. The low light through the windows gave the building an air of quiet contemplation. She wished she felt the same.

She heard a noise from behind her.

She turned and saw, standing some distance away, a child. It was a boy of about three years old. He had his back to her, his arms by his sides, looking at the ancient map of Lychford and its surroundings which was once again on display and featured on the list of points of interest in the church's tourist leaflet.

This was a bit odd. There'd been nobody on the path outside, and she was pretty sure there was nobody else in the building. "Hi," she called.

He didn't reply.

Lizzie walked down the length of the church towards him, not wanting to scare him. As she approached, she heard he was muttering to himself, in the way toddlers did. "Say hello, everybody."

"Hello," said Lizzie again. She'd put on her brightest voice. She didn't want him running away. She realised that, oddly, some part of her was also feeling . . . afraid. There was something not quite right about . . . what?

The boy turned to look at her. His expression wasn't the excited interest you normally expected from a child of that age. It was a look of terrible, lost pain. It was an expression that should only appear on a much older face.

Since having the waters of the well in the woods thrown over her by Judith Mawson, Lizzie had seen some extraordinary things. She could now sense what those who lived in the everyday streets of Lychford seldom saw, the effects and creatures of . . . she hated to use the word, but of *magic*. She realised now that here she was seeing something else of that world. This little boy wasn't quite here. She realised that, now she was up close, she could see through him.

This was her first ghost.

The feeling was almost one of relief. That this wasn't a real child who demanded her immediate care, but one for whom that care was . . . too late? But no. Here he was, right in front of her, his expression demanding . . . something. This was no Victorian urchin. This boy had a Thomas the Tank Engine pullover, and those tiny trainers with lights on them.

"Not Mummy," the boy said. "Where's Mummy?"

"Are your Mum and Dad about?" she said, helplessly. Did she expect there to be a ghost Mum and Dad? Wouldn't that be cosy?

"No hurting," he said. It was half a plea, half scolding.

He was literally radiating anxiety, a coldness she could feel on her skin. Lizzie squatted down and reached out to him, encouraging him to come to her. He backed away. She was scaring him. Was it just because she wasn't his Mummy? A second later, without any sense of movement, he was gone.

Lizzie got slowly to her feet. She realised she was shaking. She herself had never wanted to be a mother, but the way that small boy had needed *someone,* to get him back to where he should be, wherever that was—

She jumped at the sound of the church door opening.

It was Sue, carrying an armful of candles. "Sorry," she said. "Hope I didn't disturb you."

It's probably not real," said Judith, who was sitting exactly where Lizzie had expected to find her, behind the counter of Witches: The Magic Shop. These days, the old lady seemed only to venture away from her post among the potions and unicorn figurines and crystal balls to reluctantly head home, and that was often late in the evening. The elderly witch complained bitterly, to anyone who'd listen, about her new situation as a "shop girl," but spent so much time in that shop that Lizzie could only think she protested too much.

"Those are not words I ever expected to hear you say," said Lizzie, who'd been relieved to have had provided for her a cup one of the shop's more soothing herbal teas.

"Well, of course it's a bloody *ghost*. Your church *is* haunted."

"So by 'not real' you mean . . . ?"

"A ghost isn't often a person. It most probably don't have feelings you can hurt or soothe. It's just a . . . whatchamacallit, a symbol. Like the green man on the traffic light."

Lizzie tried to get her head around the idea that that frightened little boy might appear in her church as often as the sign at the pedestrian crossing turned green. "So . . . is it sort of an architectural feature, a recording of something that happened, or is it there because . . . ?" *Because of me,* she wanted to say. Where had that thought come from?

Autumn, who owned the shop, and was, as always, dressed as if she'd staggered out of an explosion in Next, brought the pot of tea over, a concerned expression on her face. "Ah, now, wait. I've read a lot of texts that say ghosts are the souls of people who are prevented from getting into heaven—"

"I don't believe anything *could* prevent them," said Lizzie. "If there *is* a heaven, about which Biblical sources—"

"—but I was about to add," finished Autumn pointedly, "that since I don't believe in an afterlife, I don't think that can be true."

"It's not like there's a vote on what's real," said Judith. "It don't matter what either of you believe, the world just gets on with it. Still, at least you're agreeing on summat, which is that it's probably not real either way. Might be a recording, like you say. Might be summat else."

"However," Autumn stressed, "I'm trying to train Judith in the correct approach to customers, and, Lizzie Bizzie, you are, at this moment, a customer."

"I haven't bought anything," said Lizzie, feeling now vaguely as if she should.

Autumn ignored her. "Judith, what have I told you about addressing the feelings of customers first, before getting into the details of why they're visiting us?"

Judith glowered. "Summat annoying, I should think."

"I *am* paying you to work here."

"Only because you're now *my* apprentice and you want me here so *you* can learn from *me*."

"You still have to actually do the job. And I'm trying to teach you how. We have a Christmas rush on." Autumn gestured at the empty shop, completely without irony. "It's time you learned about customer satisfaction."

Judith carefully took out her hanky, spat into it in disgust, then put it back in her pocket, as if this were the epitome of etiquette.

"Well, this has been informative," said Lizzie, just as exasperated by the impossible situation these two had set up for themselves as she had been on the last few occasions she'd visited. It was always good to see her friends, but it wasn't as if they could understand her situation, when Autumn still sometimes referred to Lizzie only working on Sundays. And now they'd used her child ghost as just the basis for another row. She made her goodbyes, threw her scarf round her neck, and just about managed to avoid slamming the door.

That evening, Judith Mawson left the shop rather earlier than usual, and headed up to the marketplace, then up the road to St. Martin's churchyard. At the start of December, the church had had a neon star put on the top of its tower. Now Judith looked up at it and snorted. "Bloody Christmas," she said. She couldn't be having with the sort of uncontainable, overexcited enthusiasm the Reverend Lizzie displayed for such a tiring season. She pushed herself forward on her stick and headed for the church door.

Judith knew there were at least a dozen things a ghost could be, including, well, she didn't like to call such things souls, that being ecclesiastical territory, but yes, summat that was still a person. She didn't like being vague to just about the only two individuals in this town it was possible that in a few years' time she'd get round to calling friends. However, there existed a worrying possibility about what this was, and she didn't want to burden Lizzie with that thought until she was sure. It was possible that the Reverend had been cursed. Perhaps not with . . . something as personal as Judith's own burden, but certainly with something that had scared her, badly. Despite her trying so hard to be Ms. Vicar and not show it. Bloody Autumn had, of course, remained oblivious. But the wise woman had seen.

Judith tried the door, found it to be still unlocked, and stepped into the empty church. She sniffed the air. Nothing she hadn't expected. The flavour of the air was slightly different, as churches always got at this time of year, as different belief systems crowded in. Was that something sinister, right at the bottom of the range? Probably just the occasional deeply unrighteous individual, only to be expected in a big crowd. A village witch like her was always a bit lost when presented with people in numbers. She put that thought aside and addressed the air. "Right, then," she called out, "what are you?"

She didn't really expect an answer. Not in words. The tone of her voice had been calculated, through experience, to reach whatever had started roosting in this place. There was, in reply, just a slight movement of air.

It was hiding from her. Through fear or malice? Not sure. Judith tasted the air once more. She knew things that had been born out there in the dark beyond the bounds of the town that could conceal themselves, could even lie about their natures, but she knew most of the flavours of that deceit.

She was startled to suddenly find a new flavour on her taste buds. This wasn't something that was . . . here . . . as such, this was a connection to something somewhere else. She flexed her old fingers painfully and drew it out of the air in more detail, rubbing it between her numb fingertips. She grew worried at what she felt. There *was* something of it that reminded her of Lizzie. So there was an association between the Reverend and this child, not a curse, but it was . . . complicated. Mixed-up. It would need a working of magic to explore in more detail.

To Judith's surprise, the ghost now appeared, looking at her from around the edge of a pew. That lost, demanding face. Judith looked sternly back. Yes, she could see how that would get to the soft girl. "You go on home, then," she said. It had come out more gently than she'd intended. "If you know where that is. I give you permission to do so and I give you strength." She winced as the little pulse of life left her. She hadn't meant to give up so much of that either. She'd regret that moment on her deathbed.

However, the thing didn't collapse into cold air, as she expected it to. It just kept looking mournfully at her, and then, as if it had decided she couldn't provide it with whatever it was seeking, it once more faded.

Judith found she had a catch in her throat. Half of it was that she felt tricked. Half of it was that it was the oldest trick of all. The trick of affection. She was getting soft herself. "Stupid old woman," she whispered to herself as she left the church. "Stupid."

"Stupid," said Autumn to herself, sitting at the PC in the room above the shop that doubled as her office and bedroom. Her finger was hovering over the "delete profile" button on a dating website. It had been hovering there for about a minute now, as she watched the number of messages coming in increase. Twice in that minute she'd taken a quick glance at those messages. Both times she'd gone right back to wanting to delete the whole thing. The genius of this site, she realised, was the bait of hope. One of the men trying desperately to contact her might turn out to be able to string a sentence together, one that wasn't immediately blunt or abusive. She felt she had somehow let herself down in having ventured to this online location, to the realm of the desperate and deranged. Christmas always did this to her. It emphasised how alone she was. There were, as far as Autumn could work out, exactly two single men of around her age in Lychford. She ran into them every now and then down the Plough. One of them seemed only interested in her as a possible cleaning lady, the other—though in this town he was probably never going to admit it even to himself—would only ever be interested in her as a shoulder to cry on. The other possibility was for her to get herself out to the bright lights of Swindon or Cirencester; but the idea of getting done up, then driving alone to stand in some bar, not even being able to have more than one glass of wine to give one an excuse for being there, while the contents of this dating site sloshed around the room in person . . . She stood up, not liking the direction her thoughts were going, and had to take a quick walk around the room. It was either that or throw the PC out of the window. How did anyone ever meet anyone? How was it the human race hadn't gone extinct? Jolly thoughts for Yuletide.

She felt relief, therefore, at the *bing* of an incoming email, and sat down again to open it, hoping it was from Lizzie, who she really should talk to about all this; only it was coming up to Christmas, so she'd be busy for at least a couple of days every week, and Autumn didn't want to spoil how joyful the season seemed to be making her friend, except . . . now that Autumn thought about it, it seemed that Lizzie had actually been freaked out to a weird degree by seeing that ghost. As if it hadn't been just one of those things that those who had their gift had to get used to, but was . . . personal somehow. Well, that would give her a good excuse to visit and share their worries over some wine. How about she just went over there right—

She stopped as she saw who the email was from, at a service

provider's address which . . . no, even if she squinted, she couldn't quite read it. It was like her screen couldn't handle the language it was written in, so it didn't matter whether or not her newly empowered eyes could have deciphered the original. Her new senses, incidentally, had only added to her dating problems, because now some of the men she encountered came with added visual baggage that was literally hanging around their necks, and—

"Would you please just bloody read me?" said the email.

Autumn leapt back in her chair. A voice had actually come from her computer. A horribly familiar voice. Then the face associated with that voice appeared, looking out of the corner of her screen, incarnated as a cartoon version of himself. "You seem," said Finn, "to be having trouble opening an email. Can I help with that?"

"No you bloody can't. What are you doing inside my computer? Here, can you see my downloads?"

"I'm only 'inside your computer' in the sense that I'm an email. Can an email see inside your computer? Hey, what's in here, anyhow?"

Autumn was in no way going to answer that. She'd once got very drunk with Lizzie and started talking about her very specific tastes in fan fiction, and thank God the Reverend had claimed in the morning not to remember a thing. "How do I get you out of there?"

"Well, if you click on the email—"

Autumn, not being able to stand his patronising tone any longer, did so before he'd finished the sentence. To her surprise, the cartoon figure leapt out of the screen and became his real, solid self. Well, as close to solid as Finn, Prince of the Blood, from a land Judith sometimes called "where the Fairies live," could get.

"—then," he finished, "I will appear."

Autumn pulled her dressing gown tighter. "If I'd known you were going to appear—"

"You would have known, if you'd let me finish my—"

"And what are you doing here, anyway? I haven't seen you since—"

"I have been deliberately staying away, not infringing on your boundaries. I mean both those of Lychford and your own personal ones. Since you three got together and reinforced all the borders, my lot have slept a lot more soundly. So there wasn't any urgent need for me to come and see you. Besides, since I became aware of it last time round, I've gotten a taste for this Internet thing—"

"You're on the Internet? You've got a computer?"

"Yes and no, in that order. I tasted it when I came here last time, so reached under the border and started swigging it from the air." He made a gesture as if he were drinking a pint. "And that's when it dawned on me: the menfolk you have in this world are shite."

Autumn cocked her head to one side. "Oh," she said, "what an extraordinary revelation. Mind blown."

"Yeah!" He nodded excitedly. "I knew if I pointed it out, you'd be quick to see it. You're clever like that. And when I was drinking in the Internet, I saw everything they're doing to ladies, all at once, and I was horrified. And then turned on, quite a lot. And then horrified again . . . when I realised I should be. Because last time out, I behaved a bit like that to you. By accident, largely. And that's when I decided to stay away entirely. To avoid doing that again."

Autumn stared at him. Oh God, he was serious. It wasn't like she'd wanted him to stay away. She thought they'd gotten things sorted out. Although a bit of her was pleased that just for once *she'd* managed to freak *him* out. He wasn't going to be all guilty and try to sympathise his way into her affections now, was he? She shook her head. He was running her in circles already. "You could just . . . avoid doing that again. Whatever it was."

"I could." He nodded.

She waited for the other shoe to drop, but as always with Finn, it failed to. It was like he only wore one shoe. "So . . . if you'd decided to stay away, why are you actually . . . back?"

She'd half expected him to be affronted by that, but he kept with the serious. "Because something's going terribly wrong. With reality, I mean. Listen, let me tell you everything. In the form of three songs and a list."

"Could you maybe just—?"

"The list summarises the songs. As always, I've thought of everything."

The next morning Lizzie went, as she did on the same morning every week, to stand by the gates of Jonathan Canter, the Lychford school of which she was an ex officio governor, and welcome parents and children as they blocked the roads for miles around. Jonathan Canter, Sue often said, was the main reason for the bypass. The churchwarden had known the man the school was named after, back in the day, a local property magnate whose trust still owned a lot of local land, particularly, it seemed, anywhere Lizzie and her team might want to expand the burial grounds into. That his lasting memorial was traffic congestion would, Sue said, have delighted him.

Lizzie hadn't slept very well the previous night. Months ago she'd taken the pillows from the other side of her bed, put furniture on the side of the room that she associated with her deceased partner, and managed to find a sort of college dorm room ambience that had allowed her to rest. Before the stress of the last few weeks. Now she couldn't get the face of that little boy out of her head. It was like he was demanding something urgent of her, and she should know what it was all about, but she didn't. She made herself be attentive as she said hello to the incoming mass of children, and had a couple of conversations with parents about baptisms and the weather and how lovely it was that Christmas was approaching, and wasn't it nice that The Pogues and, yes, there we go, Greg Lake were back in the charts, and it must be getting so busy for her, now that she had to work for most of the week. Lizzie found she was searching the children's faces as their breath billowed around them in the frosty air, mentally matching the little boy's expression with their hopeful ones, all of them full of Christmas. Full of the thought of presents and food, that was. Full of what money was doing to them and the world they lived in. She shouldn't be thinking like this, she knew, when she should be full of—

She realised she was looking right at him.

She was looking at him, the boy from the church; there he was, looking right back at her!

He was standing hand in hand with what must have been his mother as she, and what must have been his elder sister beside her, talked to Roz, the deputy headmistress. The boy had a quizzical expression on his face. He was wondering why she was staring, she realised. It was definitely the same child. He was even wearing the same pullover and shoes. Only he had none of that cold loneliness about him. There was nothing her newfound senses found odd about him at all. This was no ghost. This boy was flesh and blood.

Lizzie must have made a sound. The boy's mother looked round. Lizzie briefly considered what she could say, what she could ask. The mother had long brown hair, was in her early thirties, harassed and loving, also utterly normal. Lizzie decided the best thing she could do was to turn her expression of sudden horror into a cough. Which allowed her to strike up the briefest of conversations with Allison Dunning, as the boy's mother turned out to be called, about how there was a lot of it going around.

As Allison led the boy away, Lizzie kept staring after him, and he looked back, seemingly as puzzled about her as she was about him.

Like I said," Judith maintained, poker-faced, from her perch at the Witches till, "not real."

"He's an actual, living child, Jamie Dunning, goes to nursery at Magic Carpet. How much more real can you get?" Lizzie was pacing, having not been offered tea, since Autumn was still apparently busy upstairs. Lizzie had come running here, when actually she should be doing a host of things related to her actual job. Because this felt somehow more important.

"I mean what's in your church isn't a real ghost. It's an apparition of the living. A doppelgänger."

"Trouble," said Autumn, entering from the stairwell.

"They can be," said Judith. "They're usually either a warning of an approaching event, an attempt to stop it from coming to pass, or, when they're playing nasty buggers, something that can cause that event to happen, a self-fulfilling prophecy."

"I mean," said Autumn, before Lizzie could ask her urgent questions, "we've got trouble with the borders. Something's trying to sneak over. I've been . . . communing with the fairies."

"Have you really?" Lizzie asked, unable to stop herself from placing a rather adolescent emphasis on the last word of that sentence.

"And he sends his regards," said Autumn. "He says his people can feel a sort of . . . shakiness to the boundaries, as if something's messing up the system. He provided me with this list of points of where they've felt things are getting weird."

Judith took the piece of paper and tutted at it. "Bloody fairy geography. They have no idea how to talk to us about where things are."

"And that's the translated version. You should have heard the songs. Anyway, he said they can't work out what's going on, and so, without consulting his father or anyone else, or so he says, Finn came to me to get us involved."

"They'd never be seen to ask for help from humans," said Judith. "Not as a nation. Not directly. He's actually been sent by his father to get us onside, and he wouldn't have been unless . . ." She paused. "As a mere employee, am I allowed to swear in your shop?"

"You've been swearing all the bloody time."

"I mean *really* swear?"

"Why would you want to swear?" asked Lizzie. "What have you just thought of?"

"The doppelgänger in your church might have been caused by some enormous trauma of the borders, the map being shaken up by something. Time sometimes gets muddled up a bit when that happens. And since there's some connection between you and the ghost . . . oh, I found out there was. Should have told you before, I suppose." She held up a hand to once again stop Lizzie's questions. "That's all I know. It's something that's going to take a bit of biting down into. We should walk the bounds tonight."

These days, Lizzie found the woods that surrounded the town to be in equal parts beautiful and fearful, especially at night. As she kept a slow pace to match that of Judith on the path that went under the bridge and up into the trees, the taste of the air spoke of forthcoming snow. Autumn was wrapped up in a fake fur that looked like something Marianne Faithfull would have rocked in the 1960s. On anyone else it would have been white, but somehow her friend's way with clothing had touched it, and there were hints of reds and purples. Autumn was wearing the sort of frown that Lizzie usually associated with her arriving on the doorstep in the early hours. Whenever the subject of Finn came up, there was a flash of that look. She herself was still full of worrying questions, but she'd already had all the answers she could get. Part of her feared those answers.

It was already dark by the time they got up to the ridge the locals called Maiden Hill. There was now a new line of a few saplings, still fenced off, but the trees weren't yet tall enough to obscure the view of the town. A half moon was rising over the vale, with a few scudding clouds illuminated by it. Below lay Lychford, the shape of it made visible by the lights: the cross of compass-pointing roads that met in the marketplace; the church off to one side, with alignments of its own; the new developments of the Backs blossoming out; the river the artery that ran through all of it. In the dark, the town was like a cluster of small fires that spoke of hearth and comfort, that should speak to her, Lizzie knew underneath it all, of Christmas. She wished she could find that feeling.

But here she was with her two friends, who would now always be kept by the burden of their knowledge at a little distance from that warmth. This is where the three "witches" would always be. They needed to be out here looking over it in order to protect it. Did that distance add to how she was feeling? "And you don't get proper Christmas Number Ones these days," she said. "Just whoever's won the bloody *X Factor*."

Judith looked at her and blinked like a tortoise. "What does that have to do with anything?"

"She does this," said Autumn. "She continues conversations like the eight conversations in between haven't happened."

Judith considered them both for a moment, then made a noise in the back of her throat and marched off.

Lizzie was about to follow when Autumn put a hand on her arm. "Are you okay?"

Lizzie didn't know where to begin. Now was not the time. "I'm fine."

"Come on, this is me. It always takes me a while to realise, but I always get there. And it's not like Judith's ever going to notice."

Lizzie sighed. She always appreciated Autumn's moments of empathic clarity, but this time her concern just seemed to add to the awkwardness she felt. "If I'm not fine, I don't know why. I mean . . . that little boy is absolutely not dead. I've made a few discreet inquiries about him. He's got a loving family, no trouble at home."

"But—?"

Lizzie hated the way Autumn could always do that. Her rare moments of understanding tended to go all the way. "But he doesn't . . . feel right. He feels like he's asking something of me. Or . . . blaming me for something."

"What, like the two ghosts in *The Muppet Christmas Carol*?"

"Or just the one in *A Christmas Carol*, yes."

"But what would he be blaming you for?"

Lizzie really had no idea. That was where the void was. She felt guilty without knowing what she'd done. She just shook her head. At that moment, thankfully, Judith called to them to catch up.

They found the old woman staring at a tree stump that looked as if, centuries ago, it had been struck by lightning. "I call this the dial," she said. "What do you see?"

Lizzie took a step closer and looked down onto the stump. Judith had rubbed away some moisture that would soon become frost. The concentric rings of new growth were each, to her newly skilful eyes, differently illuminated. She could feel each colour . . . and somehow flavour . . . leading down into the soil around them, and away under the horizon, where they became . . . associated with the sky. The grammar of the sentences these sensations suggested to her brain, when she tried to put how she felt into words . . . it still amazed her that she could feel and think things language wasn't designed to cope with.

"It's like a network diagram," said Autumn. "Or a nervous system."

"Yes, yes, science," sighed Judith. "Stop reducing it to it's like this or it's like that. It is the thing it is. Someone, nobody knows who—"

"You mean you don't know," said Autumn.

"—and I'm the last one who might, so that's nobody; someone grew this tree here and tied it carefully to every border that runs in every direction, worldly or otherwise, around the town. The borders were grown into it. Then, I should think as part of that process, it was struck by lightning, as a sacrifice, to give it power of its own, and felled, so everything could be easily seen on the stump. A piece of great magical art, this is. I think when whoever had the trees up here burnt, they might have been trying to get at this."

"Wasn't that Sovo?" Lizzie shuddered at the thought of the company that had set the townsfolk against each other earlier in the year. She still had come nowhere near to matching the money of theirs that she had burned rather than accept.

"I thought so at the time," said Judith. "But I've sniffed the air up here since, and it don't smell like anything else they did."

Lizzie took a tentative sniff and wished she had the same experience of the gifts of the well as Judith had. Everything to do with magic smelled the same to her: like bonfire night when she was eight.

"So what does it tell us?" asked Autumn.

Judith took off her left glove, then the glove underneath that one, and put her bare finger onto the stump. Lizzie flinched as all the colours suddenly flashed into her at once, but a moment later it was obvious that was what Judith had expected to happen. The old lady stood there, lit up like, well, a Christmas tree. Lizzie thought for a moment she had broken into a coughing fit, but then she realised it was Judith's version of laughter. "Oh," she said, "that always tickles my sensibilities. I sometimes come up here when I really don't need to, you know. Come on, you do it, too."

Lizzie looked at Autumn, wondering if this was going to be another moment like when Judith had introduced them to the well water via the distribution mechanism of a bucket. Autumn shrugged, and put her finger beside Judith's, and Lizzie quickly followed suit.

The colours that shot up her arm were definitely . . . welcome in several interesting places. She didn't want to look at Autumn now. Sharing this intimacy was right on the edge of too embarrassing to bear.

"Oh, look at you two, like unicorns at your first orgy," said Judith, for all the world as if that were a thing people said. "Get past that, and if you can't read it with your bits, read it with your brain."

Lizzie did her best to read it with her brain. She could feel a . . . lacking of something, a kind of nausea about something that wasn't working, or that had been . . . interfered with. No, more serious than that, this was like perversion, or . . . she found she was uncomfortable with the concept, but like . . . blasphemy. She tried to see or feel or work out where it was, but couldn't. She looked to Judith, and found that Autumn was doing the same, with a shocked expression.

"I probably got more out of that than you did," said Judith, taking her hand from the stump. "In terms of info, I mean. It turns out that, as I suspected from the fairies getting involved, one of the boundaries has been weakened in an impossible direction."

"You mean in a dimension beyond the four we know about?" said Autumn.

"That's what I said. Which is a bit serious, because when one of those sods steps in, things get all . . ." She did a sudden twisting motion with both hands. "They don't have to pay attention to the boundaries of mind, of memory. The fairies have a lot of trouble with the existence of beings who can do that, because, though they don't like to acknowledge it, they themselves are all about their relationship with human minds and memories, and this lot instead are all . . ." She did the motion again. Lizzie found she really didn't like what it implied. It looked like Judith was turning something inside out. "They can get into your head, mess with what you think you know. It's also harder for us to see the problem. I don't know yet how I can work out exactly what's being done to reality. It feels like it's ongoing, like something that's gathering in strength, echoing back and forth and building up. Still, I think I know a way to see where the initial distortions are."

"So is this anything to do with my ghost?" asked Lizzie.

"If it is," said Judith, "then this might turn out to be a bloody terrifying Christmas."

Lizzie took a few moments to take that in, and realised that if she thought about it at any length . . . no, she needed to keep going. She looked at her watch. "Okay," she said, "very much taken on board, but I've got the wedding couple coming. Give me a call if you find out anything else." The other two agreed that they would, and she headed off down the hill, her boots sliding on the frost that had started to form on the grass. The moon rising behind the hill cast long shadows over her as she made her way back down to the river.

Autumn watched Lizzie go, worried for her friend. Lizzie's spirituality sometimes felt like a force field that she used to keep difficult emotional stuff at bay until it all got to be too much. While for Autumn herself, difficult emotional stuff was more of an adventure playground.

She felt Judith's hand land on her arm, like the skeleton grabbing out from one of those old novelty money boxes. "You're with me, my apprentice," she said. "We're going to try summat."

"Every day," said Autumn, "you remind me more of the Emperor from *Star Wars*."

Judith considered that for a moment. "Nice to finally get a bit of respect," she decided.

Lizzie got back to the Vicarage with ten minutes to spare before the wedding couple were due to arrive, and frantically cleared up her study, which basically involved grabbing everything on the floor and throwing it into a cupboard. She always tried to make the place look welcoming, because wedding couples always arrived with several fallacies in their heads. They thought she was empowered to stop them from getting married, probably after she'd decided they weren't holy enough. But actually, though she herself didn't have to agree to marry them, she had no legal right to stop anyone else doing so, if legally married they could be. They also always thought she was going to talk to them about sex. As if anyone needed "the conversation" these days. As with everything else, they got their ideas of what she did from sitcoms, if anywhere. These were the people who'd decided to take the stress she was always already under and pile on some more.

She heard the sound of a car pulling up in the drive, and went to switch on the kettle. It had boiled before the doorbell rang. Which was right at the moment the kitchen clock indicated was the appointed time. Wow, these two were either very scared or very precise. She opened the door to the very tall Alan Bathurst, and the really quite tiny Emma Beeson, who were both wearing jumpers with Christmas motifs and matching woolly hats and grinning at her like idiots.

"Festive," said Lizzie. "Do come in."

We're going to be a little demanding," said Alan, leaning forward in the sofa in Lizzie's study, and somehow managing to loom from a sitting position. He, like his fiancée, had a rich Swindon accent.

"Oh?" said Lizzie, killing off several sarcastic replies before they could reach her lips.

"Yes," said Emma. "We hope you don't mind. We have made a plan."

Lizzie had been wondering what was in the briefcase that Alan had placed on the floor in front of them. "An order of service, you mean?"

"Ah, not just that!" Alan beamed as he opened up the case and brought out a series of what looked like professionally designed lists. Lizzie realised with slight horror that this couple had their own logo. "This is what happens before, during, and after, and where everyone and everything should be in the church."

"Do you mind?" said Emma. "It's going to take a bit of doing. But please say it's okay. It's very important to us."

Lizzie leafed slowly through the plans, holding back her every grumpy impulse. "It's . . . not something we'd usually do. What are these 'statues' you've got on the map?"

The couple looked at each other as if it were amazing she'd think there was anything odd about this. "They're from our student halls," said Alan. "You know the stupid stuff most people have in their corridors, traffic cones and all that? Ours went a bit further. We nicked actual—"

"They were nicked at the time," said Emma quickly, "but

these statues we've got our eye on are exact replicas, they'd all be bought and paid for."

Lizzie pinched the brow of her nose. She'd never had a wedding couple before who thought she was about to rule out their ability to wed on the basis of multiple counts of robbery. "What sort of statues?"

"You know, the sort you find in . . . now, don't take this the wrong way—" began Alan.

"Churchyards?" finished Lizzie.

Alan pointed at her like she'd got the right answer at charades.

Lizzie wondered exactly what the *right* way to take that would be. But still, there was nothing here that was disallowed. These two weren't attempting to marry at night or to write their own vows, or any of the other things couples couldn't do that sometimes surprised them. She took a moment to calm herself down. "Okay," she said.

"Marvellous," said Alan.

"The order of service looks . . . different. But nothing we can't do. Can you get me the text of these three poems you want people to read?"

She was not at all surprised when Emma immediately slapped paper copies into her hand. She was aware of the couple looking nervously at each other as she read them through. These were probably from some movie she hadn't seen. "All fine," she said, finally.

Emma and Alan visibly relaxed.

After she'd shown them out, Lizzie slumped against the door. A sudden wave of exhaustion had washed over her. Only to be expected. There was only so much protein in a steady diet of tea and cake, and ahead of her was the assault course of multiple Christmas dinners, most of them in public.

She was about to go and put the kettle on for more coffee when she heard the knock at the door.

She wondered for a moment if she'd really heard it. It was a very gentle knock. No, there it was again. There was something odd about it, like it wasn't a person doing it, but a branch somehow tapping against the front door.

Lizzie eased herself into a standing position. The knock came again. It had grown neither more insistent nor less. That was what had made her think of nature, rather than a person. If it were someone, why didn't they ring the doorbell?

Why was she hesitating to just have a look? This was probably an elderly parishioner, out in the cold and possibly needing her help. Chiding herself, she opened the door.

The little boy stood on her doorstep, the night behind him, the lights of the park opposite shining through him. He was looking at her. His expression was desperately in need of something.

Lizzie was afraid of him, and at the same time guilty for being afraid of him. That sense of culpability made her feel like the victim in a horror story, that she deserved whatever he'd come to do. But what was he here to do?

She wanted to slam the door closed on him. The fear was making her want to do that. Everything she stood for, though, stood against giving in to that fear. She knew, somehow, that to do that would doom her. She suddenly felt like she was on the edge of a cliff. But what did that feeling mean?

She took a deep breath, made herself calm, and squatted down to the boy's level. "You can come in if you want," she said.

The little boy looked perhaps slightly less lost, just for a moment.

Then he vanished, without Lizzie ever quite seeing the moment he'd done so, and she found she was looking only at the lights and the dark and the drizzle.

There was a sudden sound from behind her. It was a sound

she hadn't heard before. But it had only been the house settling, right? Just one of the many noises this place made, most of which she'd gotten used to.

She closed the door and tried to go back to work, but couldn't.

She went to search the Vicarage, switching on lights wherever she went. She didn't find anything, except a series of sounds that always seemed to be just in the next room, that she could never find the source of.

She couldn't help dwelling on what she'd just done, on the risk—given what she now knew about the world and what was threatening it—that she had taken.

She had invited the ghost inside.

2

Autumn had half expected Judith to lead her back to her own home, but it turned out this was yet another occasion on which the older woman was not going to let her over her threshold. Autumn and Lizzie had never, in fact, been to Judith's house. Instead, Autumn realised Judith was heading for the Plough, which was, frankly, fine by her.

The interior of the little pub had been decorated by the landlord, Rob, with his customary largesse. A small Christmas tree sat in the corner, there were three streamers on the roof beams, and, noted Autumn with a slight twinge of worry, a hopeful sprig of what looked like real mistletoe was hanging right in the middle of the ceiling of the front bar, by the log burner. "Biberomancy," said Judith, taking a seat at the bar, and ignoring a couple of worried looks from the locals.

"Divination by . . . drink?" Autumn felt a little awkward to so obviously be here with Judith. Being the owner of a magic shop had given her a rather jolly and sociable relationship with the townsfolk. She was the local eccentric from a local family, who didn't mind a bit of laughter at her expense. She'd gone along with that wholeheartedly. It was either that or . . . well, end up like Judith.

"By beer, or at least that's how I use the word."

Rob, looking wary, all seven feet of him, with a beard about as long, had taken his place behind the bar facing Judith. "Don't see much of you in here, Mrs. Mawson. What'll it be?"

"A pint of your worst."

Rob's beard visibly bristled. "I do not keep a bad ale. They're all Arkells, mind, which some people don't like, but them's that don't don't come in here. Shall I just pick one at random?"

"Two pints of 3B," Autumn said quickly.

"That'll do," said Judith.

Rob considered for a moment, then nodded to Autumn. "Because it's you, Miss Witchcraft." He started to pull the beers.

"Why," whispered Autumn, "did you have to say that?"

"Because now the beers will be given to us with emotional content," said Judith.

"Did it have to be *negative* emotional content?"

Judith glared at her. "How many times does the world have to show you, you don't get summat for nothing?"

Under Rob's wary gaze, they took their beers into the front bar to sit by the log burner. "So what do we do?"

"We get rat-arsed—" said Judith.

"We both have work tomorrow—"

"—while repeating certain phrases and gestures, and these phrases and gestures will be distorted by the inebriation in a way which directly indicates the shape the town is being bent into. So I'll be able to see where the distortions are."

Autumn liked a pint or two around Christmas time. However, she couldn't help thinking that Judith wouldn't be much of a drinking companion. "Is it okay if we chat to people we know?"

Judith paused for a moment so long that Autumn thought she'd offended her, but no, of course that wasn't possible. "As long as you keep up the incantation every ten minutes. Follow me." She started to make a series of sounds in the back of her throat, and Autumn, grateful for the Christmas hits playing over the speakers, began to attempt to copy her.

In order to fully participate in her social evening, therefore, Autumn found herself greeting the many friends who entered, getting up to stand with them in the main bar, then retreating quickly every ten minutes to huddle with Judith, claiming either that she was cold or having a coughing fit.

"Are you directing your germs at her?" asked Mick, the car mechanic. "Is this biological warfare?"

"She's working at the shop now," said Autumn. "It'd be rude not to bring her along."

"Keeps her off the streets, I suppose," said Paul the builder. "Now she can just be rude in the one place."

Other residents chimed in with similar comments, and, after a few token protests of hers turned the tide a bit—because in the end, these were kind and polite people—Autumn changed the subject. She hadn't really grasped until this evening just how disliked Judith was in Lychford. When she returned to the log burner, the old woman was looking into the fire, her face a mask. Surely, over the years, that background dislike must seep into you, must change you? Was that what Autumn was going to end up like? *Alone,* part of her said, but Judith wasn't actually alone, was she? Autumn couldn't remember, quite, what the details were, and now she thought about it, she was sure she'd once heard someone in town refer to Judith as a widow, but she was equally certain Judith had made reference to someone waiting for her at home. "How's your husband?" she asked.

"Piss off," said Judith. Then immediately followed it with the required noises, meaning Autumn had to join in.

Autumn had now had three pints. Being told it was imperative that one should drink had an effect. Like one of those social experiment . . . things. It did mean, however, that she wasn't going to take that on the nose, and when she'd completed the noises she said so. "You coming out with stuff like that is why that lot don't like you. What's wrong with me asking about your husband?"

"You're not really asking. You're just making conversation."

Autumn was about to reply with her usual compassion when the door of the pub opened. In walked a young man, built, as was obvious even through his hefty pullover and coat, like a rugby player. He had one of those beards that all the blokes had started getting a couple of years back, but it looked . . . all right. Tended to. His eyes were bright and interesting, and he had the most enormous grin on his face. Calls from local lads suggested he was known around here. "Good evening," he said in return, and his voice was exactly the right sort of posh, immediately suggesting he was somehow laughing at himself.

He was . . . yeah, on a second and a third viewing, he really was very damn attractive.

"Yeah," said Autumn to Judith, "you're right. Sorry. I'd better get on with the drinking. Same again?" She was up and heading for the mutual acquaintances before Judith could utter another syllable.

It turned out the new arrival was called Luke, and he was a tutor at the agricultural college who'd also been working on one of the local farms with Ben and Kerry Rosset, the locals who'd greeted him with such bonhomie. Autumn immediately offered to get a round in, and Luke, with just a glance to the Rossets to confirm this wasn't some drunken loony, agreed. This many pints down, and aware she'd only have ten minutes before having to withdraw, Autumn felt she had to talk fast. Perhaps a bit too fast. She immediately told him all about her shop, and Ed, who kept the tropical fish at the garden centre, wandered over and added the quaint detail that she was friends with the local vicar and employed the local crank. That one, over there. Luke actually waved.

Judith seemed to consider for a moment, then experimentally

raised a hand in response. It looked after a moment like she'd felt something on the surface of her palm, and turned it to examine it.

"She seems . . . weird," said Luke.

"She really is," said Autumn, who'd taken the opportunity of him turning around to check his finger for a wedding ring. There was none. She'd already given him several opportunities to use the word *girlfriend,* and he'd seized none of them. "So the agricultural college, they have a wild social life, we hear a lot of stories. . . ." Which got a laugh from the Rossets.

"It's all true. Not that I can partake. At the end of the evening I head sadly home to my lonely staff apartment."

Was it her imagination, or was he checking her out, too? Right, she needed to come out with something that would indicate she was on a whole different level to any farming women he might know. Something that would say she was not only matey, but full of witchy wisdom, the cunning woman of the shadows. "So," she said, "are you watching *Strictly Come Dancing*?"

A blur of conversation gradually got lost somewhere in darkness, and there was probably some . . . kissing . . . and then she must have fallen asleep because where was she now, exactly? Oh. *Phew.* At home in bed. All the familiar details of that cupboard over there; hello, cupboard. Oh . . . she felt . . . she felt . . . no, managed to keep that down. Still a bit drunk, too, so this was going to hurt even more later. Still, it was Christmas. She'd just gotten a bit too festive. But there'd been something important. Oh, right, Judith. Their magical mission. Well, she'd done her bit. Probably. She remembered Judith had said something to her, late on, had tried to get through to her about . . . right, well, maybe she herself hadn't learned anything, but she hoped Judith had.

Okay, time to slowly get moving, find out where her feet were, get some serious coffee into . . .

She felt something move in bed beside her.

She looked across and saw the naked back of a man. Whose name was . . . no, that wasn't coming to her. And it was also now suddenly very important that she was naked, too.

Oh no. *Oh* no.

"Oh, hi, are you awake?" He turned over and looked anxiously at her. At least he didn't look like the cat who'd gotten the cream. *Had* he gotten the cream? It didn't quite . . . feel like he had. She realised she hadn't said anything, and was just looking at him in a way which was getting a very worried reaction. "Nothing happened," he said quickly. "Please don't worry."

"We're naked!"

"You kind of . . . insisted on that. I tried to get out of bed a couple of times, but you'd switched the light off, and I couldn't see anything, and I couldn't find my clothes, and it was cold—"

"How do I know you're telling the truth?"

He suddenly looked very serious. "Because I would *never*—you *wanted* to, but you were about to pass out."

She wished her new senses could tell her if someone was lying. But no, she didn't need that. Just by looking at him, she could see he was offended by the mere implication, and worried for her, too. She nodded. "Okay."

"Okay. So. Would you like to . . . talk about it?"

"What?"

"This." He gestured vaguely at them both. At least she hoped that's what he was gesturing at.

She could only shake her head.

"Well . . . that leaves us with the option of one of us closing our eyes while the other finds clothes, and us never speaking of this again."

Autumn was about to agree when her mobile, on the bedside table, rang. Gathering the covers to her in a way which suddenly made her feel like she was in an American TV show, she saw who it was, hesitated, then felt she had to answer it.

"Quickly," said Judith's voice on the other end of the line. "What's going on there?" She sounded urgent. The volume on the phone was loud enough that the guy . . . whose name still escaped her . . . could hear every word.

"Nothing. Why do you ask?"

"I mean, is anything unusual happening to you?"

Autumn wanted to say really, yes, there was. But she knew this wasn't the sort of unusual Judith meant. "No."

"That young man who's there with you, is there anything strange about him?"

Autumn was about to say, yes, he seemed weirdly decent, when she felt a sudden movement beside her, and turned to see more than she should have seen, as the guy . . . whose name would come to her soon . . . was getting quickly out of bed and grabbing for his clothes. "I should be off," he said. "Sorry." He gestured at the phone. "Interestingly intimate relationship you two . . . anyway, early start. Sorry again. Really sorry."

"No, wait—"

But he was off, out of the door and down the stairs, looking back to awkwardly wave, then clearly feeling he was in the wrong and shouldn't be chancing a merry gesture. A moment later Autumn heard the shop door close. Which meant she'd left it unlocked last night.

"Well?" said Judith on the phone. "He's gone now, so you can tell me."

"That's all you're bloody getting," said Autumn, reflecting that that might as well be the title of her autobiography. "Apart from he wasn't strange at all, he was . . . great. And I'm fine. So you needn't worry." As Judith started to say something equally urgent, Autumn switched off the phone and threw it after—

Luke. That had been his name.

She heard the phone bounce down the stairs and then the sound of glass shattering. Then something dripping.

Autumn threw the covers back over her head and waited for death.

Judith tried a couple of times to call Autumn, but the phone kept going to voicemail. She would have to go over there.

In the pub, Judith had made a series of notes on a beer mat, comparing how far Autumn's magical shouts differed from what they should have been, and had thankfully gotten everything she'd needed before Autumn had abandoned the magical working altogether, snogged that lad's face off and dragged him out of the pub to, as she'd put it, "show him her wise and shadowy artefacts." The sampling she'd taken on her palm had told her something was wrong, but it had also told her it was going to take time to work out what it was.

That morning, before it was light, Judith had taken her notes and compared them to those she'd taken that summer, on a particularly placid day when she'd decided Lychford was about as normal as it was ever going to get.

That had given her a musical sense of the nature of the distortions. At dawn, ignoring what younger, weaker women would call a hangover, she'd climbed to a high place overlooking the town, and come out with a shout that approximated the gap between how things should be and where they were now. The resonances of that shout returned, to her enhanced senses, an idea of where the distortions were. As she'd suspected, they weren't fixed, but building, like water slapping back and forth as the ground underneath it juddered in a gathering earthquake.

It was where those distortions were focussed that worried her most: at the magic shop; at the Vicarage; at Judith's own home. With Lizzie and Autumn in their beds, that might mean they themselves, or, in Autumn's case, who they were with, had been got at. In Judith's own case . . . she had a horrible feeling she'd already felt the change in her own home without registering it as important. It had happened to someone . . . something . . . that was such a regular part of her life that she tended to overlook . . . him.

She would have to tell Lizzie and Autumn about this as soon as possible, but first she had to deal with her own house. Judith went to the foot of the stairs and looked up them, bracing herself. She could feel the coldness from down here, had gotten used to sleeping beside it, even. She knew she deserved this curse, for employing the darkest of workings, decades ago. But she couldn't say she'd changed. As soon as summat difficult had blocked her path, when the three of them had come together to resist Sovo, she had gone straight back to the darkness.

She put one foot on the bottom step. Arthur's voice, of course, immediately came from upstairs. "You been out already, woman! You been off with your fancy man?"

"Course I have," she called back. "We've been making mad passionate love in the dewy grass. You hang on, I'll tell you all about it." She'd been doing the minimum for Arthur in the last few days, just nodding in the direction of her duty of care. Taking care of him was a nonsense, she knew it was, but she couldn't seem to help it. Perhaps that was part of the curse. Or maybe it was just human nature. If it was, that said good things about her which she wasn't quite willing to believe. She started to climb the stairs.

"You don't even want to see me during the day. You spend all your time with that whore now. Encouraging her. Letting what she does get your juices flowing."

"Summat has to, because you can't!" Judith's mind was racing. Had that been a reference to what Autumn had got up to last night? If so, how did Arthur know about that? It wasn't as if she shared information with him.

Judith had to pause for her usual moment on the threshold before going into her bedroom and finding Arthur, or rather what she had to start making herself think of as the ghost of him, attached to his ventilator, which was, unlike him, entirely real and a burden to her electricity bill. He was, as always, watching his whodunits on Sky, the remote, which was also a real artefact, accessible to his fingertips whenever he wanted them to be solid. He met her gaze with his usual baleful expression. "Oh, you've decided to come and spend a few moments with me. I'm honoured."

"You should be." If whatever distortion of reality had touched Lizzie and Autumn had also reached out in her direction via what might well look to it like her weak point, via Arthur, then it might have also made itself vulnerable. If it had altered him, then perhaps she could learn something here. She had to make use of Arthur to seize that thing which was trying to sneak up on them all, and was building and building towards something terrible.

She made herself sit down on the side of the bed next to his chair. She watched *Murder, She Wrote* for a few moments. Some people were being very jolly about a corpse. She tried not to think about what she was contemplating. She kept her eyes fixed on the screen and slowly made herself reach out. Her fingers touched the ice of Arthur's head. There was a sense memory there, a little charade of familiar skin. That softness where he hadn't shaved for about four days. The scent of him came to her, so familiar in this place as to be normally unnoticed, but back at the centre of her senses now, the same as when they'd met. With it, the memory of dances in the town hall. That suit he'd worn with chalk on the cuffs, his lapels always so scuffed. She made the hand go further, through the skin, something she'd never before dared do. Why would she have? She'd known when she'd first seen him here that he was a punishment that had been entirely deserved. She'd never tried to escape him. Though she also longed to. Stupid.

"What you doing, woman?" He said it with the same playful tone as when she used to reach out for him in bed. He knew how to play every note of her. He was her curse. With every inch her hand reached, she felt more and more like she was compromising herself with intimacy, holding desperately to a corpse, a corpse that had infected her, had hurt her, and why, oh why, had she been so weak, so foolish, to never tell anyone? She was like her friends who didn't go to the doctor and had died out of pride. Only this had lasted much longer. She was sobbing, she realised. He was chuckling at the sound.

Her hand reached a point of nothingness, right inside Arthur. She flexed her fingers in the darkness at the centre of what had started as his body, but was now pure void. It really should have come out the other side, but there was more space inside him than looked possible on the outside. "Judith?" he said suddenly, and his voice was horribly different now. "Judith, is that you?"

"Of course it's me!" she managed to blurt out.

"I don't know where I am. I'm inside something. I can't see you. Give me your hand!" The words were still being spoken by the cold ghost sitting next to her, but they sounded distant, echoing from the impossible space inside him, and different, loving, young. Was *her* Arthur really somewhere inside this thing? How had she not realised that? Or had she always known it? Was this the change the ripple across reality from the border had made?

She was stretching out her fingers before she could even frame the thought. She was trying to reach the real Arthur.

Something brushed the tips of her fingers. A hand that was about to close on hers.

Its fingertips were cold.

She jerked away. The hand grabbed hers. She yelled, and tried to wrench out of its grasp. It had locked onto her hand. She looked urgently at Arthur, and he was grinning all over his face, which lapped like a pool of water around her arm, his features distorted by her being inside him, and he said, with that bitter, clever voice back in place again, "One down, two to go."

It was a trap, she realised, one that had been baited with love and with her own arrogance.

Judith had no time to cry out before the hand inside Arthur, impossibly strong, heaved on hers, and she fell headlong into her husband.

Over the next few days, Lizzie attended another Christmas dinner, this one at Deanery Chapter, with a lot of other local vicars all looking equally put upon, and the conversation deliberately bright and cheerful to the point of mutual hysteria. She couldn't help feeling the others were only under the normal pressures of Christmas, and didn't have to deal with whatever was weighing down on her. Then she presided over a carol service at the school, after which a mother had told her that those carols had been much better than the ones in church, not so religious.

Most nights now she was working late, trying to put out of her mind the little noises from elsewhere in the Vicarage. She was hardly sleeping. The stress seemed to be increasing every day. It was like she was missing something that was heading straight for her. Her plans for reorganising the crib service in order to bring a few more actual children into it weren't getting very far. So when she saw the familiar number on her phone, Lizzie was more than ready to give in to the distraction. Besides, she'd probably reached capacity on her answer phone. She hadn't spoken to Autumn in days, not since the tree stump. She had been unconsciously waiting, she realised, for Judith to call them all together and explain what this subtle threat they were facing was all about. She'd been ignoring the possibility that the answer might involve her. "Hey, how are you?"

The voice at the other end of the line had an undercurrent of desperation to it that it took a moment for Lizzie to realise she actually felt nostalgic about. This was Autumn as a student all over again. "Kind of . . . weird . . ." And she went on to describe her night at the Plough and the morning after and how awkward she'd felt in the days since.

"So," said Lizzie, when she could get a word in edgewise, "what did you and this guy Luke actually end up, you know, doing?"

"I may have . . . jingled his bells."

"But did you jingle all the way?"

"I don't think so, and you're smiling at having come up with that line, aren't you?"

Lizzie deliberately killed her grin. "Do we have to hunt him down and . . . actually, no, don't tell Judith about this, she really would want to hunt him down."

"I don't think he did anything wrong, I think he was kind of . . . lovely, actually, and Judith already tried to sort of warn me about him. She hasn't been in to work since, or I'd have asked her what that was about. I haven't gone after her because I kind of want to sack her, but then she might sack me, or worse, not, and then she'd be completely in charge of me."

"Did you get Luke's number?"

"I . . . found it. About lunchtime that same day. When I went for a shower. I don't know why I wanted him to write it down there. I copied it using a mirror."

"You know you're wonderful, don't you?"

"You're smiling again, at my distress."

"Are you going to call him?"

There was a long pause. "I've already called him—"

"Not at all needy."

"—eight times—"

"Indeed, 'needy' is absolutely not a word I would use."

"—and left eight voicemail messages."

"Saying what? Needily."

"That I want to apologise to him, to try to explain—"

"You once told me you always did what the Duke of Wellington said, 'never explain, never apologise'—"

"Yeah, and you told me the Duke of Wellington ended up as the most hated man in Britain. And I don't want to be like that. I don't want to keep working through a list of rom-com clichés. But I don't want to be alone, okay? And I'm fed up with . . . trying without it looking like I'm trying. He was lovely, and I've fucked it up. Like I always fuck everything up . . . I'm sorry."

"Come on over."

"No, it's fine, I just . . . I love him."

"What?"

There was silence for a moment. "I shouldn't have said that. I'm messed up. I'm going to try to get some sleep."

"Autumn, wait—" But she'd hung up. Lizzie immediately tried to dial her back, but the call went straight to voicemail. She thought about going over, but it was late. There had been an edge of weird desperation to her friend's voice that Lizzie hadn't heard before. Sleep might be the best thing for her. Like it would be for her.

"No hurting," said the small voice from the doorway.

Lizzie looked up to see the little boy again, and yet again the sight chilled her. He had both his hands up as if to hopelessly defend himself. "No hurting," he repeated, imploring.

"Are you . . . afraid of *me*?" asked Lizzie, getting slowly to her feet. If so, why had he come into her house? The movement seemed to startle the boy. He turned and vanished even as Lizzie took a step forward. She stopped, and rubbed her brow. "Coffee," she said. "Maybe some rum."

Autumn lay in her bed and tried to sleep. She had never felt like this before. She felt weirdly guilty at having let Lizzie hear a little of it. The feeling had risen up in her during the afternoon, and made her keep going back to her phone, keep trying Luke's number, over and over, until with an effort of will she'd called Lizzie instead. She was breathing harder than she normally would, a great weight of twitching anxiety in her chest. She wanted to hear Luke's voice, to have him reassure her that she hadn't offended him, that everything was okay, that she would see him again. That might lead to more. No, that wasn't the most important thing, just being okay with him, that was where it had to start.

The same set of thoughts rolled over and over in her head. She should make herself get undressed, have a hot drink. How was she ever going to sleep? She clutched the covers in order to feel something in her hands. She'd been in love, possibly, a couple of times in her life. She thought that was probably what people would call the sensation she'd felt on those other occasions: a nervousness about the bloke in question finding someone else, a desire to make sure everything was okay between them. But this was ten, twenty times as intense. She'd made herself think that he might have someone else, and she'd been suddenly filled with hatred towards an imaginary person, the agricultural-student nature of whom she'd sketched out in her mind to the point where her rival had a ponytail and a checked shirt. Like someone in a musical.

She was going to be alone at Christmas, when a tally was made of who was alone and who wasn't and loneliness became a thing everyone talked about. She was going to be alone and in love. Was this what love was going to be like for her from now on? This was so not her.

Autumn closed her eyes and tried to will herself to sleep.

Days are not days as we know them in the places where Finn, Prince of the Blood, walked and thought, far from the fields we know, and whether these were places and whether or not that was walking or thinking, these are also not exactly what we'd mean by those words.

But let's say there was a moment when he came to the edge of Lychford, and he was thinking of why—since he'd been so urgent last time, since his message had been one of impending danger—he'd heard nothing since from the three whose mission it was to protect the borders of this place.

He moved, proudly and unhesitatingly, to cross those borders himself, intending to manifest once more to Autumn and ask what progress had been made.

He stepped not through, but straight past.

Shocked, he tried again. Again, the border to step over eluded him.

Scared and furious now, he bellowed and struck where the border should be, bringing something like lightning and sunlight and gravity together all at once where his fist hit—

—nothing.

He stared at the gap in the realities. This wasn't possible. The worlds had been rearranged, entirely without the permission of his people or anyone else, to cut off the humans inside from all aid.

Finn calmed himself, then turned and said a word and ran, became a light and a hare that skipped over hills and was the wind and was the hills and would get to where his people existed at the speed of the word leaving his mouth. His father had to know of this. He had not the faintest idea what even his people might do to stop this. The worlds had been turned inside out. There might already be horrors abroad in Lychford.

With four days to go before Christmas, Lizzie got to the church early and had everything ready for the wedding rehearsal before Alan and Emma and their families and supporters arrived. At least this was something she'd gotten down to a fine art. This lot, of course, had all their added extras. Indeed, they'd brought along a couple of examples of the statues they were going to place in the church on the day.

"So why do you want . . . this, exactly?" she said, looking up at a carved face that was veined, bulbous, not really much of a face at all. The body of the thing was also not something you'd expect to stand in a churchyard without comment. Those were wings, weren't they? Sort of. Too many arms, really. The whole thing looked like a melted cherub.

"Sentimental reasons," Alan said with a laugh.

"This is exactly like the first one we, *err,* pinched, when we were students," said Emma. Her maids of honour nodded, like this was a story they'd heard often. They were an interesting pair themselves, identical, but Lizzie had been assured they weren't twins. They had eyes that were strikingly green and sort of golden at the same time. Alan's best man, Derek, was also quite something. He must have been over eight feet tall, and Lizzie hadn't really gotten a good look at him, because his face was somehow continually hidden in shadow. He was now carrying the second statue, just as ugly as the first, to the specific spot where this lot wanted it placed.

The father of the bride, Stewart, was present only as a shaft of pulsing green light, which seemed to emanate from somewhere under the floor and faded into the roof. Lizzie had been assured he was going to wear something more formal for the ceremony itself. She leafed back through her forms, worried that she was somehow missing something. But no, there didn't seem to be anything odd going on. "Where did you say you were from?" She should know that, shouldn't she? She should know that offhandedly.

"Swindon," said Emma. "So not too far to drive."

"Are we okay with the order of service now?" asked Alan.

Lizzie wanted to say that actually this was the first thought she'd had about it since the night she'd last seen them, but no, bright and professional, that was the way. She'd had no notes last time she'd read through it, eccentric as it was. She could hardly remember anything about it. She took it from her papers and noticed there was one point she should ask about. "What do you have for the moment when I have to—?"

Emma, of course, had produced a doll of a baby before she'd finished the sentence.

"And here's the other thing," said Alan, putting a very heavy ceremonial knife into her hands. "I'm assuming you won't have one of your own."

Everyone laughed. Lizzie took the doll and the knife up to the font. "And it should be up here, at the end of the service?"

"Right at the climax," said Emma.

"But on the day itself—?" Lizzie couldn't help feeling, as she stood there, the point of the knife sticking into the plastic of the doll, that she was missing something rather important. Was there a point of procedure about this that she hadn't got straight? Why was something inside her screaming that she shouldn't be doing it? She sighed inwardly. Her brain was such a jumble at the moment. Bloody Christmas.

"Don't worry," Alan assured her, "on the day itself, we've already arranged to get hold of the real thing."

Autumn tried to work. She went downstairs each morning, made herself get as far as the door, attempted to swing the sign on it from CLOSED to OPEN . . . but if it wasn't to do with getting Luke into her life, what was the point? She was barely sleeping, just finally giving in to exhaustion in the early hours.

One evening, she went over to the Vicarage, hoping to find Lizzie, who was now not answering her phone any more than Luke was. She was surprised to find the Lizzie who opened the door was looking as pale and nervous as she did. "It's not going to snow," she said, without even a hello. "No white Christmas this year."

"Can I come in?"

Lizzie gestured impatiently that she could and Autumn entered, startled about what she'd just noticed about Lizzie's hands. But no, never mind that, that wasn't important, she had something urgent to ask. "So, have you heard from Luke?"

"Who?"

Autumn held in the sudden fury she felt at that impudent question. "Luke! My Luke!"

"Is that the bloke you—? I've never met him. Why should I have heard from him?" Sounding very distracted, Lizzie led her into the kitchen, where . . . oh my God.

A small boy stood in the middle of the room, weeping. On seeing Lizzie, he instantly grabbed for her hand. "No hurting!" he shouted.

Lizzie sighingly pulled her cardigan sleeve away from him and pushed past him to get to the kettle. This, Autumn realised, must be that ghost Lizzie had told them about. Back when . . . yeah, Judith hadn't been into the shop for ages now, what was that about? But no, there were more urgent matters at hand. "I think there were some specific words I said to Luke that he didn't like, or maybe it was the way I said them. Should I go over to the agricultural college, do you think?"

Lizzie made a sudden gasp of pain that made Autumn look over to where she was washing out two cups. She'd gotten the water on her hands, and the backs of her hands were . . .

"Sorry," said Lizzie. "For some reason I've been trying to stop myself from being able to use my hands. It's the stupidest thing. I can only hurt them for a little while before I can't manage it anymore. I've tried burning them with candles, sticking them with a screwdriver. I can't quite bring myself to use the scissors but, you know, I'm going to have to get to that soon, or it'll be, I don't know, too late."

"No hurting!" yelled the boy.

Autumn was stunned for a moment by the horror her friend was inflicting upon herself. But hey, it was nothing compared to what she was going through. "You think you've got problems? I think I've now filled up Luke's voicemail. Or he's switched it off—"

"Will you just stop—!" That had been a sudden shout from Lizzie. The kettle was now starting to boil. "Sorry, sorry, I need to concentrate. Making you tea just gave me an idea. I should have seen it sooner. I'm going to try boiling water on my hands. See if I can ruin them completely."

"Why . . . why—?"

"Then I'll be useless to them. I won't be able to do the thing." She made a stabbing motion. "I've tried everything else. I don't know who this 'I' is I'm talking about. Myself, I'm fine. Just a bit busy. There's just . . . you know, something inside, trying to do something to stop all this."

"All what? If you can't listen to this important stuff I'm telling you about Luke for five minutes—"

"No hurting!"

"That can wait. This is important." The kettle was boiling furiously. Lizzie snatched it off its stand and made to pour the water over her hand.

Reflexively, Autumn leapt forward and knocked the kettle into the sink.

Lizzie cried out, pushed Autumn away, and grabbed for the kettle. Autumn, furious at her, tried to get it off her.

"Don't!" cried the little boy.

Lizzie slapped Autumn as hard as she had ever been hit by anyone.

Autumn fell to the floor, clutching her face.

"Oh no, oh no," whispered Lizzie. Then she took the kettle again and started to refill it.

Autumn was panting, feeling the anger, the adrenaline . . . breaking down something inside her. She wanted to hurt Lizzie back for this, more than anything, so she could get back to . . . get back to . . .

Oh no. Oh no, what was happening here?

She heaved herself up and grabbed Lizzie's wrists, making her drop the kettle. "Do that again."

Without hesitation, Lizzie broke free and did so.

Autumn yelled with the impact, but this time she was ready for it. This time she could feel clearly the sudden insight it brought. She grabbed her friend, and started to heave her towards the door, Lizzie fighting all the way. "Okay, you . . . you keep doing that. You keep slapping me. But you're coming with me."

"No! I'm busy! I have to hurt my hands!"

"No hurting!" the child cried desperately, turning to watch them go.

"Listen to him," said Autumn, hoping against hope she could keep this anger going. "This isn't normal. We've been got at."

Lizzie kept flexing her fingers in her gloves as her friend drove through the rain-lashed darkness. This was a complete waste of time, when she had so much to do, and her hands were still functional, and that was breaking her heart.

"It's good," said a small voice from the backseat.

Lizzie looked over her shoulder to see that bloody boy still sitting there, shivering. She was furious that he'd followed her. Only . . . she somehow felt that she'd wanted him to as well. She was doing her best, she was doing all she could do, while part of her, a stupid part, kept trying to hurt her hands . . . or was it the other way around?

"Hit me again," said Autumn. "I'm starting to . . . to go where we're going for a different reason."

"You're driving, and I'm wearing mittens, you stupid—!"

Autumn made a desperate sound, then reached over to the stereo in the battered old Ford Fiesta and shoved in the CD that had been sticking out of the player. The sound of Greg Lake erupted into the car.

Lizzie made a sound of her own and hit Autumn again.

Autumn swung the car down the driveway and past the sign saying "Hartford Lodge Agricultural College," and as she did so she began desperately to sing along.

Luke Halsall was looking forward to going home. Tonight he'd gone for a Christmas pint with his students, then he had some paperwork to do, and he'd be off before lunchtime tomorrow, down south, back to his friends. The nature of his job meant he couldn't keep his phone switched off, but he'd managed to assign that Autumn woman a different ringtone, a warning siren, and took care to let it go to voicemail whenever she called. He'd been going to call her back after the first message, but before he could, she'd left loads of them, and his guilt had turned into annoyance, then worry. That night had been such a mistake. He'd kept going over it in his head, but no, he thought he'd done the right thing. It seemed like the owner of the magic shop was the villain of one of those horror stories where one *didn't* have to do something wrong in order to have someone go the full bunny boiler on you.

Which was a huge pity, because he'd really liked her. When she'd been drunk in the pub she'd been good fun. Apart from her having to keep popping back to the corner to keep that nosy old woman company while she practiced her folk songs. That had maybe been a bit of a warning sign. Even the next morning, she'd acted in an entirely understandable way, but then . . . that phone call by, again, that old woman . . .

His thoughts had kept Luke, as he walked back across the darkened campus towards the tutors' quarters, from looking at what was ahead of him. But now, as he neared the corner of his housing block, he wondered what the odd shape was he was seeing there by his door. Was someone waiting in the shadows? Oh no, it wasn't—?!

Autumn stepped out to confront him. "It's okay," she said. "I'm not going to try to force you into anything." Another figure stepped out beside her. Autumn looked between them, as if only now realising what this looked like. "That's absolutely not why I brought along a vicar."

Against his better judgment, Luke let them into his flat. The presence of another person in his slightly personalised abode of vinyl record player and specialist coffee maker, even one as weirdly tense as this vicar seemed, made him feel slightly safer. This was surely that friend of Autumn's that people had talked about. Maybe this would be a chance to put an end to this. "Listen—" he began.

"I'm not weird," said Autumn, interrupting him. "At least, not so long as she keeps on—Lizzie—?" The vicar slapped Autumn around the face. "Thanks. Now—"

Luke took a step back. What the hell? "Okay, I've changed my mind, I think you should go—"

"Please, just listen to me, just for a few minutes. That's all I ask."

"Okay." He waited.

He realised she was looking at him with a kind of giddy joy, that she'd drifted off, but this time she stopped herself before the vicar could move in to slap her. "I understand, in my moments of clarity, that I've been pursuing you in a scary, intense way. I think . . ." She seemed to choose her words carefully. "Something's upset my brain chemistry." The vicar picked up a stapler and started to play with it. Autumn grabbed it off her. "This isn't the usual me. I was hoping that if I came to see you, you might be able to talk me down, but with how I'm feeling now I'm here, nope, not going to happen. So now I need your help in a different way."

She seemed to know what she was talking about. It was quite a relief to hear that voice he'd heard that first night. Luke had had an uncle who'd been schizophrenic, and this understanding of her own condition reminded him of how he'd been sometimes. He carefully sat down and faced her. "What can I do?"

Autumn took something from her bag. "Look at this."

She handed it to him and he found he was looking at a saucer full of some sort of potpourri, which he couldn't help taking a sniff of, and it smelled really weird, kind of—

He managed only a croak as darkness welled up into his head.

Autumn looked down at Luke's body where it had fallen onto the sofa. He started to snore. "Okay," she said, "help me . . ." She wanted to ask for Lizzie's help undressing him, but that took her back to the awful reason she'd put the sleep powders into her bag in the first place. "Roll up his sleeve. And keep slapping me. Lizzie, stay with me!"

Lizzie had a jam jar in her hands, and had been about to smash it, Autumn had realised. Now she quickly nodded, distracted beyond distraction, holding on to the same tiny thread of helping each other that was keeping Autumn herself going. The little ghost that had accompanied them here looked anxiously at them. Lizzie squatted down and administered the required slap to Autumn, which she was starting to find bracing, then the two of them got to work on Luke's shirt. Autumn found the syringe in her bag, part of the alchemical kit she always carried, fitted a new needle, and drew out . . . well, who knew how much blood was going to be enough? She was making up this recipe based on nothing more than instinct and what little Judith had managed to teach her. Oh, Judith. She'd been deliberately kept distracted from thinking about Judith. "We have to look for Judith," she said. "She must have been got at, too. But first we have to get back to the shop." She put the syringe full of blood back in her bag, and made Luke as comfortable as she could. She looked down at him on the sofa, tousled, lost. He'd been ready to listen to her, even at this extremity. "Keep slapping me," she said to Lizzie. "Slap me lots."

Autumn was well aware that the rules for "love potions" were very strict. This was one of those areas where one could easily wander off the path into curse magic and thus invite horrors into one's own life. All love potions could do, she'd told several young customers, was help make someone's mind up about what they really wanted. They couldn't influence that decision, not without terrible penalties. However, Autumn was aware that there were recipes for potions that claimed to be able to do just that. So what if you took such a recipe, but picked every opposite ingredient, and added, as always in these cases, something associated with the target of one's affections, and blood was the biggest association of all . . .

"What's the opposite of vanilla?" she asked Lizzie, as they stood in the back-room laboratory area of the shop, water already bubbling in the cauldron. Autumn had taken the precaution of wrapping the Reverend's hands in three layers of gloves, held on with elastic bands, so at least she'd have some warning if she was going to try any more self-harm. The inability to use her hands seemed, fortunately, to have satisfied her, and she was staring into space, the conflict inside her playing out only in the tiniest of tics. Beside her stood the ghost child, looking desperately between them.

Lizzie shook her head, snapped back to reality by the question. "Kinky?"

Just the sound of it made Autumn sad. It was like Lizzie's sense of humour had forced its way up out of her, but the face it came from hadn't noticed. "Tutti-frutti," she decided, and got some ice cream from the fridge to provide the first ingredient. Her own brain kept rolling around with the idea of whether Luke would like the smell of vanilla, and shouldn't she go back and see how he was, and of course the slaps were going to be a bit muffled now, so she'd better bloody get on with it. She rushed around the lab, grabbing what she could, letting her unconscious guide her. "The opposite of rose is . . . thorn! The opposite of sugar is . . . salt. The opposite of lemon is . . . lime." Which was such bollocks, but she knew enough about magic by now to know that wouldn't matter. She kept adding ingredients until the boiling mixture smelled like an industrial accident at Holland & Barrett. She added Luke's blood from the syringe and stirred it in. She was disturbed to find she felt affection even for the liquid. Now came the difficult bit. She'd only had a few lessons from Judith on the subject of projecting one's intent into matter through gesture and sound. She didn't know where to begin. If only she could just say, "and here's one I made earlier," like on the cooking shows. The three ways of empowering something were to make a sacrifice, use a sort of judo to fool the universe into doing something for you, or appeal to a higher power. Autumn didn't actually believe in the existence of any higher powers, but before she'd gained her extra senses, she had always relied on them as a metaphor, so now, as she made the basic hand movements she'd learned, she brought her own more nebulous icons of what she'd always regarded as he unconscious process in her own mind to bear on the working. The power of blood, which was meant to be mighty, would help.

It was going to have to be enough.

Judith was in hell.

That was the only conclusion she could come to. She was still aware, though it was a bit like being asleep. There was a cold darkness all around her, and she was falling. The fall was endless. So the cold kept chilling her to the point of fear, and her body kept jerking with the sudden realisation she was falling, over and over, and there was no stopping it.

She was falling through the architecture of the curse. In other words, she was falling through a simulacrum of Arthur. She felt who he'd been and his love for her at every moment, enormously, through every pore of her skin.

She was in hell.

She was aware of her body, vaguely. She felt naked. Her eyes didn't seem to be working. Or there was nothing at all to see.

Robin, her old lover, had made this curse, all those years ago. His field of study had been necromancy, that bloody awful pit of dark clothes and graveyards and loving the dead. Whoever she'd ended up with as her sweetheart after Robin, the necromancer's trap had been set for them to fall into on their deathbed. Could you fight your way out of a curse? Had anyone ever been confronted by their just deserts and said "sod you" and got out of it?

Judith was lost. She didn't know where to begin. But she got the feeling she had forever to think about it.

Autumn lowered the mug from her lips, having drunk down the potion and felt, just for a moment, sad about . . . it was going, yes, it was actually going, she was losing the feeling, and that was making her sad! Sad but . . . no, why the hell would that make her sad? It was gone, that horrible feeling was gone, banished by her anti-love potion. It had worked. She was free of it, free to act. She slammed the mug down onto the table and pulled Lizzie to her, shaking in sheer relief. "Right," she said finally. "They took their best shot against all of us, whoever they are. But they didn't get me. Now let's see what we can do about you."

"Nothing to be done. Everything's fine. Let me get back to my work." Lizzie actually shook her head as she said the words, desperately denying them.

"Can you tell me why you've been trying to hurt yourself? What's this 'thing' someone wants you to do?"

Lizzie shook her head once again. "Nothing." She was looking ashen, as if whatever was wrong had increased in intensity, just in the time Autumn had been working here.

"No hurting!" called the ghost child.

What was the connection between the boy and Lizzie? Judith had called Autumn to warn her that something unusual might happen to her. Presumably her sudden passion for Luke had been one of the distortions in reality the old witch had been trying to sense. Was the child another? She had no idea how to get rid of it if it did turn out to be dangerous. Autumn looked at the clock. It was already past midnight. If Judith had, by some miracle, just been sulking at home all this time, she'd be long in her bed by now. But no, how likely was that? "Come on," she said to Lizzie. "Let's see what they've done to her." Whoever, she silently added, as they headed out, "they" were.

Standing outside Judith's house, Autumn could feel stark coldness radiating from one of the upper-floor rooms, beyond the cold in the street and the snow starting to fall around them. It was, she realised, a sensation she'd felt before, when passing Judith's house. It was only now she'd come here on the lookout for some kind of threat that it had become meaningful. She went to the door and paused. Okay, this was a bit like a police officer believing harm was being done inside a building right now, wasn't it? She looked to Lizzie and the ghost child beside her for an approval that was met only by Lizzie's look of agonised distraction. Okay then. Autumn took a run up and aimed a flying kick at the door.

She bounced off it and collapsed onto the pavement.

It turned out that doors were a bit harder to get through in real life than on TV. And of course Judith would have the sturdiest possible door.

"Did I really just see that?" a familiar voice said. Autumn looked up to see Judith's son, Shaun, heading over, the lights of his police car behind him. "Tell you what, let's say I didn't."

It turned out that Shaun, aware that his mother hadn't been in touch for what was, even for her, a long time, had just come off shift, and had decided to come by to see if everything was all right. Autumn told him the truth about his Mum's absence from the shop in recent days, and Shaun used his own key to open the front door, which, worryingly, wasn't actually bolted. They stepped over a pile of mail to get in.

"Mum?" Shaun called up the stairs, his voice an aching compromise between professional and personal. He called twice again as he led the way up them, the former sound gradually taking over from the latter. He hadn't even asked why Lizzie was with them, and of course couldn't see the child, who was looking around himself in greater agitation the higher they climbed.

Shaun also obviously couldn't see, as they entered the bedroom, the strange sight that greeted Autumn and, she was sure from the look of surprise on her face, Lizzie. Alone in the room, there was a man, an old man, who was radiating the dark and the cold. He was standing by the window, his arms by his side, as if communing with something far away.

Shaun couldn't see him, but he reacted with alarm to the absence of Judith. He headed straight back out, presumably to mount a quick search of the rest of the rooms. Autumn and Lizzie stayed as the old man turned slowly toward them. "Amateurs," he said, in a voice meant only for them.

"She's not here," called Shaun from outside the room. "The place hasn't been lived in in days. Okay, that's it. I'm going back to the car to call it in."

They waited until they heard his steps recede down the stairs, then Autumn looked to the old man and realised she had now to say in deadly earnest a recurring joke from so many movies. "Who are you, and what have you done with Judith?"

The man laughed. "So she hasn't mentioned me? She wouldn't. I'm her husband, Arthur. Well, her ex. And what I've done has already given me a window on the world again, and is about to make me real, to set me free."

Autumn was desperately trying to get her head around what the relationship between Judith and this ghost had been. He looked like he'd been here for . . . had Judith really been living with this all this time? "Yeah, right," she said. "If we let it."

The man stepped toward them in anger. Autumn raised a finger in a basic protection gesture, the first thing Judith had taught her, and he shrank back. His bark looked to be a lot bigger than his bite. "They promised," he whispered. "They got in touch from far away, asked me. I let them inside me, let them change me, they said it'd end up with me getting away from here, being able to go anywhere, becoming a whole person, all of my own."

Autumn wished she knew more about the nature of whatever this being was. The only way she could learn was to keep it talking. "It's pretty obvious something's trying to get into the town. Why would it care about you getting away?"

"They changed what's inside me. They set it up so that when she—"

"When she what?" He'd meant Lizzie, Autumn was sure.

The man shook his head, realising he'd said too much.

Judith had never liked Autumn using the word *experiment,* but maybe it was time for just that. "So it's about what's inside you? All right." Before the ghost could react, Autumn reached out and put her palm to the surface of its skin. She could feel such cold, such . . . wait a sec, why was the man suddenly smiling?

The sudden sidelong gravity wrenched her off her feet. She

was hauled towards, no, into, Arthur with horrifying force. She threw out a hand, and grabbed, not Lizzie, as she'd intended, but whatever this oxygen tank thing was. But it lifted off the ground—

—and Autumn slammed into the ghost. And straight through it . . . into . . . where was she?! She screamed. The darkness was all around her, so dense she couldn't see. It felt like there was an infinite drop below her. She was . . . she realised she was still holding on to something with one hand. She flailed around with her free hand. She was being pulled downwards, and if she fell, she would fall forever.

She reached up, trying to blindly find with her other hand what one was still desperately clutching. She missed it. She tried again. The hand caught. She held on. She heaved. Something was coming for her from below, she realised. She felt, but couldn't see, something clutching, a hand, something like a human hand! Only it was so cold!

She broke the surface. She got her head out. She saw she'd been clinging to the oxygen tank, wedged against the end of the bed. She slapped one hand on it, then the other, and hauled herself out of the ghost, hand over hand, calling out all the time for Lizzie to help. Because if she fell back, if she didn't keep out of the reach of that hand, if she fell back, Lizzie was the only one left to—

Then Lizzie was there. She grabbed hold of Autumn and heaved.

Autumn fell onto the carpet. She looked back to what she'd crawled out of. Something was happening to Arthur. The expression on his face was suddenly horrified. "No," he whispered. "No, no, I'm real. Please, let me be real. They're closing this end of it. But they promised!"

"Who promised?!" yelled Autumn.

"The couple. The family. From out there. They got me to do that to Judith. She's still inside. She'll always be inside now."

"Are you saying that's where Judith went, that she's in there?"

But Arthur couldn't answer. His face had contorted impossibly. A great sucking vortex had developed inside his chest, reaching for Autumn and Lizzie, only it couldn't reach far enough. Instead, it was consuming him. "No," he cried out forlornly. "No, I'm a person—!"

And suddenly he turned inside out like a sock and was gone into a twist of darkness, then nothing. Something slapped onto the carpet and vanished.

Autumn lay beside the oxygen tank, panting. She looked back to Lizzie. "The couple, the family. That's what he said. That's who's doing this to us. Do you have any idea who he's talking about?"

Lizzie helped her up, shaking her head, a look of distant horror on her face. Then all at once she relaxed. "Oh," she said. "Oh. Oh God. Thank God. It's gone."

"What?"

Lizzie started to laugh. "Autumn, you did it. Whatever was trying to get across the borders, that was their way in, and somehow you closed it!" Lizzie grabbed her and held on. "Sorry I didn't help. Sorry I've been so weird. I was trying to hurt my hands, wasn't I? It was making me do that, I don't know why."

Autumn looked back to where Arthur had been. "But . . . I didn't do anything."

"Maybe disturbing the surface of that thing was enough to make it collapse?"

"Maybe." Autumn couldn't find it in her to share what felt like an odd and rather desperate sense of triumph on the part of her friend. There were still too many unanswered questions, too much still at stake. "Judith was in there. I think she's still in there. Even though the . . . door has gone."

"Oh no." Lizzie broke off and looked worried. "Can we get her back?"

Autumn sat down on the bed. “I don’t know.” She looked across at the ghost boy, who was still looking horrified at Lizzie. One thing above all was troubling her. If they’d just won . . . why was he still here?

Lizzie looked in the same direction and smiled sadly. “Looks like I’ve got a follower for life. Ah, well.”

3

The Reverend Lizzie Blackmore, vicar of Lychford, spent December 23rd merrily attending Lychford's Christmas Fayre, and several people mentioned, as she went from stall to stall saying hello and distributing sweets, that they were pleased to see her smiling again, and were also a bit surprised that she hadn't mentioned, given her past form, that there was no "y" in "fair." On every occasion, with a laugh in her voice, she told them that fair was foul and foul was fair, which tended to get a slightly perplexed laugh in return. Mostly.

That day she also took Communion in the Nine Lives old people's home, and attended the rehearsal for the crib service. This involved the junior school and nursery children, so Lizzie had to put on an especially big smile when she saw Jamie Dunning in the audience. She was even called upon, as she ran the children through their parts, to put a doll in the manger. It turned out to be relatively easy not to think about what would happen the next time Jamie was in this building. There was, since Arthur had said those words to her in a different voice while Autumn was away, now something in her head to let her deal with all that. She wasn't compelled to hurt her hands, and that was a great relief. She could barely hear that small part of herself that was still free, screaming inside a distant room in her head. The actual crib service, since it was scheduled after the wedding on Christmas Eve, would of course never come to pass. But there was no point in letting the cat out of the bag about that.

Mind you, every time she looked at the ghost boy, things still got difficult. She wished she could be rid of him. Why was he still here? What was he for? He was terrified of the presence of the real Jamie Dunning, had tried helplessly to stop her from approaching him at every point.

As she locked the church that night, Lizzie wondered distantly what the town would look like after tomorrow, after Christmas Eve? She had been told that everything would be wonderful after the change, after the breaking down of the borders and the inversion. She had been told that Christmas would never come, that it would never come again. What would that be like?

There was only one more normal service to get through tomorrow, Holy Communion at 10 a.m., and then would come the wedding, and then it would all be over, for her, for Lychford, and for the world.

That evening, Autumn sat in the Plough, Christmas happening all around her, friends filling the pub with laughter and the literal warmth of bodies. Nothing could warm her. Despite Lizzie's assurances, and nothing setting alarms off in her own extra senses, she couldn't make herself believe the danger was over. She'd spent the day researching possibilities for how to rescue Judith. She hadn't even found the terms she needed to use to address the problem. If it were possible at all, it would take years, maybe a lifetime. She'd done everything she could to contact Finn, even replying to his email, but had gotten no response. Perhaps the fairies had decided the humans were on their own.

She looked up when the door opened. It was Shaun, in uniform, his face a picture of worry. She wished she could tell him the truth about Judith, so at least he'd stop searching in the real world, but no, she decided, she would only do that if she could also offer him hope. "I'm just stopping for a coffee," he said to Rob. "Another missing person tonight. Mum was the first one we've had in a decade, then two come along at once, maybe it isn't a coincidence."

"Who is it?" asked Autumn, intercepting him.

"A toddler," said Shaun. "He was at home in his room, then he wasn't. I can't go into more detail than—"

"What's his name?"

"Jamie Dunning."

Those listening reacted, some of them knowing the parents. A mutter of worry went round the pub. But it was nothing compared to the sudden fear Autumn felt. She carefully put down her pint. "You're right," she said. "That's not a bloody coincidence."

Autumn asked a few of the locals, found out where the Dunnings lived, and went into the Backs to find their semi-detached house. The police car lights identified it from quite a way off. She didn't know what she'd been hoping to see here. The best her extra senses could manage was a sense of . . . not quite a presence, just a shadow of something having been here. The shadow felt huge, painful, askew from everything, and utterly in hiding. Whatever it was a shadow of . . . Autumn felt a chill at the thought of facing the reality, of how big that would be. It reminded her, she realised, of whatever had grabbed for her in that endless darkness. "The couple, the family," she whispered under her breath. Those were the words Arthur had used.

She told herself that the mere fact that their enemy remained in hiding, that they had tried to get rid of the stump that might indicate the most vague details about their nature, that they had closed off the literal loose end of Arthur, spoke of them still being somehow vulnerable. But that might not be the case for much longer.

Autumn got as close as she could, feeling the horror from the house more acutely as she did so. She could imagine it: looking in on a child's room to find it surprisingly empty, searching the house, at first bemused, then worried, then very quickly terrified. The impossibility of it would have hit them sideways. The height of that bedroom window off the ground. Everyday people shouldn't have things like this happen to them.

There was no way anyone was going to let her go inside to look more closely. And she was pretty certain there would be nothing more to find. Autumn turned and felt new determination as she headed for the Vicarage. Judith might be gone, but she and Lizzie were going to fight this thing. Autumn was going to go right now and get her.

Thank goodness Lizzie was back to her normal self.

Lizzie huddled in the kitchen with the lights off, listening to Autumn trying the doorbell for the fifth time. The ghost boy sat beside her, looking at her imploringly as always. "Why did I let you in?" she whispered. It would have been so much easier if she hadn't. Then she would be completely comfortable in what she was doing now. She could be comfortable. She was often comfortable. Except sometimes in the evenings, when she had nothing left to do and sleep still would not come. "They'd like me to get rid of you, but I can't. That look on your face keeps making me doubt."

The boy carefully reached up and climbed onto her to awkwardly sit on her lap, as if seeking any possible comfort.

"It's supposed to be Christmas," whispered Lizzie. "But now Christmas will never come." Christmas to her had always meant a little light, the light of the stable in the darkness of the winter. It was the hope that never died, but now it was going to. The hopes and fears of all the years are met in thee tonight, as the carol said. In the dark streets shineth . . . and now that light would be extinguished. There was a reason why people got depressed at

Christmas, because it was the one point in the year where this flawed, selfish civilisation, rotten with money, still allowed itself to face infinite forgiveness, infinite compassion; people compared their situation to the parade of home and hearth and tinsel that had been draped over that fact and instead of finding hope they despaired.

Infinite forgiveness, infinite compassion, all gone. A surrender to despair.

All she had to do was get up and open the front door, and let Autumn in, like one day, so long ago it felt, she'd been brave enough to let this boy in. Come on, Lizzie, said a different voice, a voice like a father, somewhere. Come on. It's not too much for you. There's no such thing as too much for you.

She pushed down on her feet and rose slowly, her back against the cupboards. The ghost boy looked excitedly up at her, hope on his face for the first time.

She took a step across the kitchen, everything they'd put in her brain screaming at her now to stop. Oh, they must be afraid of Autumn. What she and Autumn could do together. A sudden crippling headache turned into physical pain, racking her back and chest. What these things couldn't do, she told herself, putting one foot in front of the other, was kill her. They needed her. So she would walk herself forward into death if they pushed it that far. She wouldn't give up before they did. She'd walk right into death and away from all this and she would beat them like that if she couldn't do it now like this.

The ghost boy stepped with her, looking up eagerly at her, holding her hand.

She made it into the hallway, and realised blood was now running freely from her nose. It was like hangover on hangover was being thrown into her head. Her vision was distorting with the pain. She stumbled at the door, and as her lungs started to contort in some sort of shock, she managed to use the last of her breath to rip out the security chain and heave the door open.

"Autumn!" she cried out.

But there was nobody there. The pain had been roaring in her ears so much, she hadn't noticed when the doorbell ringing had stopped. She stood there for a moment, having given her all, staring into the darkness that had no light in it. Beside her, she was aware of the ghost boy making huge horrified sobs. The pain suddenly fell from her like the punchline to a sick joke.

She collapsed beside the ghost and held him as the rain started to fall on them both.

Autumn couldn't bring herself to stay up late watching the lovely old movies they put on the telly at this time of year. She had none of that Christmas Eve tomorrow feeling which she'd never quite lost from childhood. She was sure she wouldn't feel right again, not until she'd found some way to discover what had happened to Judith, some way to find the lost child.

She fell on her bed, exhausted, intending to get just a quick nap before going back to her research, and was surprised when she woke to light and the sounds of morning. She lay there, wishing some insight had come to her, in her . . . actually, it kind of had. What had Judith said about the ghost child, that a doppelgänger could be an attempt to stop the thing it was warning against from happening? Either that or it was trying to make it happen. And it kept saying "no hurting," as if it didn't want to be hurt. Well, if harm coming to the real boy was what it was warning against, it didn't seem like its presence was a self-fulfilling prophecy, given that it was haunting Lizzie. . . . Unless it was Lizzie who had kidnapped the real . . . no, of course she hadn't!

Though Autumn wished she knew where her friend had got to last night, because perhaps there was something still just a bit wrong going on there. So if the ghost boy was trying to *help* his real self, *then* why haunt Lizzie? No idea. And it wasn't as if the boy himself could tell her . . . unless . . .

"Oh," she said aloud. "Oh. How do you power up a ghost?"

Autumn ran into her laboratory, still in her dressing gown, and started grabbing ingredients. This, your basic passing on of power to something or someone, wasn't difficult, this was the basics. This was what Lizzie would call a blessing. She would need, again, either the judo or the appeal to a higher power or the sacrifice, but, oh, this was going to be the tough bit, that little ghost was really lacking the ability to convey much of a message. He'd need a lot of support added to him, her own rather academic internal icons weren't going to do it on their own, and this time she didn't have the power of good old-fashioned blood to give the whole thing a bit of *oomph*.

She really needed a sacrifice. What could she put into this working that was important enough to her, that she would acutely feel the loss of?

Her phone rang. She saw who it was, and was surprised to the point of astonishment, but relieved to these days be able to answer calmly. Of course, if he were calling because he realised she'd stolen his blood, then she was just going to end the call. "Luke. Hi."

"Hi." He sounded like he was being really careful. Of course he was.

"Listen, I'm sorry about the other night—"

"I don't actually remember much after you arrived." Yes, thought Autumn, that would be the effect of those sleeping herbs. "I must confess, I did wonder if I dreamt all that. Am I right in thinking you . . . brought a vicar?"

"I brought my friend Lizzie."

"What did we talk about? I remember you were trying to . . . explain?"

"You were kind enough to listen."

"I remember you making sense. You sound like you're doing okay again now."

He meant with her mental health, Autumn realised. This guy thought she was ill, but was actually willing to engage with that. "I am. Sorry again."

"I'm taking part in the search through the woods today. You know, the police are getting a lot of local people together to look for . . . well, nobody's saying what they're looking for, but we all know—"

"You haven't gone home?" He'd told her about getting back to his friends on their drunken night together, which now seemed like it had been centuries ago.

"No, I've been putting it off . . . because of you. Because I really liked that evening and I can deal with the . . . health issues, and . . . what I'm going to be doing today, it makes you think about what's important, doesn't it? Especially on Christmas Eve. So I was wondering if . . . maybe you'd like to meet up for a coffee, after, or after I get back in the New Year, and—?"

Autumn had closed her eyes. She so wanted this. She so wanted this to be the ending of her Christmas rom com. But he didn't actually know what he was signing up for. Maybe the loneliness, the burden that Judith had borne, unspoken, was the sacrifice you made to protect something you cared about. Like this was going to be her sacrifice now. "I'm sorry," she said. "You're brilliant, but I can't see you anymore." She clicked off the phone and made the gesture of adding the sacrifice to the working, and as she started to brew the potion she added to it her tears.

After she was finished, Autumn stumbled to the door of the shop and swung it open, letting the clear air of a crisp winter morning in and the heat of the brewing process out. She stood there on the threshold, wiping her face on her sleeve. She could hear the church bells ringing for what must be . . . she checked her watch . . . Lizzie's first service of the day would already be over, so that must be the wedding. She felt dizzy from having put so much of her own energy into the working. Stupid girl. What had she hoped to achieve, anyway?

She realised, as she wiped the tears from her eyes, that a small figure was standing on the pavement across the road. The ghost boy was looking at her like she was his last, desperate hope. "It's okay," she called, quickly. "It's all going to be all right!" He stepped slowly across the road, ignoring the car that passed through him and caused Autumn to yell, and finally stopped in front of her. "Come in," she said. "Please."

Autumn didn't have much experience with children, and this being a ghost child, she didn't feel able to offer him a biscuit. She closed the shop door behind him and squatted down to his level. "What's your name?"

"Sort of . . . Jamie."

He was definitely able to communicate more easily. Probably better than the real child. "Do you know where Jamie . . . the real Jamie . . . is right now?"

"I'm in a big white car."

Autumn's mind raced. That was a useful detail, but she needed a lot more if she were going to somehow find a way to tell this to

Shaun. "Can you see where you are?" The boy nodded. "What's around you?"

"People in the car. People in suits. Flowers on suits."

Flowers on suits? Like clowns?

"Men with flowers on suits. Big white dress."

Autumn stood up. That sounded like . . . and a line of connections suddenly raced through her mind. The couple. The family. No hurting! Why had this boy haunted Lizzie? Lizzie had wanted to hurt her hands, stop herself doing "the thing" which had looked like . . . stabbing. "The wedding," she whispered to herself. "Oh, dear God, it's the wedding!"

Lizzie stood at the door of the church, welcoming all the shapes and shadows that burst and fluttered past her without a word. They would be unseen to the everyday people of Lychford, she was sure. What would happen if she didn't welcome them into the church? Well, that was why she needed to welcome them. The doubts of the night were behind her. Thankfully, as she'd been getting ready, the ghost boy had vanished, too. Hopefully the real thing was being calmed about the matter of his fate. No, no, she wouldn't listen to the part of her that was screaming. She had to dab at her nose every now and then to stop the blood, but that was only to be expected. The groom was already inside the church, of course, even bigger than before and standing at a strange angle, standing with his family, filling the place and changing the space, and preventing all the things this church would normally be. He'd shaken hands with her, and his hand had been so cold.

The happy couple had been so clever. The wedding had been so well arranged. Jamie would be brought in right at the last moment, she'd been told. Any people who thought for some reason to look in on the wedding would be discouraged by the presence of the ushers, and Derek of the hidden face, who was stalking the edges of the church, waiting for victims as a best man should. Hopefully he'd be back in place when it came time to hand over the rings. The organist, who was now playing clashing, impossible chords, had been brought in from elsewhere. The bell ringers—who were now causing the bells to leap in frenzy on their ropes—had been, too. None of her usual folk who might have seen what was happening were here. Everything had been thought of.

Ah. Here came the bride. Everyone else had gotten inside in time. Emma was getting out of a white limo at the bottom of the path and was progressing through the lych-gate, her white dress and train somehow . . . hissing as they made contact with the ground, and there was just the smallest trace of smoke rising into the air as the dress ignited the last few dead leaves with her passing. Behind her walked her maids of honour, now visible as many-faceted things, their eyes reflecting glory. In her hands, the bride carried, because she was impossibly strong, the struggling small figure of Jamie Dunning, who'd been dressed in a little suit of his own, with a buttonhole, even. The light in the eyes of the maids, Lizzie knew, would stop those who'd idly gathered to watch the bride go in from seeing the little captive, from seeing that anything was amiss.

Lizzie, her teeth grinding, bowed her head as the bride approached, and was delighted to hear her laughter and feel the warmth of her breath on her face. "Is he waiting?" she asked.

"He is waiting," whispered Lizzie.

"Is the knife washed and prepared?"

Lizzie tried to make herself look down at Jamie, who'd started screaming, but she couldn't. "The knife is washed and prepared."

"And are you prepared to use it?"

Lizzie managed, just, to stop herself from replying, but her head, held in a vicelike grip of muscle control, was forced to nod.

Autumn had gotten dressed quickly and had gathered what little she could think of that might be useful for protection, with the ghost boy watching, desperately urging her on. Should she call Shaun? No, she should go to find him. He'd always known and accepted a little of what his mother had done. Maybe Autumn stood a chance of convincing him. If she couldn't, then she was going to have to do this alone. Well, apart from the boy, and what could he contribute? As she locked the shop behind her and stepped out into the street, he followed her. "No hurting?" he asked plaintively.

"I hope not," said Autumn. "But—" No, she didn't want to say aloud that she had no idea what she could do to stop this.

Lizzie stood in front of the pulpit, the bride and groom kneeling in front of her, looking out at a bizarre congregation that filled the pews like a shifting sea of light. Sea was right, she thought; she could feel it beating against the barriers, eager to soon get in. When it did, they would all be lost among it. That, she told herself sternly, was a good thing. Jamie was being held by three . . . she had no idea what they were. He hadn't stopped screaming. Derek and the father of the bride stood nearby, the latter flickering in anticipation. The two statues were in place, at odd positions inside the church, their shadows fixing everything where it had to be. Lizzie began reading the words that had been handed to her, the three poems that would prepare the shape of the changes brought by the sacrifice. It would all be over soon.

Autumn tried at the local police station, which had a small queue of volunteers at the door and a calm police officer at the desk, dealing with the public end of the operation. Shaun, she was told by those in the queue, would be out in the woods somewhere, with the search. Autumn considered for a moment how long she had, and what help any everyday person might be, even if he brought the whole Gloucestershire constabulary with him. Then she decided. It was going to have to be just her and the boy.

She marched across the marketplace, past the Christmas tree with the brass band playing, and up the road that led to the church, as excited families with children went past her, heading out for last-minute shopping at shops that were lit up and decorated. The boy walked with her, looking nervous but urging her on. Whatever the consequences of what was going on in that church were meant to be, would this lot be aware of them either way?

She looked up at the tower of St. Martin's as she approached and saw that the neon star now shone. . . . Her extra senses saw it was shining black, somehow, a glittering darkness that was pulsing, increasing, pushing against the sky. The shadows that flashed from it onto the churchyard made the frost hiss.

She walked up the path, aware that she was probably going to her death. Only the anger at what this lot had done to Judith, the knowledge that Lizzie was inside the building, let her keep going. Just a few days ago, her biggest worry had been that she was working her way through a list of rom-com clichés, but now . . . She increased her speed as she headed for the big wooden doors, ignoring what her senses were telling her about the sheer weight of a terrifying presence inside, and slammed them open to rush into the church. "Stop the wedding!" she yelled.

As everything in this . . . horrifyingly alien mass of things slowly turned to look at her, Autumn realised she might not have entirely escaped those rom-com clichés after all. But she had no time to think about that. There was Lizzie, and there was the real Jamie Dunning, both standing by the font, and Lizzie . . . had her arm raised and a knife in her hand, and she was holding Jamie with the other hand and he was screaming!

Autumn in that same moment made eye contact with Lizzie and saw such pain and helplessness in her friend's eyes. She ran at her, the ghost boy yelling in fear beside her. She was aware as she did so that suddenly smoke was pouring from her bag and from her pockets. The protective charms she'd brought along: this place was dissolving them!

Lizzie screamed herself as she swung the knife.

Autumn leapt forward and caught her wrist. She was aware of a strange noise rising from the building all around her. She was sure it was some otherworldly version of laughter. The bride and groom . . . Autumn didn't want to think about what they looked like, and now they'd gotten to their feet and were standing over the two of them, enjoying the spectacle. "No hurting!" cried the ghost boy. His real-life version was sobbing too much to form words.

Lizzie, her expression desperate, was using all her strength and some that came from beyond her to force the blade down. Autumn realised that she was wasn't going to be able to stop her. The sharp point of the knife was heading for the boy's throat. Lizzie had him by the hair. "Lizzie, stop, please, this isn't you!" But she could see from Lizzie's face that she knew, and she was already doing everything she could to stop herself. "What can I do? Lizzie, what can we do to help you?!"

With agonising slowness, Lizzie managed to turn her head. It was obviously something whatever was controlling her didn't want. She was looking, Autumn realised, straight at the ghost boy. She was wanting something . . . from him? Autumn looked back to him. He was nodding, encouraging her . . . reaching out to her.

He was moving so slowly, as if something was holding him

back. Autumn was losing her grip on Lizzie's wrist. The forces acting through her friend were just too strong.

Oh God. Oh God . . . Autumn realised she was going to have to take an enormous gamble. Let every aspect of every archetype inside her be onside now, because . . .

She heaved Lizzie back, and in the same moment grabbed the ghost boy, using all the willpower she had to actually be able to lay hands on him. She felt him cooperate with that. As Lizzie leapt forward again, knife in hand, to finish her bloody task—

Autumn threw the ghost boy at her.

Lizzie reflexively stabbed in the air at the phantom. The ghost . . . disintegrated. Its vapour shot into every orifice of Lizzie's face and vanished into her.

The only sound now was the screaming of the real boy as he desperately looked up at Lizzie, wondering what she was about to do. She still had the knife in her hand. Autumn realised: the otherworldly laughter had stopped.

The groom stepped forward, a huge shadow that made Autumn cry out as it fell across her.

Lizzie turned to face him and with one reflexive movement broke the knife over her knee. "How dare you bring this to my father's house?" she whispered.

Autumn had never been so relieved to see her friend angry.

The creature lunged for the boy, but Autumn grabbed him out of the way and leapt back so they could both stand behind Lizzie, who was now shouting out words of what must be liturgy. As the groom reached for them, Lizzie made the cross gesture of blessing.

The groom staggered backwards, swatting the air.

The church physically rocked.

Autumn fell as she felt the ocean of fury slam itself all at once against the boundaries. She clambered to her feet to see Lizzie holding back the groom, and the bride now beside him, with gesture and words and sheer anger. Where had she gotten all this energy from?

The bride and groom were once more forced back. Lizzie turned and started frantically blessing the congregation, marking out the boundaries of the church in gesture. The beings screamed, the tide slammed backwards against the far wall, and rushed forward at them. Autumn cried out as the bride and groom swept toward them at the head of the mass.

She saw at the last second what the groom was trying to do. His extraordinarily cold hand reached out impossibly across so many different directions at once, and it landed on Jamie's arm. Lizzie turned, reached out at the same instant Autumn did, completing her blessing with a shout.

But that shout made the tide turn, in one motion. Exactly as the groom must have expected. The whole congregation, the bride and groom with it, that whole mass of impossibility shot back towards the door, stretching Autumn's vision with a blur of painful gravity.

Jamie's fingers missed theirs. He shot away with the tide.

The big doors slammed. The church was whole again. The forces from beyond had gone.

But they had taken Jamie with them.

Lizzie leapt to her feet. "Come on!" she shouted. She sprinted off towards the door.

Autumn heaved herself to her feet and followed. "Where will they take him?!"

"I don't know!" They burst out of the church together and saw a blur of something snapping into the white limousine at the bottom of the path, which then suddenly started up and began to accelerate away.

They raced to the bottom of the path. Autumn saw Mick the mechanic getting out of his van by the cashpoint on the other side of the road. "Mick," she shouted. "Jamie Dunning is in that car!"

Mick took one look at her, realised she was serious, and ran back to his van. Autumn and Lizzie got to the sliding side door just as he started the engine. "They don't have a turnoff that way for about a mile!" he called. "We can catch up with them. One of you call the police."

Autumn was already doing so. At least, she thought, as they took a scary turn out into the traffic, horn blaring, here was something for Shaun to go after. She called the number she'd seen on posters asking for information, and got straight through to someone who seemed far more willing to believe her when she put Lizzie on the line. Lizzie spoke quickly but very precisely, making up on the spot a story about seeing Jamie with someone in her church, who'd fled when she challenged them. It would do, Autumn supposed. Lizzie switched off the phone when the call was over. "We've been told not to pursue them, to leave it to the police," she said to Mick.

"Yeah, not doing that." Ahead Autumn could see the limo, glimpsed through the trees as it took the curves at speed. But then, suddenly, it veered off the road.

"Oh no," said Lizzie.

But as they themselves turned the corner, it became clear that the car hadn't crashed. It had gone straight through a fence and was speeding up across a ploughed field, the mud flying from its wheels. It was heading, Autumn realised, for the woods. "How the hell did it do that?" said Mick. "I can try to take us up there, but the ditch—"

"Stop here," said Lizzie. As Mick brought the van to a screeching halt, she was already unbuckling her safety belt, and Autumn followed suit.

"You stay here, tell the police where—" began Mick, who was also clambering out.

"No, you do that," shouted Lizzie, and was out and running before he could argue. Autumn made sure with a look that he was going to stay put and ran after her. Ahead, the limo had stopped, and three figures were running for the tree line. "They're heading for the paths that the police won't find," panted Lizzie. "Only we can follow them there."

"Why do they still want Jamie? If the sacrifice has been messed up—"

"They must be able to do something with him. Only the two of them left; the others must have retreated over the border. Maybe if they make a sacrifice there, they can at least weaken the boundary enough to let them in. They were going to get the whole thing in one go, but if they do it this way they'll have to fight for it."

"You did great in there."

"I did bloody awfully. I should never have let them—"

"You didn't let them do anything. They did this to you." The figures had vanished into the trees ahead. Autumn and Lizzie got there moments later, on the paths only they could walk, and Autumn found she recognised where they were. "If they're heading for their own border, surely we won't even be able to see that?"

"All we've ever seen," called Lizzie as she ran on down the path, her breath misting on the air, "is the one border, when Judith had us walk it. Maybe that stands in all directions."

They reached a conjunction of paths. Autumn realised, at the same moment as Lizzie evidently did, that there were several different directions they could go from here to get to the boundary. "Which is the quickest way?"

"Bit of a toss-up. Damn it."

As they looked around for any sign of which way the couple might have gone, Autumn realised she could hear something familiar, a long way off. It was something she associated with . . . well, once it had been fear, but now it was confusion . . . it was a high, repetitive, six-note strain, followed by a recurring three-note summons. It was the music, the music Finn often played! "This way!" she said, and sped off down one of the paths.

After turning left and right for a few minutes, following the music, they burst into a clearing. What was normally invisible, Autumn realised, even to them, was now horribly apparent. This must be the border itself, one side of the clearing wildly fluctuating between the scene of the everyday trees beyond and . . . several different landscapes, one of which she recognised as the land of fairy. That was gorgeous, too gorgeous, but some of what she saw in those other moments . . . she wanted to close her eyes. But she would not. Because, above and beyond all that, here they were; the big thing and the little thing, now returned to their human guises, "Alan" and "Emma." Alan held, in one enormous hand, Jamie Dunning. His other hand held a Stanley knife, up against the boy's throat.

"What are you?" asked Lizzie.

"We own this land," said Emma. "We were here millions of years before you people in your swarms, with your weird religions, walked over from the continent, bringing your fairies with you. We're tired of living in the cracks. We don't like being banished. We want back what's ours."

"And that's worth the life of a child?" asked Autumn.

"Course it is! These 'lives' of yours exist only in time and come to a stop anyway," sniffed Emma. "Bunch of perverts."

Autumn was wondering what they could possibly do next. These two were clearly waiting for something, perhaps for when their forces would rally and appear in one of the many landscapes that were appearing in rotation behind them. While she was thinking that, she found herself watching those many landscapes and saw in one of them . . . but then it was gone again. "Keep them talking," she whispered to Lizzie.

Lizzie did so. "So the changing of the seasons, moments like Christmas, are nothing to you? It's all just . . . now?"

"Much the better system," said Alan.

Autumn watched again as the landscapes cycled past, and this time she saw it clearly. Approaching the boundary was some sort of army. All she could see were glimpses of light on sword and shield, but the way she couldn't quite see what was carrying the weapons was deeply familiar to her. These were the fairies, the army of the Summerland, going to war. And there, she could clearly see, because he must have let her see, there was Finn at the front of them, a look of calm determination on his face she'd never seen, and there beside him, with a sword the size of a small tree . . . oh. *Oh.* "You're going to want to start negotiating," she said to the couple.

"No," said Emma patiently, "because nothing can get across the boundary unless we allow it. Fixing that was pretty high on our to-do list."

"Yeah, but things can still go through the other way, right?" Autumn stepped forward until she was looking up at Alan. His size and presence terrified her. She was only going to get a moment to do this, and again, if she got it wrong, a child would die.

"Well of course they can. Or our forces would never have been able to fall back. Even now they'll be regrouping, ready for—"

Autumn had just seen out of her peripheral vision, as the landscapes cycled back to the land of fairy, and the army was here now, and right here, up against the boundary—

She leapt at Alan, caught him low with her head, under his centre of gravity, and pushed.

He staggered back, bemused more than anything, effortlessly keeping hold of the screaming child. He stepped back to steady himself.

He stepped over the border.

"Hoi," said a voice from behind him.

Alan spun to look.

Which was the exact moment Judith Mawson swung at him a fairy sword the size of a small tree.

The sword connected with Alan's neck. His head flew off like a coconut knocked from a shy. Autumn felt but did not see a much bigger event, the visible beheading a metaphor for a death that was harder to comprehend, a mystical sundering that could only have been completed by a weapon like that sword.

The body fell to the ground.

Jamie Dunning fell beside it, yelling in fear.

Judith inclined her head to Autumn. "How's that for customer satisfaction, then?"

"You're alive," said Lizzie, astonished.

"Just about," said Judith. "I'll tell you later. Now push her across and all." She indicated Emma. Autumn realised the boundary had stopped cycling. Whatever power had made it do that had been wrested away from the couple when Alan had died. Finn had squatted down beside Jamie and was reaching out to him with birdsong and a smile, the most human she had ever seen him, while the army behind him continued to seethe with angry intent. Autumn looked back to Lizzie, and realised she was actually hesitating.

The Reverend Lizzie Blackmore had come to this place with nothing but a desire for justice in her mind, a righteous rage at what these two had done to her, at what they'd nearly made her do to a child.

But she didn't trust that feeling in herself. She never had.

"No," she said. "Put her on trial if you like—"

"That's not how we do things," said Finn from the other side of the boundary, quite gently. He was still holding Jamie, making sure the boy didn't look at the corpse.

"Don't piss this lot off, Lizzie," said Judith. "They're here with a good fraction of the big lad's power. They could just walk in and take her."

"Then they'll have to come through me," said Lizzie, stepping in front of Emma. She gathered that the big lad must be Finn's father, about whom Autumn had told her enough to know that she'd just done something really stupid.

"I don't want your forgiveness," hissed Emma.

"Tough," said Lizzie. She turned back to address Finn, Judith, and the army. "If I give her up to you to be killed, if I don't do everything I can to stop that, then midnight tonight won't mean anything anyway. Not for me. And so this lot will have made the difference they were after. In one person, anyway."

Autumn looked hard at her, then sighed and stepped up to join her. "Me, too," she said. "Though that doesn't mean I think it was wrong to cut his head off."

"That is a bit different," agreed Lizzie. "He was going to kill Jamie."

Judith looked them both up and down. "Idiots," she sighed. She stuck the enormous sword into the ground and turned to confide in Finn.

Emma leapt for the cover of the trees. Before Lizzie could react, an enormous sound roared past her head. The tree beside Emma sang with the impact of something like lightning and exploded.

Lizzie blinked at the light and Emma had gone. She had escaped back to her own world. Damn it.

Lizzie turned back to see Judith had her hand on Finn's arm. He was glowering at her, while still smiling at Jamie with the same face. She had, Lizzie realised, spoiled his aim. "They'll be back, you know," he said. "That'll be your fault."

"No," said Lizzie. "Now it'll be theirs."

Jamie Dunning was eventually prised out of Finn's care, the fairy having asked if he wanted to stay in their lands a while, to which Judith, Autumn, and Lizzie together had quickly answered for the boy in the sternest negative terms. Finn had said they were disrespecting the cultural values of his people, and had added, more seriously, that he and Autumn had issues now; all three of them did. They had frustrated the will of his father, and brought future danger to his kingdom. As the fairies flickered away into the setting sun of late afternoon, taking that dirty great sword and the body of Alan with them, Autumn found that she really couldn't give two hoots about what Finn's dad wanted, and flicked two fingers in their direction. "And a Merry Christmas to you, too, you ungrateful sods."

"We could," said Judith, leading the toddler along the path with one finger in his hand as the early afternoon darkness closed in, "have ended up with them owing us a favour." She considered for a moment. "Which might have been worse."

"How did you get out?" asked Autumn. "How did you get here?"

Ahead of them, at the point where their path met the paths of the real world, they could see a group of police officers, locals, and dogs moving frantically at an angle to them. In a moment the four of them would emerge into their sight. "You get the lad home," said Judith. "I'll tell you down the Plough tonight." She took Jamie's hand and put it in Lizzie's.

"No hurting," said Jamie, proudly. Which made Lizzie smile.

"No," said Autumn. "Judith, you lead him out and be the hero. Go on."

Judith coughed a laugh. "You can't be the one who takes heads and be the hero, too. You'll learn that, my apprentice." And without another word, she turned and trudged off in another direction.

Lizzie picked up Jamie, and walked forward into shouts and cries of relief and, growing as more and more people arrived and the news spread, applause.

Autumn watched it all bounce off Lizzie like rain. But when Mike and Allison Dunning were called and ran forward to embrace their child, at least the Reverend allowed herself a smile.

Epilogue

Judith took a long drink from her pint, then set it down. The three of them had found a nook in the back bar of the hugely crowded Plough Inn where they couldn't be overheard. "I suppose," she said, "I'll have to start grieving properly now. So I've got that to look forward to."

"You lived with the ghost of Arthur," said Autumn, "all that time." She'd also got a pint, but Lizzie, who had Midnight Mass to begin preparing for in ten minutes, was on coffee. They'd both had to run the gauntlet of locals, Mick included, offering to buy them drinks. Mick himself had already benefitted from the generosity of those who'd heard he'd been part of the rescue effort. Shaun, hours earlier, had taken the (almost entirely fictitious) testimony of Lizzie and Autumn, to pass on to what Autumn assumed would be a meaningless search for the perpetrators. While doing so, he'd taken, first to his joy, then his annoyance, a phone call from his mum, who, Autumn judged by his reactions, told him she'd been off in London Christmas shopping. She gathered he'd been making some sort of fuss about her being away.

"You get used to things," said Judith.

"You should have told us," said Lizzie.

"Why? What would you have done? Apart from moping and telling me I should mope, too."

Autumn sighed. "How did you get out?"

"I heard you screaming when you fell into Arthur, too. That gave me a reference point, a way to start working out where I was. You giving more power to that ghost, that also had a bit of me in him, that was like a beacon, too. The structure of the curse was still there. It was powered by undead animals a certain someone had buried in the woods. Once I could see the shape of it, I gathered up all the power I could from . . . the sort of recording of the real Arthur that was in there; he couldn't help but help me, and I found my way out along the shape of the curse, to a real place, or at least as real as the borderlands are. I couldn't come out on our side of the border, so I decided to come out in fairy instead. Where I immediately had a word with the big lad. Hence them loaning me the Sword of a Billion Heads, I think it were called. Billion and one now." She laughed again, a very dark laugh.

"The sheer knowledge it took to do that," said Autumn. "Bloody hell."

Judith gestured in Lizzie's direction. "She managed to save herself without knowing a thing."

"How did I do that?" Lizzie looked puzzled.

"You kept giving your energy to the ghost lad. By letting him in, letting him follow you, trusting him. Without knowing it, you were storing it like in a savings account, protecting it by hiding it in the glitch in the worlds, so you could use it later."

"The light in the darkness," said Lizzie. "The hope out of nothing."

"Are you carrying on an old conversation again?" said Judith, clearly disapproving of the application of poetry to magic.

"Yeah," said Lizzie. "You could say that."

"Oh, hey." Autumn turned at the sound of the familiar voice. Standing in the entrance to the back bar was Luke. Autumn found herself without the power of speech. After all she'd gone through today, this was beyond her ability to cope with. "I heard what you two did. Are you okay?"

"She was a complete hero," said Lizzie, before Autumn could self-deprecate. "It was all down to her."

"You two go and talk in the front bar," said Judith. "Me and the vicar have got matters of high import to discuss."

Annoyed as she was by that blatant bit of social engineering on Judith's part, Autumn did as she was told, and let herself be bought drinks, and told Luke the (almost but not quite so much entirely fictitious) story of what had happened. She could only tell him, when he asked about her apparent former desire that he go away, that things with her were always complicated, that she'd thought she'd been doing something good, and actually had been, but sometimes doing something like that seemed to lead to good things in return that were totally undeserved. Autumn was nudged by Lizzie as she went off to arrange Midnight Mass, and she found herself, as the hour approached and they'd both had a few, with Luke under that mistletoe in the middle of the front bar. He looked as surprised as she was. He put a hand to the side of her face. "Merry Christmas," he said.

And it turned out, in the end, that Autumn really didn't mind getting to the end of that list of rom-com clichés.

Lizzie looked out at her considerably larger than normal congregation for Midnight Mass, including two relieved parents and their sleeping toddler. The crib service had been cancelled this year, due to the unexpected circumstance of the vicar becoming a local hero. People had wondered if this service would go ahead. Lizzie had told them that her not missing this had been the whole point of her day. "Welcome all wonders in one sight," she said, "eternity shut in a span. Summer in winter, day in night, heaven in earth and God in man. Great little one whose all-embracing birth brings earth to heaven, stoops heaven to earth."

She hadn't known what her sermon was going to be about until, just before joining Autumn and Judith down the pub, she'd done some random research. Tonight she was going to talk about the values underlying Christmas, and how the famous writer of what was often thought of as a sarcastic festive hit had declared he loved Christmas, but that he was actually protesting how commercialised it had become.

She wondered though, looking at the relative youth of this lot, how many of them would have heard of Greg Lake.

A Long Day in Lychford

For Lizzie at 7A and Maxine at The Coffee Post
(the coffee shops of Fairford
where parts of this book were written)

1

Marcin Przybylski was lost, and the voice in the cab of his lorry wasn't being much help. "At the roundabout, take the third exit, and continue . . ."

He stared into the darkness of the tree-lined road ahead. "Where's the roundabout?" he asked his phone, helplessly. The phone was attached to a bracket on the dashboard, and illuminated as if to underline its importance. Because right now it ruled his life. Mr. Ofgarten, who right now would be asleep in his comfy bed, had some sort of beacon attached to each one of these phones. If, when he woke up and checked his enormous tablet over his delicious morning pastries, one of those drivers was not anywhere near, in this case, the brand new Tesco distribution centre at Pilning in Gloucestershire, however you were meant to pronounce that . . . well, there would be a stream of German obscenities down the line. It was said that to be more than twenty minutes late meant automatic dismissal. At least then Marcin could tell him what he could do with his smoked sausages.

He'd got to the Oxford distribution centre for Sainsbury's with no problem. That was second nature by now. It was the combination of this new location and this "brilliant new crowd-sourced navigation app" that Ofgarten had installed that was foxing him.

A sign loomed ahead in the summer night. "Lychford," he said to the phone.

"I do not recognise the location," the phone replied.

"Of course not."

"I do not understand the instruction."

"Oh, go to hell!"

"Changing route now."

"No! Stop!"

"Stopping now." And the screen showed the moving circle that indicated it was waiting for further instructions.

Marcin managed to avoid bellowing at it, worried that might dig him in deeper. He was passing a new housing estate on the edge of this Lychford, woodlands on the other side. Was there anyone around here he could wake up at this time in the morning to ask for directions? How willing to answer their door would they be? And he didn't have much English. Did he trust his phone to translate for him?

Suddenly, the light seemed to change a little, and he jumped, worried that, despite being used to the night shift, he'd fallen asleep. But no. Still the woodlands. Maybe that had been lightning? Or was it getting light this early?

"Turn left," said his phone. Ah, it was back!

Only of course there didn't seem to be a . . . no, what was that up ahead? He couldn't see it properly, did he need glasses? The road seemed to suddenly—!

Marcin had to haul on the wheel as abruptly, impossibly, the road he was travelling on turned almost at a right angle and headed upwards into . . . what the hell was that?!

"I do not recognise this location!" yelled his phone. And it kept yelling it. As Marcin and his lorry skidded uncontrollably into what seemed like . . . nothingness.

Autumn Blunstone woke up, and gradually realised she was lying face down, fully clothed, in her own bed, upstairs at her magic shop, Witches, in the market town of Lychford, in the Cotswolds. These facts came to her one by one, introducing themselves politely.

The sun was already up. A cool breeze was ruffling the curtains. It was . . . really early still. Why was she awake?

Autumn felt . . . bloody awful. Not actually entirely . . . hungover, not yet. It was like the hangover was literally hanging over her, waiting to expand to its full dimensions, but had first just wanted to knock on her door to tell her it was getting ready to do its thing. We have a delivery for you, it was saying, and we will not hand it to a neighbour, but intend to unpack it in your every special place.

Knocking on her . . . no, someone was actually knocking on the door downstairs. Really quite loudly and urgently. At this time in the morning. And there was distant music somewhere out there. The *duff duff duff* of dance music. What was that about?

Autumn shouted something incoherent, reached out to find her robe, realised she didn't need to and fell out of bed.

At the door she found PC Shaun Mawson, in uniform and definitely on business. In the air, from somewhere behind him, faded in and out that beat of some distant, ongoing rave.

"Miss Blunstone," he said, "can I come in? It's urgent." It must have been for him to call her by anything other than her first name, or more usually just a shy nod. Shaun was the son of Autumn's elderly employee and supposed mentor in the ways of magic, Judith, but he shared none of his mother's bloody-mindedness. Thank God. He turned down the offer of tea, and made Autumn sit down in the kitchen.

"Is someone . . . dead?" she asked.

"We don't know. That's why I'm here." He got out his notebook and pen and held up a hand to gently halt her questions.

"Let's start at the beginning. Can you remember much about last night? Can you remember where you got to?"

Great question.

Worrying question.

Why *had* he asked her to sit down?

No, come on, concentrate on the question. Where *had* she been last night? Autumn had always said there was a pub in Lychford to suit her every mood. If you wanted the good company of builders and town councillors, there was the Plough. If you wanted to meet people who were just passing through, or to sit and read quietly, there was the Market Hotel. If you wanted noise, youth, and the offer of drugs in the toilets, there was the Randolph. And if you wanted a fight, there was the Custom House. That was it for the pubs of Lychford these days. A couple had closed down recently. When Autumn had been a teenager, there'd been seventeen. Over the years, her range of options had narrowed, but, neatly, so had her range of moods.

"I think I was at . . . the Custom House?"

The Custom House was the sort of pub that the town council kept wanting to find a good reason to close down. The dusty whitewash on the outside gave one a clue that here was an inn the carpet of which could have been the subject of a TV nature special by David Attenborough. As you headed for the bar, your footsteps crunched. The walls inside were bare, the cloth on the pool table ripped, though people still played on it. The fruit machine's soundboard had once had a pint tipped into it, resulting in strange, muffled, warblings. However, the landlord, Malcolm, kept the beer pipes clean, and for the Custom House's clientele, that was the only required saving grace. After you got to know people, the décor became a feature, not a bug.

But yeah, there were often fights.

"Why did you decide to go there?" Shaun's tone suggested

that no nice young lady would. Autumn tended to end up at the Custom House having had a couple of drinks at one of the other pubs, become slightly angry with something someone had said there—but not enough to want to cause a fuss—and thus decided to move on. Her light complexion, what her best friend Lizzie had once called her "had clothes fall on her accidentally" sense of style, and, she supposed, the fact that she'd always been around, all distracted from the fact that she was, as they said these days, a person of colour. So she overheard things in those other pubs: perfectly nice people who'd never use the N word still saying "chinky" and, incredibly, "pikey"; people on her own social level knowing they were being risqué when they'd had a few, making jokes that started with "Jewboy and Mick walk into a pub." When she'd been younger, she'd always spoken up at that point, and had been pleased when there'd often been whoops of applause rather than dismissal. Some of it was "oh ah, here she goes again," but some of it had always been that feeling that she was to be congratulated for speaking up for "her own people." Not that she knew, apart from her extended family in Swindon, any of her own people. Not since her Dad had passed away. She was literally the only non-white person in the entire town. That, she suspected, was the only circumstance in which you'd get that welcoming reaction, when the majority thought of you as the sole representative, and therefore harmless. Of course, in Lychford, there were also Sunil Mehra and his employees, but she'd never felt they had much in common. Sunil was part of the "reception for the Prince of Wales" crowd in this town, who'd probably see himself as "one of them," while she was . . . whatever class it was that owned magic shops.

She was aware that, as she'd gotten older and still overheard things in pubs, she'd stopped speaking up so much. Because when you stopped being a teenager, you started feeling less sure of yourself, and not everything seemed like it was life and death. And she liked fitting in. She was quite popular, wasn't she? And these were good people, really. Really. But it hadn't eased off like she used to think it was going to. It had gotten worse. It had gotten more normal. The ones being "risqué" seemed to find it easier to say.

And then last year, that bloody year.

The walk through the marketplace on the day after the Brexit vote had been like something out of a science fiction movie. And that was saying something, coming from someone who was getting used to seeing magical beings. Which of these people, she had thought, looking around herself on that market day, had voted to saw themselves off from the rest of Europe? Which of these people, in their heart of hearts, wanted a Lychford that was "just like it had been in the 1950s"? Which of the shops she spent money in were owned by people who wanted the full emulsion white paint job, corner to corner, maybe without even having thought about it enough to know that was what they wanted? Which of the coffee shops contained people who were cheering inside today? She'd never know, because this was Britain, after all, and nice people don't talk about anything that might cause trouble, and so all that day the town had been weirdly silent.

She'd gone down the pub that night, and people hadn't talked about it there, either, but Autumn had overheard things, a lot of things, and that had been the first time she'd found herself going down the road to the Custom House. In the weeks and months that had followed, she'd found herself going there more and more. And now the General Election was approaching. And she felt more worried and scared every day. She'd talked with Lizzie about how she felt, and that always made her feel better for a while, like going on the Women's March in Bristol after Trump's election had made her feel better for a while. But the trouble with talking about this with Lizzie was that Lizzie would never understand how much these things made Autumn feel like an outsider in her own town. It had been months now, and she still couldn't find a way to haul herself out of the pit that social media dropped her into every morning. She looked at the future, and for the first time in her life, the way ahead looked uniformly grim. There were such incredible things in people's lives now, like photos from space probes around Saturn, and such incredible things outside those lives, the magic only the three of them knew about, and yet still, still, these tiny bloody people with their pent-up little bloody fears—! Even if she could have put it all into words, she couldn't be sure Shaun Mawson would ever understand.

"I don't know," she said. "I don't know why I went to the Custom House."

"Did anything . . . particularly stressful happen to you yesterday? I'm wondering how worked up you were when you got there."

Yesterday had been a long, sweaty summer day, which had seemed to gather up anger within itself, ready for a storm. And, oh God . . . yeah, she remembered now, the storm had broken. During that day, she had ended up having the row she was always going to have. And, horribly, it had been with the mother of the police officer who was facing her now. It had been with Judith.

They'd fallen into it by accident. The old witch of the hedgerow, as Judith liked to style herself, both mentally and in terms of grooming, had sat permanently behind the till that day, just like most days now, glaring at any tourists who might happen to come into the shop, setting quizzes about the occult history of Gloucestershire in the sixteenth century to any of them who might offhandedly try to strike up a conversation about crystals or the healing energy of unicorns. It was like Autumn was keeping a troll behind the counter, in every sense of the word. She had wondered hopefully, in the last few months, as Judith's attitude to people had got worse, if Judith might seem like the more challenging end of the real ale spectrum, that people might start to say that was the real thing at that magic shop, that, horrible as it tasted, it was the genuine experience. But no, after the third tourist yesterday had left without buying anything, at a speed which left the shop bell bashing against its hanger, Autumn had finally dropped the idea of monetising the degree of difficulty her employee presented to the world. "Okay," she'd said, "you can't keep doing that. What with Brexit, I need to start making some sales here—"

"What about it?"

Autumn had realised that, at the end of a tiring day, she had finally let slip what she had avoided talking about with Judith all this time. She had said the magic word. Ironically. Still, she knew that Judith's grasp of economics was usually that of an elderly aunt who every year tried to bet five pence each way on the Grand National.

"Any supplies I get in from Europe are now literally worth their weight in gold, and given everything that's happened this year, the council will be putting the rates up."

Judith had made a dismissive sound in her throat. "Things'll get better."

Autumn had paused, wondering if that had meant what she'd thought it had. Judith had made grudging eye contact, then looked away. And Autumn had recalled how, according to the polls, there had been a direct correlation between one's closeness to the cemetery and how willing one was to mess up the future for generations to come. It had occurred to her that it would be just like Judith to have done what a number of the folk down the pub seemed to have done: to have taken any yes/no question from any government as an immediate reason to burn down their own house and everyone else's. "Okay, you got me. You've been working hard today to separate my shop from its customers. I'm interested in how you feel about separating other stuff. Which way did you vote?"

Judith had glared at her. "None of your business."

Which nobody on the Remain side ever said. It was only the Leavers who wanted to hide it. "Oh no. You did, didn't you?"

"Vote's private. That's democracy, isn't it?"

"But you're not proud of it?"

"I don't talk about politics or religion."

"You're a *witch,* who works in a *magic shop* and, like the car sticker would say, your other apprentice is a *vicar*."

"I don't talk about politics. Stop going on. Do you want a cuppa?"

Which had been the first time in the history of their association that Judith had ever offered to make the tea. The enormity of this distraction might even have worked, if Autumn had been willing to let it. With the sun getting lower in the shop window, the row might have faded and Autumn might have decided to let it go, let her go, let her go back to her house and annoy her neighbours instead. As the song so nearly put it. But that had been the moment, Autumn remembered now, the moment she'd realised something huge about the situation she and Lizzie were in, something that had felt in that second like sheer complicity on her part. "Oh my God," she said. "That's what you're teaching us to do."

"What?" Judith had looked at Autumn like she'd gone mad.

"We're *defending the borders* of this town. We're here to *deter the outsiders*. That's what we're all about, isn't it? That's what we *do*."

There had been a long silence. There had been, even then, Autumn thought now, things Judith could have said.

But instead, Judith had slowly got to her feet. "Do you want me to keep on working here, then?" Those merciless old eyes had fixed on Autumn. Judith had done what she always did. She had boiled down the complexities of a situation to some ridiculous basics.

Autumn had wanted to say of course she wanted Judith to stay. She really had. But in the heat of that moment, she hadn't been able to get the words out. Instead, she'd said nothing.

After a moment, Judith had picked up her bag from under the desk, and headed for the door. Autumn had wanted to call to her before she got there. She had not.

So Judith had left, and the door had closed gently behind her.

It had taken Autumn a few minutes after Judith had left to move at all.

When she had, it had been fast. She had been shaking with emotion. She had locked up the till, locked up the shop, slammed the bolts . . . and headed down to the Custom House.

"It had just . . . been a long day," she said to Shaun now. "I'd had some problems with one of my staff."

He carefully wrote that down. What was going on here? She felt like she'd just somehow incriminated herself. "Okay," he said. "Was there any trouble when you were in the pub itself?"

Autumn recalled that she hadn't been the first to set forth across the crunchy carpet of the Custom House last night. Her heart had sunk, in fact, when she'd seen who'd gotten there before her for early doors. It had been Jenker. Keith Jenkins, he was properly called, a taxi driver who'd married someone in the Backs. The Custom House was his local. Earlier that summer, when Autumn had come in complaining about the heat, he'd said something about her working on her suntan. At the time, she hadn't been quite sure whether or not he'd meant it literally, and he'd maintained eye contact, kept that innocent grin on his ruddy, aye aye, here's the life and soul of the party face. She couldn't help but be wary of him after that, though, and yeah, she'd overheard things.

"Hello hello!" he'd boomed yesterday night. "Here comes trouble."

Which would normally have been the sort of greeting she loved. But not from him. And especially not after the day she'd had. She'd nodded to him, she remembered, and ordered a pint of 6B. It would have been impossible, in the circumstances, not to talk to him, but the last thing she'd wanted to talk about was what had happened with Judith and the guilt and anger that were wrestling within her. He'd tried the normal, harmless, topics, such as football and the weather, and she'd nodded along, barely listening to his replies. With anyone else, on any other day, she would gleefully have raised the subject of the weirdness of her work at the magic shop. She liked to present what she did, at least the public part of it, to her pub friends in all its eccentricity and have them tease her about it. But she couldn't do that with Jenker. She wouldn't make herself sociably vulnerable to him.

After a couple of drinks, however, she'd taken something he said for a starting point for a conversation that swiftly turned into come on, did he feel okay with how things were now, when you couldn't say anything on Twitter without some fascist, some, I mean, literal fascist, someone who if you asked "are there any fascists here?" would put up his hand and say "actually . . ."? It had turned out Jenker wasn't on Twitter, and thought people who paid too much attention to the Internet were a bit . . . he'd made big boggly eyes at her.

Where had it gone from there? Oh God, she was starting to remember. Shaun the police officer was actually quite good at this interviewing thing, wasn't he?

After three drinks, one of which Jenker had bought her, and she'd suddenly started to wonder if he thought she was coming on to him, but no, that moment had gone past without comment, they'd started to seriously argue about what Brexit was going to mean to the economic future of Britain. He kept cutting her off and saying "nah," while making points she found she didn't have the information to hand to come back about. If you were a "crap farmer, not a good farmer," you had reason to vote to stay in, he said, but fishermen had a good reason to vote out. Then Autumn said what about wanting to keep all the brown people out, and he'd said it wasn't about the brown people, he was mates with a lot of brown people, like her, no offence, it was the bloody Poles and the whatever they were from central Europe, who couldn't speak English, taking their jobs, bringing their own shops over here and their foreign muck into our supermarkets. If she thought it was about brown people, that was where the chip on her shoulder had come from. No offence. Here, Autumn had been on steadier ground, at least in terms of data, and she'd held her own, and had actually said out loud that she felt she was one of *those* people too. *Every* sort of those people. He'd said, what you? You've been here longer than I have! He'd started holding up a finger for his interruptions, and had said they should have another pint and blimey love, you can talk, can't you, you and me must have been separated at birth, maybe I had a touch of the tar brush too, 'cos you're not full on, are you, you're half and half, so I don't see what you've got to worry about, and she'd been about to . . . explode? Yeah, hopefully she'd been about to do that rather than force a laugh, when one of the many, many people who had somehow filled the pub around them, some of whom were now looking on in glee or embarrassment, had spoken up.

Oh. Oh my God. She remembered now.

This was him. She remembered his face. An old lad, in his

seventies, newspaper under his arm. A ruddy, drinker's face, balding, a fleck of grey stubble on his chin. He was so important. Why was he so important? What had happened to him?

"There . . . wasn't really any trouble," she said to Shaun. "Bit of a row."

"Do you remember anyone in particular being there?"

She mentioned Jenker. But okay, Shaun probably had in mind this . . . weirdly important guy she'd just remembered. "Someone told me his name was . . . Old Rory?"

"Rory Holt." That seemed to be the box he'd been wondering if she was going to tick. "Did he say anything in particular to you?"

Yeah. Yeah, he had, now Shaun had made her think of it. And it had been a terrible thing. It would have appeared in her memory, sometime today. It would have popped up, to bring her crashing down. Like it had halted her in her tracks now.

She could see him in her mind's eye now, a little grin on his face as he'd said it. "Bloody good idea." That's what he'd said.

"What is?" she'd replied.

"A wall," he'd said. "Trump's got it right. We should build one too. Keep 'em all out."

Which had gotten laughs, because come on this was still Britain, and nobody, whatever their politics, flew a flag for the most ridiculous American of them all, and that had come out of bloody nowhere. But it had left Autumn speechless. It had been a one-two punch with the awkward anger at what Jenker had just said.

She had stared at the old man. He'd met her gaze, challenging her. He hadn't looked away. His gaze said, *What the hell are you doing here in my sight? Did you think we were equal? This is my home. Not yours.*

Jenker had tapped her on the shoulder. "Old Rory's been

reading the Internet too much," he'd said, and made the boggly eyes again. "Do you want another?"

Was that how furious the look on her face had been, that he'd felt he'd needed to distract her?

What had happened next? She remembered leaving the pub . . . didn't she? Had that been soon after? Had she had that next drink and lost track? Had she lost track of Rory Holt too?

"What happened next?" asked Shaun.

"I . . . I really don't know. Could you tell me why you're asking me all this?"

Shaun pursed his lips.

Like a lot of elderly people, Judith Mawson didn't need much sleep, and thus tended to get up early. She would put the television on in her kitchen and watch something stupid before the news as she made a very early breakfast, these days usually consisting of whatever half-arsed cereal the doctor said she needed to force down for the sake of her . . . heart, usually, but pick any organ. Like they said, eating healthy food might not help you live longer, but it certainly made you feel like you were. In the last six months or so, as she went through her usual ritual, she'd find herself glancing at the stairs, always thinking she'd heard a voice, when actually she hadn't.

"Stupid," she whispered to herself. "Soft."

Judith had got used to living with the spiteful ghost of Arthur, her husband, or rather, a curse that had taken his shape. The spectre might have been evil and cruel, but at least he'd been company. She was still trying to find a way to deal with the lack of another presence in the house, and thus, for the first time, having to completely accept that the real Arthur was gone. It was a strange, attenuated sort of grieving, made worse by Judith only having two people she could talk about it with: her apprentices, Autumn and

Lizzie. Well, make that one person, after yesterday. The thought of it made her stop, with the cereal packet in mid-air. She had to take a moment to control her anger, as she had so many times before finally getting to sleep last night. Of course that stupid girl had wanted her to stay on at the shop, she just hadn't been able to bring herself to say the words. And that wasn't bloody good enough. Before she set foot in that place again, before she let Autumn resume her training, she would want, at the very least, an apology. And more money. And . . . whatever bloody else that stupid, stupid—!

Judith stopped herself. Her doctor probably wouldn't approve of her getting so worked up, and what for? It had only been the sort of thing young folk did, with their emotions flooding all over the place like spilt milk. She'd lost sleep about it, but so what? She wouldn't go in today, get an afternoon nap, let the stupid girl come to her.

For the umpteenth time, she put that matter to the back of her mind. What was worrying her more right now was this note she'd found attached to her fridge by a magnet. It made no sense. The note said:

Remember that your parents are dead, you great fool.

Which was ridiculous, because Judith's parents still lived next door like they'd always done. Only . . . no, that wasn't true, was it? She clicked her tongue, annoyed with herself. That was her getting old. Joyce who had that horrible laugh lived there now, with her parakeet. So . . . Judith's parents must have moved out, but . . . they'd have told her where they were going, wouldn't they?

They must have moved out.

Where?

This bloody note, making no sense. Nothing of magic about

it, either. It hadn't just appeared. Someone had, quite normally, written it and put it there.

The weirdest thing about the note was, it was in Judith's own handwriting.

The Reverend Lizzie Blackmore groaned, and threw out a hand to hit her clock radio. It was only when her hand had connected three times to the button atop the radio, and she had only succeeded in switching it on, and it had filled the room with the soothing really very early morning sounds of BBC Radio 2, that she realised it was not actually 6:30 a.m., but a whole hour earlier. She switched it off, and then realised what had actually awoken her. The sound of distant music was wafting through her open window. *Duff, duff, duff,* dance music, so far away you could only hear the beat, then the beat changing, then back to the previous beat. She got up, stumbled to the window, and closed it. That wouldn't be uncomfortable. The Vicarage was cool in summer, if bloody freezing in winter. But she could still hear the beat, like a distant tapping. It was locked into her consciousness, specific and now just at the volume that made your ears listen out for it. Had it stopped? No, there it was. Had it stopped now? Nope.

She went back to bed and listened for about ten minutes to the changing beat, without wanting to. If it would only stay the same for a minute or two, she could have fallen asleep to it. She really didn't feel much like bloody dancing. Finally, she got up, put on her dressing gown, and grabbed from her bedside table the item which was now ruling her life. She'd gotten the Exercise Tracker for herself as a New Year's present, following that rather traumatic Christmas. The little electronic sadist was already making a bit of a difference to the size of her arse. Then she headed for the stairs, intending to make a cup of tea. She could spend this extra hour sending out a few emails, getting ahead of the day's problems. And perhaps she could play *Overwatch* for a bit.

She was surprised, and then alarmed, as she walked blearily down the stairs, to hear that the kettle was already boiling. She stopped, remembering that the burglar alarm was still below her in the hall. It was only relatively recently, after she'd been bathed in the water from the well in the woods, and become able to see the magical powers surrounding and threatening Lychford, that she'd even started turning it on. She couldn't get to the emergency button, but her phone was charging upstairs. She'd started to carefully make her way back up when a voice called from below. "Do you want a cuppa?"

She recognised the voice, and the way it had just said the most ordinary of sentences as if it was learning a foreign language, and was first relieved, then angry.

She marched down the stairs and into the kitchen to find Finn, Prince of the Fairies, appreciatively watching her kettle boil as if it was some sort of modern art installation. "What the hell are you doing here?" she said.

He turned to look at her, not his usual jovial self. "Something strange is happening. I'd have gone to see, you know, the other one—"

"You mean Autumn? Your ex?"

Finn's supernaturally handsome features creased into the most gorgeous frown Lizzie had ever seen. It really was hard to stay angry with him. Which was, in itself, worrying. "I can't be expected to remember everyone. You people keep . . . reproducing. And then I look up from whatever I'm doing and you've had a millennium and I'm like 'where *does* the time go?' and—"

"Is there any point in asking how you got in? And yes, now you're here, I do want some strong black coffee, thank you."

Finn, as if he was following the most exotic process of preparation, and looking to her for guidance every other moment, made just that, and for himself poured hot water onto a tea bag it looked like he'd brought along, because Lizzie was pretty sure she didn't own any that glowed green. "I got in by walking down past the walls, which was really hard, as expected, because the Vicarage still has about it some of the old shapes of protection."

"I thought that in Lychford the vicar and, you know, magic people were always on the same side?"

Finn took a long drink from his mug, and glowed slightly green himself for a moment. "You church folk are indeed usually allies with the wise woman of the town, but the nation of my father, we're not always friends with humans. This is reasonably easy to grasp, surely? Human beings still have different nations. You have borders even from your allies, right?"

"True."

"So those who built the Vicarage made its shape to defend against people like me slipping in and out without a lot of effort. Hence this." He pointed to his mug. "Keeps my strength up. Like I said, I'd have gone to see one of the other two for preference, but the old one's got some serious 'keep away' hoo-hah round her place these days, and Autumn's got a guest over."

"Oh?" Lizzie realised she'd put the wrong note in her voice and changed it to a more neutral "Oh."

Finn raised a frankly delightful eyebrow. "How *are* she and that new lad of hers doing?"

"How do you know about that?"

Finn just pointed at himself.

"Has that question got anything to do with the sort of company she's got this morning?"

"Not sure. Probably not. So how *are* she and Luke doing?"

Lizzie noted that he knew Autumn's boyfriend's name. "They

have their ups and downs, but they're still together. He's off on some teaching thing up north."

"Probably for the best."

"Why?"

"Because of this strangeness that's been going on. As I was about to say before I was so rudely interrupted, today it wasn't just the shape of this place that made it hard to get in here. Something has happened to the borders. Leaving fairy and getting into Lychford is normally just about taking a step here and a step there. This time it was like stumbling down a hill. I felt like I'd crash any moment, and I don't know what crashing would even involve. When I get back, everyone'll be yelling about this."

"That is worrying. Okay, thanks for—"

"But that's not why I came here! I only found that out on the way here! And now I think of it, maybe the two are connected, because this is damnable, this is unconscionable, this I was sent from the court of my father with urgent diplomatic condemnation concerning!"

Lizzie held up her hands, amazed at the sudden fury which had taken him over. It was as if he had remembered that he was supposed to be officially angry, and in that moment, took on that emotion for real. Once again, she'd been reminded that though a fairy like Finn might resemble a human being, he was actually very different. "What?!"

"*What,*" yelled Finn, pointing out of the window in the direction of the repetitive beats, "is that bloody *music*?"

Lizzie could only shrug in agreement. "I know." Then she realised she was representing possibly the entire human race in an official diplomatic negotiation with another . . . species? If that was what fairies were. Not a situation she expected to encounter while still in her dressing gown. She made herself straighten up and adjusted her robe. "I mean . . ." she said, more carefully, "I don't know."

Finn sighed. "I now have a new winner for our 'stupid things humans say' board."

"Do you really have a—?"

"What you're trying to say is: *you* don't know what that music is either?"

"I know *what* it is." And before he could scream in frustration, Lizzie quickly explained the concept of illegal raves, from the perspective of someone who'd last gone out dancing two decades ago.

Finn seemed relieved to at least have an explanation he could take back to his father. "Well, normally I'd be all for that, and good work there with the mind-expanding drugs, because at least someone here's *trying*, but how is the sound of it getting into fairy? We've got stuff to do, you know. We need the sleep of ages under the hills. We can't be having with *dush dush dush* all the time."

"So the dance music is . . . keeping the fairies awake?"

"That's what I just said. Try to keep up."

"Well, our local police, such as they are, will be out trying to find it, I should think."

"Probably, though I've seen a few of them this morning doing other things besides. But what worries me most is, since I got here I've had a bit of a look for where the music's coming from, and I can't find it. And I have the nose of a bloodhound. In my pocket." He took something that Lizzie really hoped was a felt novelty of some kind from his jacket and showed it to her. "So your police won't be able to. You put that together with the borders getting messed up, and it's big trouble for everyone."

"You're right. I'll tell the others."

Finn seemed satisfied. "Excellent. This is what the three of you are for." He threw back the remains of his tea, then glanced suspiciously at Lizzie, carefully washed out his mug, and retrieved the tea bag. "Good luck with it. Now I have to go home and listen to everyone at court getting worked up all over again. Let's hope you can deal with it before that boils over into, you know, the collapse of reality. Or whatever." And with a gesture that seemed somehow dismissive as well as functional, he vanished. Then there was a sudden *clonk* sound from somewhere inside the walls, and a cry of pain, and then a motion of air that Lizzie somehow knew meant that now he'd actually gone, on the second attempt, and that the Vicarage's old defences were still good for some things.

Lizzie's first impulse was to go and see what sort of company Autumn had at this time in the morning, but no, Judith was who she should go to find.

She went back upstairs, pleased at having added an unexpected flight of steps to her fitness tracker's records, dressed, then headed off to Judith's house.

As she walked up the hill from the marketplace, that distant sound of dance music was still drifting over the town. It was indeed weird that, if that was an illegal rave, the police hadn't found it and closed it down by now. Something that loud couldn't be legal, could it? Wouldn't she have had a warning letter through her door, or something?

There didn't initially seem to be anyone at home at Judith's house. But that was often the case these days. Lizzie knew Judith had been grieving in a manner that was, quite possibly, unique in all of human history. Lizzie had been doing her best to help, because comforting grieving widows was very much part of her skill set, but Judith had been, as expected, one of her more challenging subjects. The old lady's desire to not say anything to anyone about anything unless it was somehow offensive had reached a new intensity in these last few months. It took a bit of work for anyone dealing with her to realise that she'd changed, because she now bore an entirely different burden than the one she'd borne for years before. And that burden had been made worse, of course, by its own potential for change, that someday Judith might bear no burden at all. The weight on her shoulders had grown to be part of her, had informed the malice that often seemed, to those who didn't know her well, to be what kept her going.

At Lizzie's third ring of the bell, the door opened. Judith stood there, looking even more grim than usual. "I was just about to come and find you," she said. "Summat terrible has happened."

"I know—" began Lizzie.

"No you don't," said Judith.

We're dealing with two missing persons cases this morning," Shaun had said, when Autumn had pressed him for details. "We think you might have particular insight into one of them. Rory Holt is missing."

"Oh no." Autumn had felt a horrible tension building in her stomach. She'd tried to keep her expression steady.

But Shaun had looked at her as if that reaction had been meaningful. "His daughter, who lives with him, called it in in the early hours. She thought she'd heard him arrive home, but when she got up to go to the bathroom, the door to his room was open and his bed hadn't been slept in. He was nowhere in the house. She thinks he must have actually gone missing between leaving the pub and getting to their doorstep. Right now, we think you were the last person to see him."

"Why do you think that?"

"Because there's security camera footage of you two . . . continuing your altercation."

"You got to see security camera footage this early in the morning?"

Shaun had sighed. "I do sometimes wish the public didn't

watch so many detective shows. We saw it because it was from the security camera on the front of the police station."

Autumn had indeed watched her share of police procedurals, and had thus suddenly been very aware of what this meant. She'd been the last to see the victim . . . and she'd been arguing with him. "You're saying I'm some sort of . . . suspect."

Shaun had looked awkward. "A Detective Inspector's coming up from Swindon, about both cases. The brass are wondering if they've somehow got anything to do with the illegal rave that's been reported. We were told to go out and interview everyone who might be . . . involved." A buzz had come from his phone and he'd looked at it, then looked up. "She's here now, and I'm to ask you if you'll come in for interview."

Which was how Autumn now found herself inside Lychford police station, waiting to be interviewed. She'd immediately taken up the offer to have legal representation present. The solicitor in question seemed businesslike, a little remote. Autumn numbly listened as she'd filled her in on the basics of what was going to happen. She'd never been inside Lychford police station before. It was seldom open these days, a tiny adjunct to the trading estate. Now it had a cluster of police cars and vans in front of it, and there had even been a reporter from a local radio station, with a power pack, a microphone, and a look on his face which said this was the biggest thing with which he'd ever been involved.

Shaun had sighed again as they'd made their way across the car park. "More of those'll be on the way." He was looking at her, Autumn had realised, like she'd let him down, like she was part of his world which wasn't behaving as he wanted it to. Most coppers knew, from long experience, she remembered reading, that the obvious suspect had usually done it.

The reporter had seen Autumn and moved quickly, had taken a picture. She'd been caught staring, she realised, wondering if trying to get a hand in the way would make the image look worse to whatever friends and relations might see it.

She'd been given a cup of black coffee, which had been welcome, and left in this interview room with the solicitor. The guilt and the anger and the hangover were now all one thing. Oh God, she should have called Lizzie. She should have called Luke. She was remembering more and more now. And it was all bad.

A female plainclothes police officer entered, with, again, that look of businesslike distance about her, and introduced herself as D.I. Pearce. She began with some legal formalities Autumn really didn't like the sound of, telling her she was going to be recording the interview. Then she started the tape decks running. Pearce led her through the same chain of events Shaun had, referring to his notes on occasion. She kept it so by the book that Autumn's solicitor kept nodding along. Autumn felt, horribly, like the two of them were workers in an industrial process and she was their raw material. She said the minimum, agreeing with her previous version of events. Then they got to the point to which Shaun had taken the narrative. "When you left the pub, where was Rory Holt?"

"He followed me. He was shouting at me."

"What was he saying?"

She could remember every detail now. "He was using . . . you know . . . hate speech."

"What *exactly*?"

So Autumn was forced to put those words in her mouth. They made her feel sick all over again. To voice them felt like she was being made to bully herself. She watched the face of the D.I. for any sign of sympathy, but she remained utterly neutral. Autumn talked as, moment by moment, the memory unfolded in front of her, of how Old Rory had pushed past her and so, yes, damn it, she'd followed him, up past the police station, with him turning to spit on the ground and yell back at her.

"Just past the police station, I yelled at him one last time, and I thought . . . this sounds so stupid now . . . I thought yeah, that showed him. I turned around and walked off, talking loudly so I . . . couldn't hear what else he was saying. Like I said, stupid. I . . . must have gone back the other way, not past that camera again."

She looked into Pearce's eyes, hoping to see some sign that she believed what Autumn now was pretty certain was the truth. No response.

There was a knock on the door, and Pearce called to enter. A uniformed officer came in and whispered something to her. Pearce seemed to gain a certain tension across her shoulders. She excused herself, and left, leaving the recorders on. The solicitor said that some new development must have occurred, as if that wasn't obvious. Autumn was barely listening, she was so relieved at having found this exonerating memory, so giddy with that release.

So why did she still feel guilty, somewhere at the back of her mind?

It was the hangover. It must be. And, okay, yelling in the street at a pensioner, even at a racist pensioner, perhaps not her finest hour. And she could never feel certain that the police would agree with her newfound proof of innocence.

After half an hour, Pearce returned. She asked a couple more questions of a general nature, and wrote down her contact details, at which point Autumn realised she was actually going to . . . not get away with this, where had that thought come from? To justifiably be let off the hook. Her solicitor broke into a smile that seemed to be about this taking less time than she thought it would.

Autumn stumbled out of the interview room, trying to restrain her trembling. In the reception area, she found Shaun, who now looked a little guilty himself. He gave her a significant look, waited until another copper had walked past, then moved close enough to whisper to her. "Just doing our job, you know."

"It's okay." Because now she was in a mood to be charitable, and he'd been fine, honestly. He couldn't help . . . unconsciously condemning her. *No, stop thinking like that, Autumn.*

"Turns out an old lady called it in. You woke her up. She saw you walk off just like you said you did, and saw Rory go the other way. And bless her, she stayed awake and kept watching."

"Oh thank God."

"She was afraid for him, and thought from what you'd been yelling that you might go back after him."

It took Autumn a moment to process that. "From what *I'd* been yelling?! Didn't she hear what *he* was—?!"

"It's not me saying this."

"No, no you're right. Sorry. Hey, you said two missing persons. Who's the other?"

"A lorry driver. The transponder on his vehicle said he'd swerved off the road, then it stopped working. Which is often a sign the rig's been hijacked. Hard to see how it all fits together. I suppose it's possible that three different illegal things this big have happened at once by coincidence. But that'd be three times more than we've ever had in any given year. Still. Maybe times are changing." That beaten down look had returned to his face. At least now it wasn't about her.

"Thanks, Shaun. Listen, if you see your Mum—"

"What?"

Autumn paused. No, maybe not. That was something she should do herself. If she was going to do it at all.

Lizzie had been looking open-mouthed between what was on Judith's kitchen floor and Judith herself, as the old witch had told her what it meant. Then she'd had to have a sit down, and Judith had told her where to find the tea to make herself a cup. "We'll need to wait a while before the stupid girl can get here," she'd said.

'Where is she now? And don't call her—"

"In the circumstances," Judith had muttered, "I intend to call her a lot more than that."

Lizzie had spent the next hour or so walking up and down the kitchen, avoiding the pool of liquid, worrying and checking the step count on her wrist. Finally, the doorbell rang.

It was indeed Autumn, who entered with her hands above her head, exclaiming, "You would not believe the morning I've had."

"We would," said Judith. "Look." And she pointed at the floor.

Autumn stopped and stared too.

On the usually spotless kitchen floor, as Lizzie had discovered when she first got here, was a pool of water, only it was reflecting the sunlight more brightly than ordinary water would. Judith poked the pool with the toe of her fluffy slipper. It rippled, and on its surface suddenly appeared a frozen image of Autumn outside the police station.

Autumn closed her eyes. "You have no right to—"

"Let's not start about who's got the right to do what," said Judith sharply. "More important, there's this." She picked up a washing-up liquid bottle from her sink and squeezed something onto the surface of the pool. The picture changed.

Lizzie was once again looking at the image Judith had shown her before. It was the wall of someone else's kitchen. On it was a wobbling red circle, like a heat haze made flesh. "Only we can see that," Lizzie explained to Autumn.

"Where is this?"

"Don't you recognise it?" asked Judith.

Autumn was frowning, deeply upset. "No," she finally whispered.

"What about this?" Judith kicked the image and it swung

round to reveal the black silhouette of a person, with limbs flailing in all directions, that was embedded in the opposite wall.

"And only we can see that too—" Lizzie began.

Autumn cut her off. "I don't need a running commentary. Where *is* this?"

"I think," growled Judith, "you two had better come with me."

Autumn walked briskly beside Judith as they headed to her shop. She didn't want to think; she didn't want to let her memory go where it wanted to. That kitchen in the picture had seemed horribly familiar, and she was starting to realise . . . oh God no, it couldn't be true. That distant music was still beating away, meaninglessly.

She unlocked the door of the shop and the three of them went inside, Lizzie with that terrible calm on her face that she reserved for the ordinary horrors that vicars encountered. She kept trying to make reassuring eye contact, but Autumn couldn't bring herself to accept that comfort. Judith led them through toward the back room, the workroom.

The smell hit her as they approached. The smell from what was inside.

And Autumn started to remember the last time she'd come here.

She rushed toward the door to her lab. She had to get there first. She flung it open.

She fell against the wall inside, coughing.

The stench was overpowering. In the past, Judith had worked on the rest of the shop so that the smells in here wouldn't escape to where the customers were, or rather, to where her own nose usually was. Ingredients bags and boxes were lying open all around. Autumn saw that some of what was causing the smell was still bubbling on a pot by the sink.

Judith went over to it, looked at it like it was the enemy, picked up a pan lid with the corner of her cardigan, and slammed it down on the pot. She looked to switch off the heat, then realised at the same moment Autumn did that the cooker wasn't actually on. "That'll need cleaning," she said. "Cleaning with the proper stuff." Meaning, Autumn realised, stuff that wasn't to be found in any mundane kitchen cupboard.

Lizzie went to the pot, made the sign of the cross, closed her eyes, and mouthed some words. She opened them again and saw Autumn looking hopelessly at her. "Couldn't hurt," she said.

"What . . . what is that stuff?"

"You made it," said Judith. "Didn't you?"

Autumn recalled now marching back from having yelled at Rory Holt in the street and bursting in here, stumbling from cupboard to cupboard, only her anger keeping her going, her head in a fog. She'd made something completely instinctively, with her brain switched off, like when she'd made that potion at Christmas to save herself from a spell, but this time with nobody in the driver's seat but sheer emotion. "Yes," she said. "I made it. What does it do?"

Judith put a hand on her shoulder, and roughly turned her to look at the opposite wall. On it, the still steaming black goo had been painted into a rough circle. Autumn remembered now the physical action of making the shape with the brush.

"It's . . . the same shape as the one we saw in the pool," said Lizzie.

Judith went to the sink, turned on the tap, and put her hands under the water. Then she threw what seemed an unfeasible amount of it onto the floor. She took the bottle from the pocket of her cardigan and squirted whatever that was onto the surface again. Autumn thought distantly that she wouldn't like to risk doing the washing up in Judith's kitchen. Judith's idea of potion storage relied on her formidable memory and a make-do attitude that was like a magical version of *Blue Peter*. She banished the thought. Too happy. She couldn't allow herself that comfort either. She was going to have to face what she'd done here. And she had a terrible feeling she now knew what it was. "What . . . we saw earlier," she whispered. "Was that Old Rory's kitchen? Did I . . . was that his silhouette?"

"All light still exists, somewhere," said Judith, ignoring the question. "You just have to find it and get on the right end of it." An image of that kitchen formed, and Judith once more touched it with her toe. "There. Now let's rewind."

She spun the image anticlockwise and it dissolved into a rainbow. Judith seemed to judge how long she had to wait, then put her toe down again. In the pool, Autumn saw Rory Holt in what, yes, must be his own kitchen, walking about, maybe intending to make tea. He looked drunk and furious, slamming cupboard doors.

He turned at what must have been a sound and stumbled back, incredulous.

Into the picture stepped Autumn. She also looked drunk and furious.

"I'm sorry," said Autumn now.

"Be silent," whispered Judith, in a voice Autumn had never heard from her before. It had sounded utterly condemnatory, with the experience of centuries behind it.

"You must have used magic to get in," whispered Lizzie. Still keeping up that running commentary. As if it was the only help she could provide.

In the image, Autumn advanced on Rory, yelling at him, pointing at him. He started to yell and gesticulate back, to indicate he wanted her out of his house. He grabbed for a saucepan and brandished it like a weapon.

"You . . . thought he was going to attack you—" began Lizzie.

But Autumn in the image didn't look threatened. "Don't, Lizzie."

In the pool, Autumn turned on her heel, and triumphantly stepped back out of frame. Rory looked alarmed once more. He put down the pan.

He flew backwards.

He hit the wall. The black ash burst from where he hit, in his shape.

Autumn looked up from the pool and at the faces of her friends. "Did I . . . disintegrate him? Or did he go through the wall? No, they . . . would have found him if he went through—"

"You didn't kill," said Judith. "Though I'm glad you're feeling the weight of that. What you really did is summat that you might find harder to understand. Summat worse."

"How could it have been worse?"

"Watch." Judith used her foot to manipulate the image again, going back to the moment when Old Rory flew backwards. Then she spun the picture once more, to find . . . nobody there.

"So I'd gone?" said Autumn. "I mean, did I leave the moment after I . . . I blasted—?"

"Hold on." Judith held the view where it was and "rewound" as she had before. Autumn saw herself triumphantly step back through the hole in the wall, stick two fingers up at Rory, and vanish, the hole closing, leaving only the circle. Judith froze the image and spun it again, to show Rory in the act of putting down the pan.

And *then* he flew backwards.

Autumn felt sheer relief surging through her.

Until Judith stepped right up to her, furious. "Don't look relieved, you idiot!" she bellowed.

"Hey! I didn't hurt him!"

"Oh, didn't you? Look!" Judith threw something at her from

out of her pocket. It was some sort of dust. Autumn flinched . . . and then realised nothing about her had changed, or . . . no, looking down, something seemed to now be wrapped all around her. Had that old witch . . . tied her up? No. No. She couldn't feel whatever this was, she could only see it.

She went to the full-length mirror in the corner and saw what it was. All around her were wrapped . . . they looked like fibres made of light, hundreds of them, in different colours. They led off from her in many directions, taut, attached to unseen anchors, fading where whatever Judith had thrown on her ended its influence. She was so wrapped up in them it was surprising she could move. She put a hand to them, and it went right through. She could move because they were still intangible to touch, as they had previously been to sight. Even to her own magically enhanced sight.

Judith marched up to her again, grabbed her by the shoulders, and wrenched her round to face her. "Last night you marched right through every line of force attached to the town's borders. You did what fairies do, walk to what's inside places, only you had no idea what you were doing. The gestures and words we use when we do magic are sometimes about *limiting* what our emotions want to do. The worst of us realise that emotions can connect straight to magic and let that go to their heads, don't try to regulate it, and that's what you did last night. You smashed through everything in your way, and now you've got the boundaries wrapped round you like a . . . bull in a knitting shop. The boundaries. They're . . . what was I saying? No, shut up, this is important." Autumn watched, bemused, as Judith stepped away and took a moment to lean on something.

"Judith, are you all right?" Lizzie asked.

Judith just shook her head. This silence, this effect on the old woman, was scaring Autumn more than the yelling had. But before she could start to argue, Judith had turned again and raised a finger to resume berating her. "Do you see? When you heaved off out of his kitchen, Old Rory was caught in the backlash and sent flying like he was on a catapult, off into who knows where. That's probably what's happened to the lorry driver that's gone missing. It might be what's happened to however many bloody people were at that dance or whatever it is that we're still hearing. And it's why the prince had so much trouble coming to see the reverend this morning. That's why I say what you did was worse than murder. You might or might not have hurt Rory. But you've hurt all the rest of us. Maybe everyone in the world. You've done what nobody's ever done, messed up the borders around Lychford. Now every dark thing that's out there, soon as they realise, they'll be heading here to mess with us. Some of the great nations too. There'll be summat happening among the fairies. And I don't know if there's anything we can do about it. All because you'd had a few!"

Autumn looked to Lizzie. She didn't look away, but was there something on her face of what Shaun had had in his expression earlier? "Well . . . what are we waiting for?" she shouted, her guilt bursting out of her as anger. "If it's so bloody urgent, shouldn't we be out there finding those people?" *And not in here accusing me of something I'm utterly guilty of.*

"Don't you take that tone with me. Don't you take any tone now." Judith was still blazingly angry. "I'm only waiting for—" There came a buzzing sound from the pocket of her dress. She put her hand in and pulled out a kitchen timer. "—right. My defences are ready. Come on."

And with that Judith headed for the door, and Autumn was horrified to see that she was actually running.

2

Lizzie would normally, for the sake of her exercise tracker, have been grateful for the opportunity of an impromptu jog, but when it was across the town, following a pensioner who was now displaying an astonishing turn of speed, with the future of everything at stake, well, that wasn't really one of the workout settings. Judith was sprinting, and sustaining it. There were cheers and laughs as they dashed past the locals. That could not, Lizzie was sure, be done without supernatural help. It must have taken some restraint, in her younger years, for Judith not to have tried out for the Olympics.

But restraint was what Judith was all about, wasn't it? And the lack of it was the great sin she was judging Autumn for. But was there something else, alongside that? Lizzie had a good ear for the interactions between people experiencing trauma, and beneath Judith's fury at Autumn, there seemed to be some unspoken anger, something personal. How gently, she wondered, had Autumn been dealing with her employee's grief? Or had she heard only stubbornness and replied in kind? And what about in the other direction? Autumn had been down and put upon for months, and Lizzie really hadn't been paying enough attention to that.

This was what their lives were now, that Lizzie not being there for her friends often enough might have led to the end of the world.

Surprisingly, since she had mentioned her defences being cooked, Judith led them not to her house, but up the hill to the Tatchell farm, baked mud flying from her sensible shoes. The sun was now beaming down on the three figures as they rushed up the spine of the bare hillside, along the track beside Tatchell's field of ripening wheat.

Judith staggered to a stop, stretched out her arms, and spun slowly, as if seeking something. Autumn just about fell beside her, until Lizzie grabbed her and managed to get her to her feet. But then Autumn started to throw up. Only another intervention by Lizzie stopped it from going over Judith's ankles.

"Over here," said Judith, not bothering to notice. She pointed and marched off across the corn, not caring about damaging the crop.

"Are you okay?" Lizzie asked Autumn, helping her to follow. At least the visible threads that had been wrapped around her had faded in the last few minutes. That dust, presumably, was wearing off.

"Of course I'm not bloody—! Sorry. What she was saying, about what I'd done, how . . . I guess, bad magicians? How they use this stuff? Am I going to 'the dark side'?" Lizzie could hear the irony she'd put into the words. "Like I'm becoming the stuff we're keeping out. Which is . . . what they've been saying to me, or not ever saying out loud. What they've been thinking."

Lizzie didn't like the sound in her friend's voice. "You've been under a lot of pressure, and I haven't been listening enough."

"I want to confess."

"Well, we don't do that very much in the C of E, but absolutely, you can confess to me and I can—"

"I don't want to be absolved. I want to take responsibility for this. Do you think there's some sort of . . . magical court, maybe with the fairies?"

"Shut up!" called Judith from ahead. "Move faster." They came to a grassy patch in the middle of the field, which stood out in the middle of the crop. Now they'd stopped running, Lizzie could still hear the distant dance music. Judith squatted slowly down and picked up two spades, which Lizzie was pretty sure hadn't been there a second before. "Dig," she said, "quick."

Autumn grabbed a spade, and set about digging. She was trying to demonstrate her commitment. "Those threads you saw wrapped around me," she said, "won't me moving about keep on disturbing them?"

Judith made a tutting noise, like this question was an unwanted burden. "The web of them is loose now. Dun't matter what you do."

Lizzie saw pain pass across Judith's face once more. "Are you okay? Doing all this, running like that, you have to pay a price, don't you? That's how it works."

Judith gave her a look that said further questions along those lines would be most unwise.

Lizzie sighed and started to dig. "How is there a grassy patch here?" She wasn't going to let Judith or Autumn lapse into brooding.

"Paul the builder is one of that lot that goes out with metal detectors. He thinks he found summat huge out here a few months back. He's got an agreement with Joe Tatchell to not sow on this bit, and he'll poke around after harvest."

"And what's that got to do with what we're doing?"

"He found an illusion I'd planted at this spot so he'd do all that. In case we ever had to do this. I'm up for fighting the powers of evil, but I'm not so stupid as I'd take on a farmer."

"But what happens when he realises it's not here?"

"I know what that lot with the detectors are like. He'd have kept poking around for it, year after year. So the spot'd stay put. Right. That's deep enough." She took from her cardigan pocket a tiny cloth bag with thread knotted at the top. "I kept these in the freezer. I had to put them in the oven when I realised what she'd done."

She'd addressed that explanation only to her, Lizzie realised. It was as if Autumn had become useful only for digging. Autumn had realised that too, and was looking helpless. "And they got into your pocket how?" asked Lizzie.

Judith gave her another look. "What do they call him, the green chap?"

"Is that someone we know, or—?"

"On schoolbags. He were on television when I were younger." It took a bit of interrogation before Lizzie realised Judith was talking about The Incredible Hulk. "Right. Him. If I go like him, knock me around the head with the brown-handled spade. That should fix it." And before either of them could ask any alarmed questions, even about why it had to be that particular spade, she'd put the cloth of the bag to her lips and started to blow into it.

Lizzie and Autumn looked at each other. "You've got the brown-handled spade," said Lizzie.

Autumn quickly swapped spades with her.

Judith's face was changing colour, but it was turning bright red rather than green. She seemed to have been blowing for an impossibly long time, drawing air from who knew where. Lizzie took a covert look behind the old woman and saw that her floral dress had flattened against the back of her legs, as if being pulled in by . . . no, she really didn't want to think about that.

Judith finally stopped, staggered, righted herself, and, with a little cry of pain, threw the bag into the hole. Light burst from where it struck the soil, and a pillar of it shot up into the sky, a light only they could see. Then it began to slowly fan out, dissipating into a vague glow that followed an arc.

"Basic defence," panted Judith. "Until . . . if . . . we can knit the boundaries back into place . . . it'll have to do."

"So now do we go after the lost people?" asked Autumn.

"In a bit." Judith looked like she didn't like speaking directly to

Autumn now. She also looked on her last legs, her face grey with effort. "We've got three more of these to do first."

They raced around Lychford in the heat, putting the cloth bags into prepared sites that were, in order: inside the bole of a tree; by the side of a road, which needed a paving stone to be heaved up and got them curious shouts from drivers; in the playground underneath the slide, which required more digging. All the while, the distant beat of the dance music continued.

"Does it have to be here?" said Lizzie, about digging under the slide, aware that if anyone saw her she'd have some serious explaining, or rather lying, to do to the town council. At least she was getting her steps in today.

"I'm not responsible for where the cardinal points are. I just did my best to get these within twenty feet." Judith had done the same trick with the bags at three sites now, and now she embarked on it one last time. Lizzie seriously wondered if it would kill her.

Finally, she dropped the last bag into the hole and they filled it in. The light this time flashed up, connected with the other beacons, and from this angle they could now see they were inside a barely perceptible dome, which faded. But Lizzie could still feel the slight sense of added safety its continuing presence imparted.

Judith sat down on the grass. "Right," she said. "Now we can . . . can find those . . ."

"Let us do it," said Autumn.

Judith was silent for a long moment, her eyes closed. Lizzie hoped she'd say something comforting, but when she finally spoke, it was as bitter as before. "You've done enough."

"Do we know if anything's got through?"

Judith opened her eyes and started to push herself up. "It will have. Maybe a few things, at random, shunted here like Rory Holt and the lorry driver and the rave were shunted elsewhere, or maybe loads of 'em, deliberately, if they were waiting ready to seize their chance."

"Refugees coming over the border," said Autumn. And now her voice was as hard as Judith's had been.

Judith finally looked at her. "It's not a bloody metaphor," she said. "Everything isn't about you."

She'd hauled herself to her feet and set off before Autumn could find a reply. Lizzie put a hand on Autumn's arm. The look on her face was a battle between anger and absolute guilt. "Just let me try to fix it," Autumn whispered. "Please. She has to let me try."

As the three of them marched down the river toward the route to the woods, Autumn kept looking at Judith. She kept waiting for the old woman to say that Autumn was no longer her apprentice, that after the lack of care she'd shown, she wasn't worthy. Autumn would have welcomed that. She would have got angry at it too, she couldn't help but react like that, but . . . oh God, when was Judith going to say it?

What would Lizzie be thinking now, if she'd been the one who'd done this? Would she be seeking judgment? Would her guilt be so extreme? How much had the town Autumn had grown up in made the feeling seep into her skin that, being the only black person here, anything abnormal might be her fault? But no. The thought that she'd allowed this to happen because of how this place had treated her . . . that was a luxury she couldn't allow herself. Not if she wanted to retain her mental health. That was what other people liked to think of people like her. She wanted to take responsibility. She would find a way.

And yet, that whole circle of awful thoughts was something that would never even have occurred to Lizzie.

They entered the woods, and after a while came to the signpost that marked the point where some routes seen only by those such as them headed off in directions that could never be recorded on any map. It felt . . . different now. Judith sniffed the air. "Borders have moved here too," she said. "Right, so, we have at least one thing that's continuously leaking across the boundaries."

"What?" asked Lizzie.

"That bloody music." And yeah, there it was, still. "So that's the first thing we can work with. Try to figure out where it's coming from."

The three of them looked around, and managed, between them, to triangulate a direction for the varying beats. They set off that way, through the woods. "Time might be different where they are," said Autumn, remembering her own experience of journeying to fairy. "They'd have shut down the music and gone home by now otherwise."

No reply from Judith. It was as if she hadn't spoken.

After a while, they came to a halt as they all realised, just about at the same time, that the direction the sound was coming from had suddenly shifted, moved to somewhere behind them.

"It's like in a video game," said Lizzie, "when you're right on top of the marker you're trying to find, and it kind of slides away around you."

"I dunno what that means," said Judith, "but now I see what's gone on. The . . . rave, is it? It's caught in what we call a knot, a little loop of border stuff that she made when she went crashing through them."

"I think you should start using Autumn's name again," said Lizzie.

Judith ignored her. "There'll be different knots all over the place. The ends knit when they're thrown together, so they form little bubble worlds. I saw it once before, when I were younger. In . . ." She paused for a long moment, and a frown crossed her face. "Don't remember. Don't matter. Where was I? Oh ah. The rave might be in one, the lorry driver in another, Rory Holt in another."

"Do we know how many of them there are?" asked Lizzie.

"Dunno. Could be half a dozen, could be thousands. What worries me most is, are those people alone in there? These aren't just bits cut off from this world. She made the borders fly about, get mixed up and connected to each other, so there'll be bits of the other worlds in there too. There might be stuff that's got into the wrong places, dark things we've been trying to keep out, but have fallen into the knots."

"I think we really should try to find another word for 'evil' other than—" began Lizzie, who'd obviously seen the look on Autumn's face.

"Words I use aren't what's wrong. What she did is what's wrong."

Autumn took a deep breath and shoved it all down inside her once again. "Okay. How do we get into these knots?"

Finally, Judith addressed her. Because she knew what she was about to say was arrogant and annoying. "You can't get there from here."

"Then how—?"

"Not by walking, not by knowing stuff. We need to be lost. Close your eyes, put your fingers in your ears, and start walking."

"What about our, you know, other senses? The ones we got from the well?" asked Lizzie.

"They'll be what get us there. But not if we let our normal senses get in the way. This is like . . . looking for summat really small. Summat that's curled up inside summat else. We need to concentrate. And not. At the same time."

Autumn did her best to follow those ridiculous instructions. At last she could do something. She put her fingers in her ears, closed her eyes, and took a hesitant step forward, muttering "one potato, two potato . . ." to drown out any external noise. She let her feet lead her, moving slowly, expecting every moment to walk into a tree. She didn't know where Lizzie and Judith were. She realised, after a minute or so, that it was actually quite amazing that she *hadn't* walked into a tree. The air around her seemed to have suddenly got colder.

When she reached one hundred potatoes, she decided now would be a reasonable time to stop. She opened her eyes and took her fingers out of her ears.

It was suddenly night.

She was still in the woods, but now all was illuminated by a full moon. Yeah, it had been a full moon last night. And it was a summer night, but it was still bloody freezing compared to the brilliant day she'd been in a moment ago, and she was only wearing a dress.

She looked round for Judith and Lizzie, who she'd assumed would be somewhere behind her, but . . . no. She took a couple of steps, called their names, and realised she would have seen them by now.

She was . . . alone here.

And she didn't know how to get back. Because Judith hadn't told her that part. Perhaps it would be just about retracing her steps? Yeah, okay, let's go with that for now. So, she had to find if anyone else was in here with her. And hope like crazy that nothing . . . she refused to think of it as "dark" . . . that nothing with evil intent was in here too.

She hugged herself. So she'd successfully entered an area that still looked like it was part of the woods, but where it was still the night before. Because, right, time must be running more slowly in here. So this was . . . probably . . . hopefully . . . a knot that had got snipped off of their own world, and was somehow stuck in this previous time. How was she moving and breathing, then? Nope, can't answer that yet.

She realised she now couldn't hear the dance music at all. All was silence. So the illegal rave wasn't in here. Tick that off the list.

What if Rory Holt was here? How would he react if he saw her? That would be an interesting conversation. Please let him be alive for that.

Cautiously, she started moving through the woods, listening, alert for any sign of movement. But all was still under that big moon. At least moving kept her a bit warmer. The sweat from all that running about was swiftly cooling off.

After a few minutes, she saw something strange ahead of her. Along the top of a ridge, a number of the trees had fallen, a great fan shape of them, with soil tumbling from their exposed roots, turning the climb ahead into a slippery slope. It was as if something had knocked them over. She heaved herself up, stepped carefully over the timber, crested the ridge, and saw that, somewhere in the hollow below, obscured by fallen trees, a cluster of artificial lights was shining. "Hello?" she called.

She thought she heard a sound in reply. Perhaps a call for help. Cautiously, Autumn began to pick her way down the slope.

Lizzie took her hands away from her face and looked round, startled at the sudden proximity of the dance music. Judith was standing at her shoulder. The sky was light with approaching dawn, the full moon of last night on the horizon. So, right, they'd gone back in time . . . or something. Ahead of them, flashing lights shone through the trees, the music blaring from that direction. She looked quickly around and then turned back to Judith. "Where's Autumn?"

Judith looked, if anything, more shocked than Lizzie felt.

"She . . . she must have walked far enough ahead to stumble into . . . another knot."

"Right," said Lizzie. "Okay. Can we get her back?"

Judith shook her head. "When we unpick this, iron out the boundaries, we'll find her then, maybe . . ."

Why was the old witch suddenly looking so uncertain? "So if we just went back the way we came, then walked as far as she did—?"

"You don't just go backwards to get out. It's a whole other thing."

"What other thing?"

Judith's face was now a complete blank. Lizzie wondered for a moment if she'd stopped recognising her. Was this the toll for what she'd done today? If so, it had come at entirely the wrong moment. "Complicated," Judith said, finally.

Lizzie was damn sure she wasn't going to take more than a step away from Judith before she explained. She wanted to say if Judith hadn't been too angry to talk directly to Autumn she might have done the responsible thing and told both her apprentices how to get out of what she was leading them into. "Couldn't you have stopped her?"

"Not my fault if she walked off that quick."

"You do get that she's trying to prove herself?"

"Dun't matter. I can't train someone that goes and does this."

"When you were her age, you messed up so badly you ended up being cursed!"

Judith glowered at her. "I don't have to keep you on, either."

Lizzie was suddenly very calm. Which was what tended to happen when she got to the end of her tether. "Right now, especially, you need someone telling you the truth. You *hate* that you just let your apprentice walk into danger. I know you do. You're on your last legs. There's clearly stuff you're not telling me. You need our help. And you and she really need to sit down and talk about all of this—!"

"Don't you lecture me!" Lizzie was taken aback. She'd never heard Judith bellow like that before. The old woman took a few steps back, her fingers flexing, as if making a great effort to control herself. "I have never, ever, in my life, been spoken to like—"

And then she vanished, like she'd suddenly fallen backward through an invisible wall.

Oh no. Oh no. Lizzie swore out loud several times. "Judith?!" She stepped quickly forward, muttering a prayer, eyes closed and fingers in her ears . . . and stopped when she hit a tree. She was still in the same space. She'd walked right over the spot where Judith had vanished.

She tried a few more times, but it wasn't working. Maybe it was just that the sound of the rave was too great to ever be entirely blocked out of her ears.

She had no choice but to give up. She turned and headed toward the rave. She had no idea what she could do to get these people out of here, but at least if something nasty was in here with them, then . . . okay, she'd cross that bridge when she came to it. Damn it.

Judith spun round, and yelled in anger. Then she turned again, reflexively. Gone! The reverend was gone too! No . . . actually, it was Judith herself who'd gone.

Stupid old woman. Where had she—?

Wherever it was, it was extraordinary.

There was nothing about this place that was like a place. It was like . . . a bunch of echoes, of sound and of light, rebounding endlessly, arcing all round her. She could breathe, but she felt it when she breathed in, it was something that was only trying to be air at the moment it hit her nose and mouth. There was nothing deceptive about that, it was a desperate attempt to welcome her, to keep her alive. But it didn't feel like there was thought behind it, either. It felt like . . . a fairground ride, summat automatic, summat that was creaking, that was being pushed too far.

She took a step, and the light and sound changed around her again. The thick air slid past her hands, maybe only skin deep. Fire, the place said, fire was near, only the world was shielding her from it, keeping her alive when she shouldn't be here.

She closed her eyes, trying hard not to panic.

She was so tired. It felt like she was going to faint, and if she did, she didn't quite know how she was going to wake up again. She'd been using it up today, burning it up so fast . . . No. She made herself shake her head and found that place inside her where she would always be tough with herself. *Come on, girl. Hold on. Those two need you to get out of here and find them. Not that they deserve . . . no, enough of that. Enough. Now. Where have you got to?* It didn't seem like she was in the worst of the many possible situations she could have ended up in. There were worlds which had informed . . . and she'd had conversations with a couple of Lizzie's predecessors about this . . . the human idea of hell. It wasn't that they were all pitchforks and fire. It was that they were *about* the person who'd stumbled into them. Those worlds responded to people's fears, or even to their desires. If this was one of them, well . . . that would make her life into a fine shaggy dog story, eh?

But no. She was pretty sure this world was genuinely trying, with all its strength, to help her. The problem was that it didn't have much strength left.

She opened her eyes again, and made her mind seek . . . land, a horizon, summat to get a fix on. And then, slowly, there were shapes, she was making herself adjust, and the land was helping her, showing her ways to see. The light rolled around her and showed her how far everything was in every direction.

Oh. It was a bubble. A literal bubble. A piece of space from another world, then, where time continued as normal, but which had been sealed off from its surroundings. This would actually be the easiest sort of knot to explore, to find anyone in. Of course, if there were a nasty in here, it would also be easy for it to find her.

How had she come here while absolutely not blocking out all the noises and sights of a world that had had a rave in it?

Oh. It had been anger, damn it. For the first time in decades, she'd let the pure force of magic run through her, uncontrolled, as she'd been thinking about how to traverse the knots. She'd only gone and bloody well done exactly what Autumn had done. This individual knot, still taut, had burst open to let her in. At least no more harm could be done.

She took a few steps forward, and then, sure she was now calm and aware enough to not fall into any knots within knots, she began to walk more confidently. She wished she had brought her stick. The physical energy she had mortgaged against her future well-being was slowly leaving her.

A flat surface, black like obsidian, but not reflecting, had appeared ahead of her and under her feet. She'd made it come to her. This place knew it needed help. In the "sky" above, the light was still whirling and rebounding. So little space for it to play in.

Ahead, on the surface, she saw something.

A set of footprints was materialising. There was someone else in here.

Judith gave a little groan and made to follow.

Autumn had stumbled down into the hollow, and had immediately realised what the lights were. At the end of a trail of destruction, where it had carved a road for itself across the wooded hill, a huge articulated lorry lay on its side. She'd run to the cab, managed to put a foot on one of the wheels, and had climbed up onto the side of it. She'd looked inside, and tried the door. When it had clicked open, she'd managed to haul it upwards and look down into the interior.

There sat a battered man, in his thirties, stubbled chin, donkey jacket, cropped hair. He had a kind, frightened, bemused face. He was out of his seat belt, having managed to heave himself into an upright position. He looked up at her in relief. "Thank you. Where? What happened?"

Was that a Polish accent? Autumn decided she couldn't answer his questions very well in any language. And even then, the undercutting voice in her head added, she'd have hesitated to get to the point where his plight was her fault. "Are you hurt?"

"My leg, maybe broken. Hurts like . . . hell."

Autumn was moved that he'd felt the need to spare her delicate sensibilities from a swear word even in a situation like this. She swore in reply, and he managed a smile. In the movies, lorries in these circumstances would always explode, but she was pretty sure that didn't really happen, and there was no petrol smell, and if he'd been here an hour already it would probably have happened by now. If they'd been back in Lychford, she was pretty sure the best thing would have been to leave him where he was and keep him company until the emergency services got here. Pity she didn't have that option. "Have you seen anyone else?"

"I thought . . . someone moving. About ten minutes. I have been shouting."

Autumn raised her head out of the cab and looked carefully around. Everything was silent, apart from the wind moving the trees. The wind and the moon . . . she realised that this pocket she'd created couldn't be cut off in space, or the area cut off must stretch to the moon, and she was pretty sure it would have been missed. So that must mean it was . . . cut off in time? Or something? The moon didn't seem to have moved since she'd got here. What would walking through this place be like for someone outside the knot, who hadn't carefully got lost to find it? Would those unaware hikers suddenly hop to a moment later, a moment that was missing from the world? Would they even notice?

These were the sort of questions Judith never liked her asking. Mainly because the old . . . witch didn't know the answers. Magic let you jump over the "why" and make use of what was hidden, all from the comfort of your kitchen sink.

She didn't think she'd ever stop needing to know why. Maybe that, too, didn't make her a very good apprentice. Just as well she wasn't going to be one for much longer. That thought gave her an ache she knew she deserved. She dismissed it.

She ducked back down into the cab. "Does your radio work?"

It took a bit of miming and explaining to translate the word "radio," but when he got it, he switched it on, and Autumn listened to a single sustained note of early hours music on Radio 1. It took her a few moments to realise it wasn't the more experimental end of the dance spectrum, but that it was going to go on like that forever. She switched it off again.

She looked back out of the cab. She couldn't put this off any longer. That "first aid for small businesses" course she'd taken was finally going to pay off.

"Okay," she said, "it's going to hurt, but we have to get you out and mobile."

It had turned out the rave was in an abandoned building that looked like it had once been a cattle barn, a building that Lizzie had walked around a couple of times in the last few weeks when she'd been trying to get her steps in. A large generator on wheels was chugging away outside, and a crowd of young people were milling around, while more had been visible through the barn entrances, still dancing. Lizzie had heard a DJ shouting encouragement. It had seemed like the party was still in full swing.

Most of the crowd outside had been smoking or snogging or sobbing, doing what the people outside clubs always did, but a few of them had seemed to be talking urgently, looking worried. Those were the ones who'd looked up, surprised, as Lizzie had approached. As if they'd been hoping someone would arrive.

One of them, a young man with a big grin and a bigger beard, had stumbled over to her, his arms outstretched. His friends had followed. "It's a vicar!" he'd cried, and, to Lizzie's surprise, he'd moved in for a surprisingly sincere hug. Sincere, but, err, he'd obviously been dancing all night. There was a certain moistness. She'd gently disengaged herself. "I'm not religious," he'd assured her, loudly and immediately, "but I love that you are, like these woods are, like those birds are. Those starlings. They're religious."

Lizzie had never previously encountered someone who, prior to asking her name, had ventured theories concerning ornithological theology. "I suspect," she'd shouted over the music, "that you may have been on more than the cider."

"Oh no! You got me! Will I go to hell?"

"I tell you what," Lizzie had said, "you tell me about a few things, and then take me to whoever's in charge, and I'll do my best to make sure we avoid that."

Which was how she was taken into the presence of a man who she was told was "Stewie, just Stewie," who'd been standing at a little distance from the barn, toying with his phone.

He laughed when he saw her. "Here we go! Is this a delegation from the town?"

Lizzie didn't want to get into whos and whys. "How long do you feel you've been up here?"

"Look, we'll be off as soon as it's dawn. This isn't up for discussion. If I see you reading number plates or taking photos, churches have stained glass windows, right? What's that they say about people in glass houses keeping their noses out of my business?"

The bearded lad who'd brought her over stepped in, his hands raised. "Hey. Hey. No need for that."

Stewie just smiled as one would at the actions of a toddler.

Lizzie found herself just a little bit pleased that she knew more about this situation than Stewie did. "What if dawn never comes?"

"Is this, like, a metaphor you're going to use in your sermon?"

"No, listen, Stewie, something's going on up here." The lad was insistent. "That's what we've been trying to tell someone. We can't get to the cars."

Stewie was about to go back to playing with his phone, but Lizzie put a hand on his arm, and he looked pleasingly startled at the force of her grip. "How about you show us where the cars are, and then I promise I'll wander off home to my quaint little church?"

Judith had been following the footprints that were being shown to her. She could feel the morning's exertions sapping her strength every moment, but would she notice it getting to her noggin as well? She was better in the afternoons than the mornings. After lunch was when she tended to write angry notes to herself and attach them to the fridge.

She'd lost so much strength today, so much that she'd never get back.

If she bloody lost track of what was real . . . *No, don't think about that now, you stupid old woman, find who made these prints.* They were made by a bloke's shoes, by the look, but you couldn't be sure of that these days.

She turned at a sound. And realised she had company. Floating in the light above her were five extensions of that light, like weird, shifting interruptions of her vision. Arcs of light flew between them, blazing and extinguishing in a moment. Maybe this was the place migraines came from.

Judith knew that the real world of magic wasn't like Harry Potter. Everyone had different names for the beings that came from the other worlds that bordered on theirs. And the degree to which those things recognised and understood human beings depended on how much they'd interacted with human cultures. The fairies, for instance, had a long tradition of cultural exchange. Which usually went one way, mind you, but at least their lust and avarice and anger meant they took the time to magic up human languages.

This lot . . . well, she had so little to go on. "Good morning," she said. Which was more polite than she'd be to most human beings.

They moved closer, interested, worried, maybe aggressive.

"Do you like mints?" She reached into the pocket of her cardigan and brought out a rather old packet of black and white striped ones. "They're very bad for me."

A jolt of light hit the packet, grabbed it, and threw it aside.

Judith was about to start telling the damn thing off, because it was either that or lose control of her bowels when there came, from behind her, something that was a mixture of a bellow and a scream.

A figure leapt out of nothingness, grabbed her, and hauled her away in a moment to an area of the black surface where the beings were no longer present. She was pretty sure, mind you, that in a space this small, they hadn't actually lost track of her, but had held back from following.

The man, because it was a man, looked around urgently. He

was shaking with fear. But now Judith had realised who it was. "Rory Holt," she said.

"Judith Mawson? Oh, that's right, you work for her, don't you? Did she get you too?"

Judith didn't know quite how to answer that.

"We should be safe this far into the bush," he continued. "She teleported us to another planet, like on *Star Wars*."

Judith realised that his senses, limited, unlike hers, to what he'd been born with, were making an entirely different sort of sense of what was around them. "If that works for you," she said.

"What the hell did you think you were doing, offering those monsters sweets? I hid as soon as I saw 'em. You reckon she'll come back to finish us off? All right, we can't talk here, come back to my camp and you tell me everything you know."

And he grabbed her hand and hauled her off. He couldn't perceive how small the world he was in was, Judith quickly realised. They were actually walking like two idiots in some theatre show, pretending to go for miles with big, silly steps as the ground rolled beneath them.

With much yelling on his part, Autumn had managed to get the lorry driver, whose name she'd learned was Marcin, out of his cab. She'd taken his weight and basically let him fall on her to get to the ground. He lay there, sobbing with pain, as she got to her feet and looked around again.

Still the silence. Still nothing moving. Still the feeling there was something out there.

She'd already found a suitable stick, and taken a roll of strong tape out of the back of the lorry. She knelt beside Marcin, and started wrapping the stick to his leg. As she worked, she tried to stay aware of her surroundings. But as she was pulling tight the last piece of tape . . . what was—?

Something was standing right beside her.

She leapt up, spun round. But there was nothing there. It had been just in the corner of her eye. But she was sure something had been there.

"Did you see anything?" she asked Marcin. It was obvious he hadn't.

She shook her head, checked the binding, and carefully helped him to his feet. The splint held.

"Good," he said. "Who are you? What do you, about—?" He indicated what was around them.

Autumn decided she had to tell him something. "Good witch," she said, pointing at herself. Not that she believed that in any sense of the words.

To his credit, Marcin only boggled for a moment. He put a finger to his nose and wiggled it. "Dee dee, dee dee . . ."

Autumn was glad she'd seen clips from *Bewitched* online. She joined in with humming the theme tune for a moment. "Yeah, and her spells kept going wrong too, with hilarious results."

"Witch with doctor, leg?"

She felt awkward. Not so much. "I try to do science too."

"Get us home, okay?"

"Okay—" And there was the thing in the corner of her eye again. This time she managed to stop herself from jumping, and tried to look sidelong at it. This was something that could keep itself just about hidden, even from her extra senses. It was just a white blur, a furtive figure, the same shape as a human being, but . . . no, she couldn't see any features.

She leapt back, sure that in that second it had moved to touch her. It had been the jerk of a predator striking. She felt like it had only just missed.

She grabbed the startled Marcin and heaved him up. "Come on!" she bellowed.

She was sure he could just about hobble along. But where could they run to?

Stewie had sighingly headed with Lizzie and the bearded lad to the makeshift car park. It should, it seemed, have been at the end of the lane that ran up the other side of the hill. But as they'd made their way through the trees, Stewie had got increasingly confused, had even stopped to look at the map app on his phone. Whatever he found had just made him swear. "How can we be lost? It was just over here."

Finally, having walked in a straight line, they'd returned to the barn.

"No," he'd said, turning slowly round. "No. Who put something in my water? You think that's funny?" He'd swung to point at Lizzie, his hand going to his back pocket, where he may or may not have had a knife. "Who are you?"

Lizzie had seen two large individuals in high vis jackets coming over to see what was agitating their boss, and had decided to put her cards on the table. "I'm your only chance of getting home."

It had taken some doing, but in the end, once the big lads had also gone to find the cars and returned from the wrong direction, startled looks on their faces, Lizzie had got Stewie to listen. He'd gone to the tent, got the DJ to switch everything off, and had shepherded the crowd, who were now sure the police were arriving, into an audience around them.

Lizzie had told them the truth, or as much as they needed to know, and had found them, perhaps unsurprisingly, pretty easy to convince of just about anything. Not that what she was telling them hadn't created its share of sobbing, shouting, and hysterical laughter. At least while she'd been talking she'd come up with the start of a plan to get them out of here.

She pointed back to the tent. "We need to get that PA started up again."

They showed her how they did that, and she got up behind the DJ's mixing decks, on stacks of crates at one end of the barn. Thank goodness nobody was taking a photo of her. She would look like the worst possible trendy vicar. The DJ, who looked like she was about twelve, couldn't stop staring. "Could you turn up the volume to full?" Lizzie asked. She bent to the microphone. "Testing," she said. "This is Lizzie, calling Finn. Come in, Finn. Or anyone in the Court of the Unseen. Come in."

"It's not a radio," said the DJ, obviously wondering if the newbie knew anything at all about the world.

"But," said Lizzie, "I know the people I'm talking to can hear it."

Judith, getting tired of being dragged along like she was in a half-arsed mime troupe, had finally shouted to Rory Holt to stop. She'd been about to tell him that she was here to rescue him, but then, over his shoulder, Judith had seen something appear out of the nothingness. She'd grabbed Rory, put a hand over his mouth, and, while he was wetly yelling into her palm, spun him round to see.

A group of the flying beings had gathered. More of them this time. Too many to count easily as they shifted and melted into each other. Between them was . . . this was their version of a device, she realised. It was a solid golden sphere that shot between them.

Rory stiffened in horror. "They've brought their cooking pot. That's meant for us."

Judith didn't believe for a second that that was what was going on here. "What do you see of what they're doing?"

"It's some kind of native religion. We're in Ooga Booga Land here."

Judith wondered what sort of books Rory had read when he was growing up. If they could see these beings now, it was because they wanted to be seen, though Rory was now miming parting foliage with his hands, as if he was spying on them at the edge of a clearing. "I think," she said, "these might be what some call sprites. There are loads of different ones. They're summat to do with elements, not like iron and whatnot, more like principles. This lot are fire sprites. Back when we lived in caves, they're meant to have come over and started campfires. To be on speaking terms with one was summat people boasted about, or more often kept to themselves. Then we get electricity and—"

"What are you going on about, woman?"

"—suddenly they're from 'Ooga Booga Land.'"

"But you can see them right there, see them with your own eyes."

"But we're seeing different things."

Rory was looking annoyed at her. "Here, I'm on your side, remember? You sound like her. She sent us here, so this is probably where she's from. She's been hiding among us, pretending not to be an alien, but now we know."

Judith didn't feel like arguing with this idiot. "Right," she said, and stepped forward to address the sprites. "Afternoon," she said, doing her best to put on her posh voice. For some stupid reason. "I think maybe we got off on the wrong foot." She looked over her shoulder and saw Rory hadn't followed her, but was still "hiding in the bushes," gesturing urgently for her to come back. "That one can't see you properly. But I bring the right tribute." She reached into the pocket of her cardigan and found her big box of household matches, the foundation of any good witch's pocket contents. She struck one, and solemnly held it up toward the sprites.

They seemed to confer for a moment, and just before even Judith with her Teflon fingers had to drop the match, the fire was sucked away to join their light. Judith looked between them. They'd taken care to position themselves to all get a bit of that flame. Judith took out match after match and lit them, letting them take the fire, until she only had a few left. She showed them those in the box. "Do you want to save some for later?"

From behind her, there came the noise of Rory slowly "stepping out of the bushes." "Wise woman make fire," he said. "Very powerful."

Judith sighed. If only he knew. "Can you understand me?" she asked them. The sprites paused for a moment. Then the golden ball flew at her and stopped an inch in front of her nose. On its surface was an image of a diminishing ball . . . or bubble. It got smaller even as Judith watched.

Judith swore under her breath.

"What is it?" said Rory. "Are they still thinking about eating us?"

Judith didn't know how to put it in terms he'd understand. This knot was collapsing. Very soon it would vanish out of existence. And they would almost certainly vanish with it.

3

Autumn had heaved Marcin along, putting all her hungover desperate strength into keeping him moving. Whatever was after them seemed to be like one of those predators in wildlife documentaries that circled their prey, then rushed in. Maybe her putting up a fight that time had made it wary. What did those documentaries say about facing a bear? Make yourself big and yell? Or was that for a mountain lion? Living in rural England, she hadn't paid much attention to those bits.

Marcin had been yelling questions at her, only about half of them in English. What were they running from? It hurt! He got to the point of actually fighting her off, and so, finally, she'd been forced to drop him. Now here they were, on a slight rise among some close trees, which Autumn hoped might give her some idea of when the thing approached. Marcin was lying on the ground screaming insults at her in Polish, and she was looking around, trying to watch out of the corner of her eyes. Which was really pretty bloody difficult. It kept making you want to just keep turning your head.

How the hell was she going to get him to close his eyes and put his fingers in his ears? Would the pain of his injury even let him lose concentration? Assuming that was actually how they could get out of this.

She needed to be able to see her enemy. What could let her see it better? What could let her see something the extra senses given to her by the well in the woods didn't let her see?

She realised. Today she had already experienced just that.

That dust Judith had thrown over her. If she could find some . . . She looked desperately in her pockets, ran her hand through her hair. Thank God. Here was just a trace of it on her fingers. The dust that had actually worked must get used up as it did so. She had no idea what this stuff was, so she could only hope that Judith activated it just by thinking some magical power into it.

But, what could she actually do with it? She could throw this tiny handful of dust at whatever this thing was when she was sure it was near. That would give her something of it she could see. But having to let it again get that close . . .

Oh. Oh, she'd just thought of something awful.

No, she couldn't hesitate. If Judith had shown her anything, it was that magic was about sacrifice.

She held open her left eye with one hand, and with the other . . . she quickly rubbed the dust into the eye, thinking magical power into it as she did so. She could hear Marcin make an uncomprehending noise of fear.

The dust was very fine. It didn't hurt as much as she expected—

Her eye was suddenly on fire. She screamed.

She blinked and slowly the pain subsided, and the colours washed into half of her brain, and she had to close the other eye for a second, because now she could see . . . everything!

The knot they were in, she could see the lines of force all around it. It was really small, and it was . . . getting slightly smaller, all the time, she could *see* the tension in the coloured threads. She could see them moving. And oh God, they were, they were moving inwards!

She looked down and saw the threads that still wrapped round her, how they loosely led off to connect to . . . she could see the connections now. They ran off from her body in all directions, linked into a great weave that was wrapped around the knot, that was the knot, that also went beyond it. All she had to do was to concentrate on one particular aspect, the shrinking or the relative tension, or one colour, and there it was, at the front of her mind, clear to her sight.

She turned and looked at Marcin. He was swimming with colour, all the flavours and influences that had made him. She could see his family, their history, the big moments of his life, intimacies that she shied away from and regretted seeing, but . . . okay, overall feeling, here was a good guy, so thank all the gods she didn't believe in for that at least. She didn't know what the individual threads meant, she'd been seeing stuff at random, had no idea how to discern that part of it. That would be the next level of this deep structure, that lived underneath their own special senses, that Judith knew about and could access if she wanted to, but that she'd never bothered to . . . no, when had Judith not done what had to be done? It must be more like she'd never needed to examine it.

It was like Autumn had a tube map, but without any of the names of lines or stations.

Still, hell of a map.

She heard a sound behind her that she was pretty sure she couldn't have heard before, because the warning signal flared in her new sight too, a sudden burst of threads into her eye. She spun round.

And there was the creature. Right beside her. It had the shape of a man, but was almost a silhouette, a few lines of a sketch. Only it was stark white. It had no features, but Autumn knew it was looking at her.

Suddenly, it hopped from one side to the other, then back again. That was something that predators did, wasn't it? It was getting its eyes lined up on her, and it wasn't sure how strong she was.

Neither was she.

Slowly, keeping her eye on it, she reached down and helped Marcin to his feet. "You're . . . seeing a thing?"

"Yes, and it's real and it's right in front of us." She managed to get him upright, and was about to reach down to pick up the biggest nearby stick when she realised she was trying to get her hand past one of the coloured threads to do it, that she could feel them now, by touch as well, feel them wrapped around her like she was covered in a sort of . . . electric pullover.

This ability to see and feel the threads wouldn't last long. But it would last longer than they would if that thing attacked. However, it was planning to do that. She could pick up the stick or . . .

She didn't know what any of the threads meant or where any of them led. But now she could see how they fitted together. So if she just—

The creature leapt forward.

Autumn grabbed the nearest thread and heaved.

Lizzie had tried calling Finn's name into the microphone, and all the other names she'd heard associated with him. She'd waited, but no response had come. Of course, it was perfectly possible that he could hear her, but couldn't get inside the knot. Given how he'd walked into her house, however, despite the collapse of the borders into new shapes, she rather doubted that. The problem had previously been that he hadn't been able to find where this was.

So she'd started to describe their location, both geographically, talking about the old barn and the track that led up the hillside, and temporally, trying to precisely describe where the full moon was. Because, and a quick peep outside the barn had confirmed it, that moon was staying put.

Now she was elaborating on those details. The bemused DJ was looking on, convinced that she'd flipped. And yeah, maybe a lack of faith in her sanity right now would be appropriate. A shout came from outside. Then a whole bunch of yells and cheers and even screams.

Lizzie got up from the mike and ran for the door as the DJ did also.

Outside, the crowd were staring at . . . oh, there was a circle of day, bright summer day, blazing into the night of the woods like a searchlight. Lizzie squinted, blinked; she could just about see something in the light. Figures. Oh, and now the light was expanding, as if heaving against something. Great, this must be Finn; they were being rescued!

Suddenly the light burst through, and the night collapsed around them like a stage curtain, and they and the barn and the generator were all standing not in the woods, but in a bright, open summer meadow in broad daylight, with the most beautiful, invigorating fragrances blasting into their nostrils.

But Lizzie was now not so reassured. Because they weren't home. She knew this exaggerated version of her own world from distant sightings. This was the place Autumn had been left so scarred from visiting. This was a meadow in the land of fairy. And standing in it wasn't, as she'd hoped, a relieved and/or petulant Finn, but a trio of strange, thin beings who seemed to be reflecting the sunlight in mad, angular ways. She could just about perceive that they were wearing armour, an armour of green and gold, and had in their hands swords that were making the air around them sing with their sharpness, that were somehow breaking the very air that drifted across them.

She saw all of this with the new senses given to her by the well in the woods. She had no idea what the others were seeing, but whatever it was, it was making them huddle together and back away in alarm.

She took a look behind them. More of the same endless

summer meadow, around a circle of mulch from the forest floor. The knot had collapsed, or been forcibly demolished, more like, and they'd been dropped into the middle of fairy.

The shouting from around her made her turn back. The three figures had stepped forward. Their shadows had suddenly lengthened and fallen over the cowering humans, deliberately, a show of force. Where the hell was Finn? He must work so hard, she thought, must have observed Autumn and the rest of them so closely to even pass as human. Because these fellows of his who weren't trying . . . they were something completely Other.

"You!" the lead figure bellowed, the word seeming to twist into a translated version as it got to Lizzie's ear. "This is our land now! You are inside! We want you out!"

Rory had been gesturing angrily at the sprites. "You send gods home, or gods get angry, gods strike you down, capeesh?"

Judith had wanted to ask what language, exactly, "capeesh" came from, but she'd suspected he didn't know. The sprites had been twisting in urgent conference. Rory had kept trying to get through to them on his own, limited, terms.

She'd been hoping the sprites might offer her some power she could use to get out of here. She'd been putting that off until she absolutely had to do it, because, though the spell she had to cast was clear in her head, she was terribly afraid of how much of her strength it would use. But no, these poor things could barely feed themselves, and no other solution was going to present itself, and she was feeling weaker rather than stronger, so . . .

What had she been thinking about? She put a hand to her brow.

Why had she been hoping the . . . whatever they were called . . . why had she been . . . ?

Oh God. Oh God. What were all these . . . things?! Where was she? Was she having a nightmare? Who was this old man?

Where was her family? "Dad?!" she called out. Was this Dad? No, he didn't look anything like . . . but what did Dad look like? She should be able to remember!

The old man was looking at her in horror.

Autumn had heaved her way through a glowing web of colour, rushing through it, grab and run, grab and run, one-handed, holding Marcin with the other, pushing all her rage and frustration into just getting past something she could finally connect with, something she could finally . . . rip through!

And then she was through it.

She stumbled out onto a . . . grey, empty expanse. She looked around. It wasn't quite a world. Distant . . . mountains? No, they faded again. They kind of shied away. It was like they were asking if she wanted to have mountains there, and when she'd mentally questioned that, they'd shyly retreated.

Marcin was gasping. She looked to him. He was looking round in horror. "Work," he said. "Work, all, nothing else, all life." She had no idea what his eyes were seeing. The expression on his face was that of someone who was in their own personal . . .

Suddenly, walls sprang up around them. Bare walls with peeling paintwork, a smell of stale beer that made her once again want to vomit, a bar overflowing with ale pump signs for unreal brands all about bulldogs and Spitfires, and everywhere around her, Union flags and the cross of Saint George, and red, white, and blue bunting and suddenly hemming them in on every side, fat, white men in Union Jack waistcoats, wearing flat caps, laughing their heads off as they chinked their handled beer mugs together, the foam splashing over her in great waves. Their laughter urged her to join in, join in, join in.

She pulled Marcin, who was looking up and down at where to her there were gaps, seemingly in an entirely different world, to the door. She flung it open, but outside there was just more of the same. A television was on in here, and an ecstatic posh-voiced commentator was shouting, "It's us against the world now! The sun will never set on the land of hope and glory!"

Autumn slammed the door. She mustn't lose control. She had to think. That moment of mountains had been this place sizing her up, testing out her mind before finding out what sort of world she *didn't* want to be in and then flinging it at her. This was . . . oh God, this was actually hell, right? For anyone who came here. *A* hell, anyway. But how could there ever be anything more definitively hellish than torments that immediately suited themselves to you personally?

She looked back to the exact place they'd been when they entered, and now, to her shock, a new figure was squeezing its way through the laughing men, the thin white shadow that had pursued her earlier. It must have been so close behind them it had come here, too. It was cringing, its fingers clenching and unclenching, staggering, spinning around as if looking for release.

Oh God. It was suffering in its own private hell too. Whatever surrealism that involved, Autumn couldn't imagine.

She gathered all her courage, and heaved Marcin along to stumble toward it. Okay, it was time to make use of the rage she felt at everything that was crowding in around her here. She concentrated again on seeing the threads that underlay everything, while she still could, and sure enough, there they were, and seeing them made her stop in shock for a moment. Here they'd been twisted into a web that looked expertly woven, that wrapped round the heads of all three of them, that looked like they were the captives of some enormous . . .

She locked away that thought before this world realised how terrifying it was and made the fear real. She grabbed the threads and heaved.

And heaved . . . and heaved . . . and now she was simply pulling more and more of the stuff out of the air, building it up around her, wrapping it around her, trapping them more and more every second, and now it was billowing out of where she was pulling it, uncontrollably, and she realised that this place had latched on to that part of her fear too.

Okay!" Lizzie had shouted to the leader of the fairies. "We're all for that! We want to get out and get back to our world as soon as possible!" Because, after all, this wasn't usually the problem with humans and fairies. The problem was usually that the fairies wanted the humans to stay. "But how do we do that?"

The fairies had been silent. Then they'd just taken another threatening step forward. And those shadows had once again lashed out with a sort of internal visual . . . roar.

"This isn't happening," Stewie had whispered beside her. "This is some . . . hallucination!"

"Then we're all having it," the bearded boy had whispered. He'd looked to her. "Who are they? What can we do?"

"They won't even tell us the rules!" the DJ had yelled.

Because, Lizzie had thought, there was something a bit stagey about all this. Was what happened here going to be related back to Finn's father, the king, as some sort of border incident, perhaps something Finn, as the go-between, should have prevented? The most worrying possibility was that if they were going to be portrayed as an invading horde, then their deaths might be a useful part of that portrayal. Not that the court were ever going to hear their version. Could this incident be used, even, to start a war? That was something the whole human race was unprepared for, never mind the three of them who supposedly guarded Lychford and now had not much in the way of boundaries to help with that.

She spoke up, aware that, following the lad's lead, more and more of these kids were looking to her. "We need to work out how to get out," she called to them. "How about we start by backing up to the edge of this?" She pointed to the ground where the circle of woodland soil and mulch around the barn, with trees still standing inside it, was a plain indicator of the area that had been in the knot, now not wrapped back around itself, but obvious against the shining green of fairy grassland.

They ran together, away from the fairies, to the edge of the circle. Lizzie quickly stepped across it. Nothing. There must be a way, a way which would be obvious, probably, from the fairies' own point of view, because otherwise how could they characterise this as an aggressive action?

She walked round the boundary, the others following her, hoping clearly that at any moment something magical would happen. Stewie was shaking his head, yelling that whoever had done this to him would pay, but the bouncers who'd come with her had serious looks on their faces. Those guys knew when they were in trouble.

Lizzie felt a vibration on her wrist. She looked at her exercise monitor. "Congratulations!" a tiny scrolling text read. "You've doubled your target!"

What? But she couldn't have gone further than . . .

She quickly stepped back over the same spot. Her wrist vibrated again. This time the device was ecstatic with the news that she'd trebled her target. If she did it again, the thing would probably give her the number of the nearest hospital. Whatever else happened to her today, she could die happy in the knowledge that she'd almost certainly beaten every other vicar in the weekly Diocesan Steps League. "Here," she said. "There's something wrong with space just here. I think this is the way out."

They all gathered round, eager and hopeful. But, given that

she hadn't immediately vanished home, what could she do with that knowledge?

Judith suddenly realised someone was talking to her, talking to her like she was a bloody idiot. It was Rory Holt. He was staring into her face. "My wife went like this. Couple of years before she passed on. I know there's no getting through to you, but I have to try. Now's not the time for you to be away with the fairies."

Judith bridled at the expression, grabbed his shoulder, and hauled herself to her feet. It wasn't his words that had brought her back; her brain chemistry had just happened to sway in the right direction. She fought down a tremendous surge of panic. How much smaller had the bubble become? Oh no. Now it was like standing in a greenhouse. The sprites were clustered near them; soon they'd all be crushed into each other. What was the spell she needed to recite to get them out? She was so stressed she still couldn't think how it started. She reached into the pocket of her cardigan for some more of that dust that would at least let her see the threads here, but she'd thrown it all at Autumn. "Stupid woman," she whispered. "I'm so stupid!"

"It's not your fault. It's that girl who sent us here." The sprites reacted with sudden light as the wall lurched in on them and Rory followed that with the nastiest words about Autumn that Judith could possibly imagine, all about her colour. "All her fault!" he spat again as the sprites rushed in fear around him. Heaven knew what he could see of them. Judith didn't want to know.

If it was the end now, Judith realised, she wanted to say summat true. Summat she'd only just started in this moment admitting to herself. "It's not her fault," she said, "it's mine. Mine a long time back. She made one mistake, I did exactly the same, and I was cursed for it, cursed for it so I suffered so long it took its toll on my noggin, and that's why you're stuck here, Rory Holt, because *I* made one mistake, and maybe you made a few too!"

The sprites cried out in light as the roof of the world fell in on them all.

Autumn had tried to think as the material that made the borders of the worlds . . . what this place was *pretending* was that material in order to scare her . . . had flooded over her. But she'd quickly become lost under it, her world just chaos, nothing her flailing hands could grab hold of. No baseline to put her feet on, no rules.

But, she realised, that was what this place was trying to tell her, to scare her with, wasn't it? There were rules, she just had to dig deep and find them. For the sake not only of herself, but for helpless Marcin, who she could feel as if at a distance, shaking with his own fears. She even had to do it for the sake of that thing that had followed them. She had to do it for the sake of Luke, for everyone who . . . cared about her.

How could she get past the fear? What was her experience telling her to do?

Bloody bite it. Chew it. Rip it up.

She snatched at the material with her teeth, grabbed it and held on, wrenched it from side to side. Was this achieving anything? Only satisfaction, but . . . there was a taste here . . . what was that? Taste, like every other sense she had, had been changed by exposure to the water from the well in the woods, but it wasn't often she got to make use of it. There was a kind of . . . meaningfulness under the emptiness she had in her mouth, a sense that . . . yeah, put her tongue on it, get more of it . . . a sense that something real was here underneath.

Okay, what had she got to lose? She grabbed a handful of what was turning into a void of meaninglessness around her and started to gulp it down. Started to take it like it was a drug. Come on, let her body and brain process this stuff, let it poison her, let her actually start to see what was . . .

She realised she'd started to see the real fibres again. That now they were leading right into her body, that she'd actually managed to randomly pull some of them into her. What if she went beyond being able to pull on them, actually got . . . ? She grabbed a great handful of them and shoved them into her mouth, and into her brain, and it pulled her open, and she pulled them open in turn, and she forced her way inside. She abandoned the idea of her brain making sense of what she was visualising, and went with the impossibility. She reached a hand out of the impossible knot that was impossible to get out of and grabbed Marcin and the white being and hauled them in after her.

Suddenly all three of them were in a sort of kaleidoscopic rollercoaster, colours rushing past at an impossible speed. Marcin was yelling, his hands trying to find purchase on something, but at least now he was reacting to the same thing she was. The being had just curled in a ball. But she herself . . . she was surfing this now. She had no control, but she could stand, and face forward, and see what was coming, ready to deal . . .

There was ahead a jumble of infinite threads, all colours, which she couldn't make sense of. The point where all the boundaries met, where all the borders were pulled tight. This was what someone had made, centuries ago, around Lychford. It connected the worlds as well as holding them apart. It wasn't a great work of art, it was an organic mess of compromises and solutions and traps.

Autumn fell into it yelling.

"What the bloody hell," said Judith, "are you doing in my head?"

Judith hadn't actually expected to be alive. She was annoyed to find that she'd grabbed hold of Rory Holt as if to shield him from the collapse, just as he'd grabbed hold of whatever he could see of the sprites. They were all curled together in a tiny preserved bubble of a world, light flickering around them.

"Holding the roof up," said Autumn, from where Judith normally had an internal voice telling her to remember she'd put the kettle on or that *Gardeners' Question Time* would be on soon, "and hey, you're welcome."

"Just . . . don't look around, now you're in there!"

"I can't help it. I can . . . see . . . no, I'm feeling, I'm experiencing, like they're my memories too . . . oh . . . oh no, oh Judith, I'm so—"

Judith wouldn't have been able to stand her pity if they'd been in the same room, never mind when it was coming from between her own ears. "Get out!" she whispered.

"If I do that, there goes the roof. I didn't choose to be in here, I just landed in the centre of . . . I think it's where all the boundaries are attached . . . and I saw you here and I threw my . . . my sort of hand . . . out to save you and here's where I ended up."

"How the hell . . . ? No, never mind that. Can you get us out of here?"

Judith felt Autumn's presence sort of . . . shifting in her head, like she was now looking at summat else apart from every intimacy of Judith's life. The other thing Judith didn't like was . . . oh, yes, she could feel Autumn's existence too. There was an outsiderness that Judith recognised, but that with Autumn was both of long standing and recently, sharply, deepened. Judith found they were suddenly thinking a thought in both their inner voices at once. It was that if she wanted to, Judith could move to another town and fit in, while Autumn would always have a certain number of people who stood between her and that release.

To share a thought . . . when she was younger, that would have been so good. But now it hurt so much. That outsider feeling was something Judith so did not want for Autumn, and she saw with great guilt how she had contributed to it. That guilt was reflected back by Autumn's thoughts about how she'd treated Judith, given how Judith . . . *was* now.

Oh. Oh no. What could be worse than this shared pity?

What could be better?

Judith bellowed internally. "Can you stop being so bloody soft and just find what you need to—?!"

"You don't get to order me around while we're the same person."

"I order myself around all the bloody time, you stupid woman!"

"We are going to have a talk about this, when . . . if I can get us home."

"What are you going to do about this one?" Judith mentally pointed to Rory, still curled up, holding on to the sprites like they were soft toys. "He's in your power now."

"So I can't just save you and the . . . sprites?" She'd found what they were called inside Judith's knowledge. She hadn't wanted to think that harsh a thought, but there were no barriers between the two women now.

"Oh, don't lie to yourself when someone's sharing your brain. You won't leave him here to be crushed."

"I just wanted him to know I had the option. I'm in his head too."

Rory looked up, suddenly furious. "Get out!" he bellowed. "Don't touch me!" And he started to scream every epithet he knew. Everything about race, everything about gender, everything about anything he was not.

There was a long pause. Then, without another word inside Judith's head, something changed.

The three fairies had suddenly reacted to something Lizzie didn't understand. As one, they'd shouted something guttural, and crouched. Then they had charged.

Lizzie hadn't hesitated. She'd grabbed the nearest kid and shoved them at the point where she'd encountered the anomaly, praying fervently as she did so, trying to push emotion into the act of pushing physically. The kid went straight past the anomalous space, and so Lizzie shoved her hands into it, calling out to anyone and anything who could help her in that instant, giving all her emotion to that in a way which she was used to in prayer.

She didn't have more than a moment. Then she'd have to get herself between the others, who were already starting to scream, run, push forward, and the danger that was coming for them. She'd wave her arms and try to look powerful, she decided. Oh God, she was going to die here.

"It's okay, Lizzie, I see you now!" a familiar voice shouted. In the centre of her own head. Kind of where she was used to God being. "Thanks for calling me. The fairies had put some sort of . . . curtain . . . in the way."

"Autumn?!" said Lizzie, boggled.

But in that second the shadows of the fairies hit them all, and the screams of panic turned to sheer terror, as Lizzie felt rather than saw the swing of three swords—

The swords passed over her.

And the others.

Lizzie felt a great sense of closeness to her old friend as they fell into darkness together, a voice and an intimate presence in her head, an astonishing embrace.

And then they were all standing there in the woods above Lychford on a late summer afternoon. Lizzie looked round and was relieved to see Judith, and Autumn, and with them Rory Holt, looking round, yelling as if he'd just been struck, and a man with a splint on his leg who was blinking, stunned, slowly getting to his feet, and all the ravers, and the DJ, and the lad who'd hugged her, and Stewie, and his bouncers, and half their generator, which was steaming and sparking where it had been cut in two, and no sign at all of the barn, which was now presumably lost somewhere in the great beyond along with the DJ's equipment . . . and floating in the air, a group of . . . perfect, smiling, giggling cherubs.

Rory Holt looked up at the creatures and broke into a gap-toothed grin. "That's what they really were," he said. "Little angels. They must have saved us."

Judith looked awkwardly at the other two. "Cherubs," she whispered out of the corner of her mouth. "Sprites, cherubs, I knew t'were one or t'other."

Autumn nodded in the direction of the cherubs, looking pointedly at Rory. "It looks like we brought some refugees over the border."

"What are you talking about?" He looked angry at her. "What have they got to do with that? They're little angels."

Lizzie found herself remembering certain lines from scripture about the need to treat strangers as if they might be angels.

Autumn's voice stayed calm as she addressed him again. "But you have me to thank."

Lizzie looked to Judith, but the old woman now had her hands stuck deep in the pockets of her cardigan, her expression unreadable, her body language saying she was deliberately taking no action.

"To thank for what? You got me into whatever that was. Probably drugs in my pint or summat. I'm going to tell the police."

He looked fearful for a moment, as if Autumn might attack him. Then, reasonably certain he could turn his back on her, he started off down the hill, looking back over his shoulder from time to time, an expression on his face of valiant, infringed dignity.

"What an enormous wanker," said Stewie. And, thought Lizzie, he should know. She looked around at the kids from the rave. They were a mixture of angry and uncomprehending. They, like her, must all have had Autumn in their heads, and knew what she'd done. To them, that was all that mattered.

She turned back to see that Judith was watching Autumn to see what she would do next. Lizzie saw that the younger witch was holding in her hand something that Lizzie could only dimly see, a handful of glowing thread. "I can do maybe one more thing with this," she said.

"You could send him back," said Judith.

"But then," said Autumn, "the cherubs wouldn't get to go home."

And she opened her hand. In a blur of motion like released elastic, the cherubs vanished.

The man with the splint put a hand on Autumn's shoulder. "Good witch," he said.

Autumn turned to look at him with an expression which said she still wasn't sure.

When the human witch had burst into the knot at the centre of the worlds, the shardling had seen the path home and seized its moment.

It had been relieved to take three steps and then find itself once again where it had been conceived, inside the long shadow that had fallen across the barrow of the court of the fairy king.

It relaxed. It had completed its mission.

It had been one of many sent out to map the disturbances of

the boundaries, to swiftly bring back the information the king needed, now he was in the shadow, the information that would lead to war.

Because in the moment before it had left, it had seen the witch build a simple, single boundary. It was nothing like what had been there before. It would be easy to breach. The shardling felt a moment of satisfaction at having this information to return to its master.

The mind of the shardling only lasted for a moment longer before the king reached out and absorbed it back into himself. The knowledge was shared. The moment of satisfaction became a moment of anticipation.

The preparations for the attack began.

As the bells of the church chimed six, Autumn slowly and carefully unlocked the door of her magic shop, her two friends beside her. She felt like a different person from who she'd been the last time she was here, that morning.

Marcin had hugged her, and had thanked her profusely in English and Polish, had shown her a picture of his family, who she now felt she knew really well, having already experienced them inside his head. Now he could return to them. Even though . . . he'd made steering wheel gestures and Autumn had had to take a while to explain that his lorry was still lying there now, miles from the road in the real woods, the moment of time it had been trapped in having expired. It hadn't been left in fairy like the barn had been. Autumn felt dimly that she'd managed to arrange that on her way out of the structure of threads. Judith had got Lizzie to call Shaun on her mobile, and had taken the phone from her and sternly told her son that the lorry driver had been found and fought off some hijackers, heroically getting injured in the process. Apparently they'd used a helicopter to lift the . . . no, she'd interrupted his incredulous outburst, this was one of her sort of things, and so was Rory Holt, who was alive and well and would by now be back at his house and ready to tell a story that nobody would or should believe, and all the ravers were fine too, and did he have any more damn fool questions?

So Marcin, to Autumn's relief, had been able to go on his way with a reasonable future ahead of him. Result.

They sat down at the table in Autumn's workroom. Which was now clean, she realised, with nothing boiling itself on the stove. "Thank you," she said to Judith, now feeling unable to look at her. The old witch must have given some of her remaining energy to do that.

"Thank *you*," Judith replied, as though the words were from a foreign language.

"Well," said Lizzie, "this is better."

"Isn't anyone," said Judith, "going to make some bloody tea?"

So Lizzie made the tea. And listened, as she did so, to Judith and Autumn continuing to thank and apologise to each other, like nations who'd been at war and didn't quite know why. That was always, in her experience, the most wonderful sound. Judith was still an employee, Autumn still an apprentice, and who'd ever thought otherwise? Judith wanted to emphasise, Autumn having seen inside her head, that she'd been in her right mind when she'd voted, but no, she still wouldn't say which way that'd been. If Autumn didn't know already. Then Autumn, having moved swiftly past that, in whispers, was trying to persuade Judith to tell Lizzie something, but Judith was hesitant. That was okay. From the glimpse Lizzie had got inside her friend's head, she could guess what sort of thing this might be.

She put the mugs and teapot and a packet of Hobnobs down

between them and decided to ask about wider issues. "What about all the people who now know about magic?"

"Nobody's going to believe those kids," said Judith, "and the smart ones won't try to tell anyone. Same for the lorry driver. He seems to know which side his bread's buttered. Rory Holt's going to tell everyone, for the rest of his days, and nobody will believe him, which sounds like the world's worked out a curse for him. Surprising how often there are just deserts."

"Or not," said Lizzie. "Can we find out what's happening in fairy?"

"I'll send messages to Finn," said Autumn. "I'm worried about him. What happened to you isn't something he'd have been up for, if he knew about it."

"If he could stop it," said Judith. "It wouldn't be the first time there have been ructions in fairy. If they war on each other, we'll know about it. So will the world if we're not careful."

Lizzie went to point three on her short mental list. "And what are we going to do about the boundaries?"

"I tried to build a very rough one," said Autumn. "Okay, let's say it out loud, I ended up building a bloody wall."

Judith actually chuckled. Autumn immediately looked angry again. Lizzie looked sharply at Judith. Her smile was as thin as the smile on a fish, but it looked genuine. "I hadn't thought of that," she said. "I didn't mean it was your just deserts. Well, maybe a bit."

"I don't want it," said Autumn, still clearly requiring some terms and conditions here. "I want a proper border that treats all these worlds with respect and works on a case-by-case basis. I mean it. Not joking."

"Well, this'll be up to you, won't it?" said Judith. "What you put up, with what we put in place, will hold until someone has a real go at it. But we can't leave it. And we can't wait until I've got my strength back." If, thought Lizzie, privately, she ever did. "So you two will have to sort out what you want and build it. Soon."

Autumn looked a bit taken aback. "Okay," she said. "Thanks for . . . trusting—"

"No, we've had too many thanks already," said Judith, "soft, both of you. And of course I trust you to . . . listen, you've made me say it, 'cos I'm going to have to start saying a lot of things now. This was why you messing up like that hurt so much—"

Lizzie looked to Autumn, but she shook her head, she wanted to hear this.

"—you, girl, are my choice to continue when I'm gone. To be the wise woman of this town. You'll have help from the vicar here, and maybe others'll come along, but someone'll have to do the lifting, and it won't be me forever. You and your . . . science," she let the word slip out like it was sour, "maybe that's the shape of what's to come. And the give and take of someone your age, that room for mercy, that'll be needed too. I just need you to . . . to not fly off at every enormous wanker, to be strong enough to be looked at like you're odd for the long haul."

"I . . . think I'm qualified—" Autumn was trying hard not to cry, and failing.

"Now I've seen in your noggin I know that. I know that you had a head start with that. Oh my girl. My girl. I don't know how long I got left." And Judith had to put a hand over her mouth and close her eyes. But she left one hand on the table. Autumn and then Lizzie put theirs on top of hers. And they stayed like that for a long time.

Acknowledgments

As well as my wonderful editor on all three of these books, Lee Harris, I'd like to thank Jaine Fenn and sensitivity reader Dee Mamora, who's given me excellent insights. Go find her on Twitter, you can hire her too!

About the Author

Lou Abercrombie

PAUL CORNELL has written episodes of *Elementary, Doctor Who, Primeval, Robin Hood,* and many other TV series. He has worked for every major comics company on series such as *I Walk With Monsters, The Modern Frankenstein, Saucer Country,* and *This Damned Band,* as well as runs for Marvel and DC on *Batman and Robin, Wolverine,* and *Young Avengers.* He is based in the UK.